Safe to Say

James Ward

Safe to Say

ISBN 13: 9780988542723

Library of Congress Control Number: 2012955078

Cover design by All Things That Matter Press
Published in 2012 by All Things That Matter Press

for Barbara
she knows why

PART I

Harmon

workhorse — double checker — farm fresh — a game

His father said there were two types: show horses and workhorses. If you heard him say it, you'd know which he preferred. Harmon heard his father's preference expressed a lot, from his little league baseball to his big league job. The sentiment stuck and now, as he sat in his private office, he thought, again, how it was that simple lesson that got him there.

The office was small and windowless, identical in its dimensions and furnishings to the others that lined the interior walls of AC&C's headquarters complex, but he had the luxury of a door to close and, allowing for a generous definition, the right to call himself middle management. Upper management had the spacious windowed offices, lower and non-management had the open floor cubicles.

It was just after eight p.m. and the end of another thirteen hour day. He flipped his desk calendar one page. June 16th, 1989 would be ready for him and he for it, early the next morning. He sunk back in his chair and took a deep breath. For his colleagues, management and non-management, the end of the workday meant a gleam in their eyes and a bounce in their steps from escaping a labor of necessity for the pursuit of pleasure. He was different. He always felt a familiar letdown, as if he were suddenly without purpose.

***

With stuffed briefcase in hand he stepped into the hallway and pulled his door closed; the lock's metallic click a comfort. An inveterate double-checker, he turned the handle and pushed, making the door rebuff his effort. As a Project Manager for the AC&C Corporation, he was privy to proprietary information. The last thing he wanted was for security to check and find his door unlocked. That was one of his fresh nightmares: coming in some morning to find a bright red violation sticker, stuck right in the middle of his door.

Before leaving, he reached out and touched his nameplate, as if needing tactile assurance that it was still there. *Harmon Wolcott*, embossed in silver on black paper and slid inside a see-through plastic holder, the paper easily removed, the name easily replaced. Life at AC&C was tentative; a good reason to be bedeviled with departure rituals.

He made his way down a narrow aisle, flanked by monotonously gray, fabric sided cubicles. All were empty and instead of the usual babble of voices and ringing of phones, the only sound was the thrumming of a vacuum cleaner, a couple aisles away. Adornments of all kinds used to hang outside the cubicles and he had liked that, for the glimpse into people's varied passions, but last holiday season someone put up an Advent calendar and after one complaint the building manager instituted a new bare walls policy, with no exceptions, not even the local sports teams, because it was too easy to offend.

On the stairway to the underground parking garage it was time to start the game he played at the end of every workday: His worry game. It was a peculiar exercise that he kept to himself. It would seem foolish to anybody else, even his mutually stressed and strained coworkers, but the game, with its regularity and intricacy, had a serious purpose: it gave him some sense of control over his worst fears.

He didn't look like a worrier. Tall and thin, he had a quiet manner and a face rosy cheeked and boyish enough that it better fit a carefree high schooler than a young executive. On his arrival at AC&C, an admiring secretary had dubbed him *Farm Fresh*. Without intention, his manner rebuffed hers and all other advances, subtle and direct.

His paternal genes shaped his face—his father was fifty-six and looked forty something. His upbringing shaped his manner, a country boyhood among stoic country people, with a father to provide unambiguous direction and a mother to agree to it. A way of life that, like his farmer neighbors and their farm institutions, he thought would never change. He could have been content with that.

***

The game's first step was to add any new worries from the current day's events. He could concentrate when on the stairs, which were hot in summer and cold in winter and that, along with their aerobic challenge, made them his alone. Everybody else at headquarters rode the elevators. It showed. One of the younger managers called headquarters *the land of elastic pants*.

He started where he always did, with his current boss. She had supervised him for only nine weeks but already overflowed with ideas on how to stretch him—how to force him out of his comfort zone. She was one of AC&C's Leadership Candidates, hotshots recruited and targeted for rapid advancement. Prominent on her office bookshelf— *Pulling Your Own Strings, Thriving On Chaos, Atlas Shrugged*. She particularly cherished the concept of stretching—stretched objectives, stretched thinking, stretched people. In the Middle Ages she would have made a great rackmaster. Just this afternoon she insisted on a ceremony, first thing in the morning, to celebrate his fifth service anniversary. A little thing, but still a worry. He didn't like being the center of attention, not even for a few minutes and a few colleagues.

Another consistent worry generator was his one and only directly-reporting subordinate, an Assistant Manager named Joe who had been at AC&C for forty-two years, earning the nickname *Jurassic Joe* for having begun his tenure sometime near the second period of the Mesozoic era. Instead of deferring to Harmon, Joe treated him as if he were a summer intern. Just that day, at lunch, Harmon had hoped aloud that his boss would be sent away, believing any replacement would be better. Given the frequency and zeal with which AC&C reorganized, his hope for a change was not fanciful. But Joe crushed his hopes. "Kid," he said, loud enough for the whole table to hear, "don't count on a new boss being any better. This company's got ass-holes it ain't even used yet."

Another worry—that morning he had brought some work to the word processing group. He needed fast turnaround. All his projects were critical. Late in the day he checked on his document's progress. Half the word processing group had recently returned from a two-day *Stress Buster Seminar* and he found his document still in their deep In-Box and his assigned typist lying on the floor with a little pillow under her head and a book on her stomach, demonstrating for her colleagues the stress busting effects of diaphragmatic breathing. On her exaggerated inhales the book sunk and her ample chest rose. He tried not to stare. He was long abstinent but not sexless. He retrieved his document and, anxious as he was, the snowy-bearded toy figures that hung from the side of the in-box seemed to mock him. Unsympathetic Joe laughed and said word processing's in-box was, "The place where elephants go to die."

***

It was time for step two when he reached the garage. He parked his pickup truck in the same convenient spot every day, a benefit of arriving by seven a.m. First, he said goodnight to the security guard. The guard was new and nodded and said in a heavy foreign accent, "Good night, mister sir." That kind of deference made Harmon uneasy but he stayed quiet. The guard seemed short on English and any attempt at folksy camaraderie could make matters worse.

In step two, he ranked his worries in order of seriousness; this while winding his truck through the dimly lit underground labyrinth, the all-terrain tires squealing at every twist and turn on the smooth concrete. Despite his creeping speed, his overactive conscience would tell him, *slow down.* He decided today's new worries ranked near the bottom. He could handle a little celebration. Joe was Joe and always would be. He could come earlier or stay later and do his own word processing. He had bigger things to worry about, responsibility for initiatives with insuperable obstacles and impossible timelines, but upon the success of which his success depended. All his work complicated by the circumstances of the new AC&C, where project management was a Sisyphean chore.

The new AC&C emerged just six months before he started. On January 1, at precisely the stroke of midnight Eastern Standard Time, as if it were an execution date, the government had stripped the old ACC of its longtime monopoly status. It was deregulation that opened the door for newcomers like Harmon. Traditionally, upgrades and transfers from craft received preference for entry level management positions, but the new CEO changed that. He meant to seed management with college hires better equipped for the competitive market's challenges. That new blood might help in the future, but now, under assault from new and nimble market driven competitors, the company's cobwebbed products, systems and leadership were unequal to the challenge and the resulting droppings rolled downhill in the form of layoffs, incomprehensible upper management missives and a constant state of stomach wrecking uncertainty. A bad environment for a perfectionist and a worrier.

Step three commenced when he topped a ramp and was free from the garage, his truck popping up outside like a prairie dog checking its surroundings. He flipped the sun visor down. With the long days of June, some light remained; most of the year he arrived and left in the dark. Step three meant packing his re-ordered worries into an imaginary bag. He pictured it as an old sea bag, like the one his uncle brought home from the Navy, *Wolcott* stenciled across the center of it. He started packing as he drove under the great thirty-foot high statue that stood as sentinel over the main entrance. Officially christened the *Spirit of Progress*, everybody called the statue *Golden Boy*. In fifth grade, he had done a report on the seven wonders of the ancient world and passing under *Golden Boy* always made him think of the *Colossus of Rhodes*, the enormous statue that once bestrode the harbor at Rhodes in ancient Greece. His report won an award and was read aloud at a PTA meeting. That was one of the times his father said he was proud of him. For the whole week after, Harmon slept with his award. The little plaque still hung on the wall back home, in his unoccupied bedroom.

His worst worries resisted the bag. They were matters that no amount of thinking could fix, but his mind couldn't dismiss. That's why the game had specific locations where the steps must be completed—the rules were to make up for his weakness.

Along the tree-lined entrance to the interstate, he pulled the bag's drawstring tight. That completed step three. He began to accelerate and the momentum triggered step four. In that final and most fanciful step, he lifted the bag over his head and, timing things just right, flung it onto the big green and white road sign that spanned the interstate and announced 287 North. The plan was for his worries to stay there, safely sequestered so they couldn't crawl about his consciousness, ruining his evening and his night's sleep. He would gather them up again the next morning, on his way back to work.

***

The game was foolish, the seabag imaginary, but his worries real. Some days it seemed as if he had just been locked onto and beamed away from his previous life; that he had been mysteriously transported smack into the middle of the pressure-packed alternate world of corporate America. Chronically homesick, on those days he felt as if his journey had taken him beyond his ability to pretend.

Riley

interviewee — take your daughter to work day — rats — HQ

The morning of her AC&C interview, Riley O'Brian had coffee and raisin toast in her apartment's tiny kitchenette. She kept busy lining up her refrigerator magnets and tightening her row of ceramic canisters. When nervous, she longed for order.

She was taking the interview too seriously, making it more important than it really was. She kept telling herself that, even though she didn't believe it. The AC&C interview was important. An administrative job in a large corporation could open doors; doors she wanted to walk through. She knew herself as a late bloomer and her adult life was about wanting to succeed to the limit of her abilities. She relished that challenge.

For the walk to the bus stop she wore sneakers and carried her medium-heeled dress shoes in an expandable business bag, just like the professional women in Manhattan. Jersey City's streets would be double tough on dress shoes. Jersey City's streets didn't get the attention of Manhattan's.

There were only two other people at the bus stop, but she didn't sit on the aluminum bench for fear it would stain her skirt. You never knew what took place on those benches at night. She resisted the urge to pace. She didn't want to make a spectacle of herself. Instead, she thought of her mother.

Twelve years ago, she and her mother had waited together at that very same stop, but for a different bus. That long ago bus didn't go into the mysterious suburbs like today's would. Instead, it took her and her mother deeper into the city, to her mother's job at an anonymous brick building. It was the morning after she had first talked about quitting school. She was fourteen then but already an iconoclast at heart. She was drying plates with a dishtowel and she said, "Mamá, I'm wasting my time in school. I don't learn a thing." That wasn't smart. Her mother wasn't one to mess with. "Okay," her mother said, surprising her with such easy agreement. Riley had expected an outburst. After a moment, her mother said that if she was ready to quit school she must be ready to work. Riley nodded. What else could she do? Her mother had a million ways to outsmart her.

The next morning her mother shook her awake. It was dark and the digital alarm clock read 4:59. Riley could still relive that moment as if it happened yesterday. From that day on there was something shiver educing about 4:59 a.m. It stuck in her consciousness as the most ungodly hour. "You come work with me," her mother had said. "So we not waste you time today." Words heavy with a Spanish accent and without contractions because, smart as she was, her mother never mastered English contractions.

She told her mother she had changed her mind, she was going back to school. Then she dug deeper under the sheet and her mother's handmade quilt. She felt as if she could stay there forever. "Oh no!" her mother said, and with one fierce pull stripped away quilt and sheet, leaving Riley squirming like an unearthed worm. "Tomorrow, if you want, you go school. Today you have commitment. You no change up the mind about commitment." Her mother tossed the quilt and sheet into the corner, as if it were laundry day. Her mother lacked contractions but not convictions.

Riley pouted all the way to the bus stop, dragging a train of attitude with her. The stop was crowded and everyone knew her mother. They all stood under a yellow tinged streetlight and with each new arrival there were nods and a harmonious, but subdued, *Buenos Dias*. Standing at the stop and sitting on the bus Riley felt every eye on her. She knew she stood out, olive skinned but with auburn hair and freckles — the half Irish, half Dominican daughter of her all Dominican mother. Back then she hated her hair and freckles and half-breed look. Half and Half. That's what the kids called her. Once, putting her gloves on after school, she found *Half n' Half* creamers stuffed into the fingers. Her hair and freckles were the only thing her father bequeathed her, beside her surname, that she would have changed to her mother's maiden name of Mercedes, except her mother forbade it.

She took the bus with her mother just that one time. Her mother rode that same bus for thirty-one years, never missed a day of work and was never late. Not once. Colds and flu and a painful bout of shingles, a fractured foot from stepping off a crumbling curb, she went anyway. With maturity came understanding and now Riley knew why. It was all for her. She had a single mother with a single purpose.

***

When her suburban bus came, she found an empty seat near the back so she could check her face and teeth in her little mirror. The ride should take forty minutes, with more local stops to pick up a full load of workers and then the highway zoom to New Jersey's affluent towns, home of the cleaning, cooking and clerking jobs.

Today she would have to be at her best. More importantly, she had to speak well. People judged you by how you spoke. They made snap judgments. Say *you know* and *like* and *ain't* and they figured you for an uneducated fool, especially if you had even the slightest accent and didn't look all American. Say, *I am most impressed with the efficiency of your organization* and you surprised them and they figured you for smart. Riley was smart. Whatever else she doubted about herself, she never doubted that. And she enjoyed surprising people.

At a fork in the road, the bus went left. The bus to her mother's old workplace would have gone right. She craned her neck to look down that street and to catch a glimpse of the building. It was still amazing to her, but back then, before she was forced to learn, she had only the dimmest idea about her mother's job. She knew she worked at some kind of research facility and that she was some kind of cleaning person, but that was it. Now she wished she knew everything about her mother's life. Though she had been there only that one time, long ago, and though the neighborhood was even worse now, she thought sometime soon she would go back to her mother's workplace, even if it were just to walk by and maybe touch the brickwork. Her mother had been gone almost five years now, dead at the age of fifty from what started as a simple cold, but with her mother's refusal to rest, advanced to a deadly pneumonia. For the mature Riley, her mother's workplace had become a shrine worthy of a pilgrimage.

***

After twenty-five minutes swooshing along the big interstate, the bus was off the highway and passing through a succession of little towns. "This," the lady across the aisle said to her seatmate, "is the nicest part. People think they know New Jersey, but they don't." It was nice; little picturesque towns with small wood-framed post offices and white steeple churches. Some change from Jersey City.

At each stop her nervousness grew. She had known about the interview for a week and it had seemed as if it would never get here. But here it was. Her favorable reviews with the temporary agency had led to this opportunity. AC&C was one of the clients the agency needed to please. "Play your cards right," her placement counselor said, "and they might hire you for a permanent position. The pay's good, they have great benefits and opportunity for advancement. Plus, you can commute by bus."

Her stop was at a dedicated entrance road marked by an understated, but stylish sign, gray letters etched into black marble: AC&C *Headquarters*. Two cleaning ladies got off with her and the bus rumbled on into the countryside. She walked away fast to distance herself from the ladies. She needed the time alone.

The road curved around a thick stand of trees and she strode to the chattering of birds. In calmer circumstances she might have enjoyed the bird talk, but now the interview ahead of her seemed daunting. To put things in perspective she thought about her mother's job.

She never forgot that day or those rats. Her mother had led the way down a dark narrow stairway, Riley two steps behind and not hiding her reluctance. When they reached the cool, cinder block walled basement, her mother flipped on the overhead fluorescent lights without having to feel for the switch. Metal cages filled the far side of the room, set on tables and stacked three high. It looked like a miniature prison. "This is where I work," her mother said. "*Mi oficina.* I *jefe grande* here. Boss of the rats." It turned out her mother cared for lab rats, feeding them, cleaning their cages, disposing of the unsuited and the dead—the rats bred, nurtured and sacrificed for research. Her mother had never talked about it. Maybe she was waiting for her daughter to ask.

Excited by her mother's presence, the rats stood on their hind legs. It seemed they missed her. Her mother made her come close and then opened a cage, stuck her hand in and without the least hesitation pulled out a rat, dangling it by its long, hairless tail, right in front of her girl's face. Riley jumped. Even now, at just the thought of it, she shivered. "No like?" her mother said. "Well I touch a lot of them. Yesterday, today, mañana. Seven to three-thirty, I touch." The rat was white as bleached flour, its tiny eyes red, its feet pink like its nose. It had amazingly long whiskers and ears so thin that light went right through them and you could see the red veins as though you had x-ray vision. When it stopped squirming the rat stared at Riley and twitched its nose in concentration, finding her interesting. Then, like an Olympic gymnast, it swung itself up and sat on the back of her mother's hand.

"We," her mother said, emphasizing the plural pronoun, "got to move them out of dirty cages and in clean ones. You do them by the tail because that the way you do it. It not hurt at all. They know it and they know they go to clean cage." Her mother stared eyeball to eyeball at the rat, as if it understood and might confirm all this. She put the rat in a clean cage. "They know what good for them. They smarter than some people I know." Riley stayed still. "So you no want to do?" her mother said. "What I do every day, while you in school, learning the nice stuff. Well, today, maybe you just clean cages. After I switch them. You clean straw with the poop. That be some help. Maybe someday I get you here. We see. Maybe when you eighteen. I work hard so they like me here. Maybe they give you the chance. With no high school, who can know? You might get lucky. The other kids, high school and college, they got upstairs jobs."

***

That's what Riley wanted so badly, an upstairs job. She cleared the trees and there it was, the headquarters complex. It was further away than she thought. Bigger, too. She slowed to take it all in. Set against distant hills, the seven interconnected buildings loomed like a great fortification, the morning sun reflecting off their red tiled roofs. She felt intimidated. It was a long walk, but she had allowed plenty of time. She passed meticulous gardens of beautiful flowers she couldn't name. She would like to learn the names of all the flowers and the birds, too. She'd like to learn their Latin names. Esoteric knowledge intrigued her. The air smelled of some kind of fertilizer and her chest tightened. She feared it was her asthma flaring up—the last thing she needed.

Tall stainless steel flagpoles stood as sentries to the main entrance. One pole flew the American Flag that her mother had taught her to never pass without putting her hand over her heart; the other flew AC&C's own flag. She didn't know a corporation could fly or even have its own flag and she didn't know what kind of salute it deserved.

There was also a water fountain surrounded by a concrete retaining wall; the fountain was the kind you would see in an old town square. As she drew closer she could hear the water and had the feeling someone was watching her, that she was a trespasser. Behind the water fountain, a giant statue stood; a naked and muscular winged man, the sun just touching his golden head, its reflection like an electric crown. If it were all meant to radiate power and make her feel microscopically small, it worked.

The big glass doors were just ahead.

Anniversary

ceremony–a gift–birthday boy–opportunity

At nine a.m., dutiful Harmon sat in the second floor conference room along with eleven sleepy-eyed district mates, everybody waiting for the boss and the little ceremony to follow. Harmon, the guest of honor, was still not happy about it.

Time to kill and at the table's far end, Jurassic Joe, who was an old hand at that line of work, made a show of twiddling his thick thumbs and humming his favorite frittering tune—Freddy Fender's country song, *Wasted Days and Wasted Nights*. Harmon squeezed his pencil. He wanted to be back at his desk, getting some of his mountain load of work done. He preferred work to celebration.

***

At 9:17 the boss rushed through the door with her usual air of hurry and urgency. "Time to celebrate," she said, her voice rising and peaking at *celebrate*. Cheerleading was part of her job and celebrate a hot word at AC&C. The hard charging CEO favored it.

"It's special day," the boss said. She touched Harmon's shoulder, a tap of recognition, then took the seat at the head of the table and lit up a smile. "It's Harmon's fifth service anniversary!"

Greeted with unacceptable silence, she lifted her hands in a clapping motion, as if to demonstrate how. Polite applause ensued with enthusiasm inverse to seniority. Harmon's face flushed, the warm glow reaching his ears. The boss clapped loudest and longest. She was younger than she looked, only twenty-eight, but already head of the Project Management District and already making six figures. The group's secretary could be counted on for that kind of information.

"In our challenging environment," the boss said, "it's even more essential that we celebrate our successes."

AC&C's challenging environment was the thematic undercurrent of every meeting, celebratory or cautionary.

Despite the boss's doctrinaire optimism, her meetings invariably degenerated, hijacked by the group's practiced purveyors of doom and gloom, forecasters of complete corporate failure and catastrophic job losses. In the doomsayers world, this was usually followed by unpaid mortgages and unfed kids, fair-weather spouses long gone and replacement jobs serving freaks on the third shift at the Dairy Queen.

That kind of talk could get to Harmon, on his bad days, provoking within him a dim foreboding of disaster, even though he had no mortgage, nor wife, nor kids, not even any debt. And, if worse came to worse, he could be back home with his biggest worry being keeping gas in his truck. Still, his mind being its own place, he worried.

"Come on people," the boss said. "Help me out here." She swiveled her chair around and bobbed her head in further affirmation of the need for celebration. Her hair bounced. With her energetic aura and sophisticated look, Harmon thought she could make a great shampoo commercial.

Eyes rolling among the attendees. Harmon's colleagues, especially the men, were tough on the boss. One said that the way she ricocheted around the office reminded him of that cartoon character, the *Roadrunner*—if the bird were on crack. Harmon often wondered what was said about him behind his back. Probably talk about his solitary ways.

"You know," the boss said, "this celebration is for Harmon." Implied but not said, *so feel free to join in because it's not for me, who I know you don't like. And it's not for the corporation that—in spite of it putting food on your tables and shelter over your heads—I know you hate.*

"Five years, I mean that's half a decade." The boss was doing her best to lend import to the occasion. Five years service wasn't much, not when the staff swelled with managers of thirty-plus years. "And you know," she added, "he's never missed a day." He hadn't. He even came in on snow days, though what was considered a storm in snow-paranoid New Jersey would hardly be a dusting back home. One joke said Headquarters once closed for two days because someone spit on Route 287 and it froze. "People, people, people," she finally pleaded, sounding more supplicant than supervisor. Still the people ignored her.

"Well Harmon," the boss said, "I have your award here." She nodded to a small tissue wrapped package on the table in front of her. "I'm just glad it got here on time. With her long thin fingers she touched the award and lifted her eyes to the ceiling. "You know Human Resources."

The guy across the table mimicked her face but Harmon ignored him and nodded appreciatively. The boss deserved some respect and, as much as he didn't want the ceremony, it was good of her to stage it. Nowadays it wasn't unusual for much greater milestones to go unnoticed. He knew a manager who liked to have folks guess how the company celebrated his twenty-five years of dedicated service. The correct answer: With doodly-squat, not even a cup of coffee. Among the seasoned managers there lived a constant pining for the old days, for custom and tradition, for anniversary celebrations held in the big conference room with half the division there; soda, coffee and the traditional ice-cream cake ensuring attendance. All that had been sacrificed to cost cutting. Now, every five years, you got to choose from a catalog of anniversary gifts, what Joe called trash and trinkets, but you needed thirty years to get a cake.

"Harmon," the boss said, "before I present you with your gift, why don't you tell us a little about your career; maybe some of your most interesting experiences and your most important successes."

He didn't want to do that. He wasn't a bragger. His father's advice, *always have more than you show.*

"Harmon," the determined boss said, "tell us what your first day was like. I bet you remember that. Everybody remembers their first day."

Harmon remembered. His first boss was surprised to see him—didn't expect him, didn't know he'd been hired, didn't know him from Adam, didn't have a desk for him, didn't know what the hell to do with him. So he gave Harmon a company issue pad and pen and sent him to sit in an all day meeting, a wearisome deep-dive into some problem with the billing systems. This made all the more incomprehensible by AC&C's peculiar language of all acronyms, buzz words and euphemisms: EBIT and EVA and MOI, change-agent, strawman, stakeholder, off-shoring, de-bottlenecking, and un-hiring.

"My first day," Harmon said, "was a little confusing."

Knowing laughter at the understatement.

"What made you choose AC&C?"

"Well," Harmon said, "the campus recruiter did a good job of explaining all the great opportunities here."

"A big company. The bigger the better." That's what his father had said. So he aimed high, at the biggest company in the world. He still liked to imagine the first time his father called him at work and the secretary answered, "AC&C, Mr. Wolcott's office." His father's toes must have curled with pride.

His father was a diesel truck mechanic, and although he respected his neighboring farmers and taught Harmon to do the same, he took pride in his own more technical skills. Pride, but not satisfaction. He expected more from his son, for Harmon to stand on his shoulders and succeed in the professional world. Harmon could still see his father, after two or three draft beers at the Deerhead Inn, the oversized tavern in the middle of their town's humble main street, going on about his boy's successes: his medals in grammar school, his high honors in high-school, his summa cum laude college graduation. The locals didn't take it as bragging, or at least took no offense to it. Harmon was one of their own. Telling of his son's achievements always brought a glint to his father's eyes and always ended with a pledge: *He's not gonna be a dumb grease monkey like me.*

"That's what sold me, too," a suddenly come awake Joe said. "You know, the great importunities."

Harmon suppressed a laugh. Joe was a gifted malaprop, especially when excited. His lingual gymnastics provided the entertainment at staff meetings; he made new trends *fabs*, to be joyful to be *aesthetic*, diligence the key to a good work *ethnic*. One time, after a site visit to a major pharmaceutical company and returning with two bags of samples for his wife, he had expressed amazement at the extent of that company's feminine product line. *You know, they even make that virginal spray.*

"Oh yeah," Joe said, "such great importunities. I started out climbing poles and freezing my Irish-Italian ass off for $40 a week."

"Joseph," the boss said. Joe shrugged his shoulders and grinned his, the truth hurts grin.

"Let's get back on point," the boss said. She liked to be on point and she didn't like Joe's old, reactionary talk. Respecting the occasion, she redid her smile and ceremoniously passed the anniversary gift to Harmon along with a large greeting card signed by her and all his immediate co-workers.

Harmon took the time to read the card and its signatures. Then he pulled away the tissue paper and opened the box to a gold plated money clip, the AC&C logo embossed on front, a tiny blue sapphire, the size of a pinhead, embedded below it. He held the money clip in his palm, assessing its surprising weight. He tilted it this way and that, but the stone wouldn't catch the light.

"Pass it around," the boss said. "So everybody can see it."

Harmon started his award on its clockwise trip.

"Is there a message in your choice of gift? Maybe something about a raise?"

"I wouldn't turn it down," Harmon said.

He said it because he knew he should. He chose the money clip, not to send a message, but as a gift for his father. His other options were a weather station in simulated wood or silver-plated cuff links. His father didn't worry about the weather and had never worn cuff links in his life, but he could pull the money clip out at the Deerhead, keeping it on the bar long enough to generate questions about his executive son living down in New Jersey and rapidly ascending the corporate ladder. His father deserved that pleasure and more.

"A raise for Harmon?" the district secretary spoke up. "Why?" She tightened her face in exaggerated bewilderment and looked around the table, as if hoping for an answer. "I mean, like, he's loaded. He's the only one I ever get complaints from payroll about. Asking, like, why don't he cash his checks! I had to tell him, man you're screwing up the payroll unit. Cash your paycheck!"

The room hooted at that, genuine wonderment that someone didn't hurry to cash his paycheck, that someone didn't have to. Harmon's face warmed again. It was hard to be an ascetic with dignity.

The boss got back on point. "Harmon, in your half decade here, when you think about it, it's amazing, you've seen so many changes already. I mean, you've witnessed the greatest transformation in business history."

A grumble of agreement passed around the table.

"Oh yes," Harmon said. "I've seen changes."

The money clip returned. Harmon opened and closed the little knife that folded from the side. He hadn't noticed it before. He tested the blade's strength against his thumb. It bent. His father might use it to clean his fingernails.

"Well Harmon," the boss said, "what's been your greatest challenge? I'd be very interested to know that."

"Oh," Harmon said, "that has to be something inside me."

"Inside you?"

The boss seemed wary, as if he were taking her someplace she didn't want to go. Harmon knew a slip when he made one. He didn't want to say anymore. But he had to. He said, "I don't want to let anybody down."

Fair enough, but his colleagues sprouted smirky smiles, the kind they saved for ass-kissers. He thought of what Joe said about AC&C's notorious brown-nosers, how they kissed so much ass that they wore Preparation H for lip balm. But he hadn't meant it that way at all. It wasn't even the boss he was afraid to disappoint.

"Well," the boss said, "you've met the challenge successfully."

He nodded. She was in too much of a hurry for further understanding or analysis and Harmon glad for it.

"And," the boss said, "you're happy now?"

"Oh yeah," Harmon said.

He wouldn't dare public consideration of that question. He didn't dare private consideration of it, except when it forced itself on him, usually in the middle of the night, when he was unable to sleep. That's when he would get up and stare out his hillside apartment's easterly window at the fluorescent Manhattan skyline. The view made his homesickness worse, for his father and mother, for their hundred-year old, clapboard sided farmhouse with the south side's peeling porch that he should get at, for working in the yard and waving to every car and truck that went by and honked.

"Well," the boss said, "we're glad you came."

She pushed her chair back. Other chairs followed; a nice, symmetrical end to the meeting.

"I know something else about Harmon," the clerk interrupted.

"What's that?" the boss said, out of her chair and leaning toward the door.

"I shouldn't say," the clerk giggled. "But he's the birthday boy, like, tomorrow."

"Harmon!" the boss said. "Tomorrow's your birthday?"

He nodded. Tomorrow, Saturday, was his twenty-seventh birthday.

"Well," the boss said, "service anniversary and a birthday. This weekend Harmon, you be sure to celebrate!"

She got up but stopped and cocked her head, as if the occasion now required more. She tapped her pen on her forehead and said, "I probably shouldn't let the cat out of the bag but I'll say this much. Harmon, I'm pretty sure that your greatest opportunity lies just ahead."

Interview

bad start — lesson learned — word of the day — an offer

It didn't help that it started badly.

"Do you have any outfits that are … more conservative?" the tight-faced Human Resources women asked.

So much for first impressions. If Riley had followed her instincts, things would have turned worse and fast. But, in an admirable act of self control, she bridled her tongue, smiled deferentially and replied, "Is there an official dress code?"

"Just good taste," the Human Resources women said, her face unscrewing some with the self satisfaction that she had gotten off a good one.

Riley smiled sweetly enough, a respectful cheek-turner. The opportunity, she repeated to herself, The experience. Mantras purposefully planned ahead, in case of meeting up with just this type, an anthropoid ass-hole on a power trip that made her want to jump across the table, grab the jerk by the throat and squeeze until she induced temporary loss of consciousness. She had to control herself. Confrontation brought out the worst in her and if she thought she was being made a fool, her mother's lessons on toughness flashed back.

The most memorable lesson involved her favorite Barbie doll, the one with the cowgirl outfit. She had lost it in exchange for a trifle, a piece of cheap red ribbon, the trade with a neighborhood girl whom she wanted as a friend. *Un tonta*, her mother called Riley. *A fool*. "You eight years old now. Get that doll back tonight or you sorry." Riley went to the girl's building and buzzed her. No one answered so she waited on the stoop. An hour later the conniving girl finally emerged, carrying the doll, cuddling it and talking to it, pretending it was really hers. When the girl saw Riley she secured the doll between her arms and chest. "It's mine now," she said. "We traded." She was a big curly-headed kid, only a year older, but twice Riley's size. Single-minded Riley ignored the fair trade argument. Instead, she grabbed a fistful of the girl's long hair and, despite being kicked in her shins and lifted off her feet, shook and yanked until only one flailing hand held the doll and she snatched it away. The kidnaper ran back into her building, bawling. Riley slid the red ribbon into her mail box, along with a big clump of black hair she found on her sleeve, to complete a fair exchange. A half-hour later someone pounded on the apartment door, shaking the walls and rattling her mother's sacred knickknacks. None fell and Riley thanked God for that. "Who so loco?" her mother shouted, from the kitchen. Riley stretched to her tiptoes and looked through the peephole. A giant woman filled the hallway, her fat sweaty face distorted by anger and the eyehole, her fists on her hips, her sleeveless dress revealing biceps bigger than the wrestlers on television. Riley hid behind the couch. The pounding started again. Her unhappy mother came from the kitchen and opened the door. Riley could only make out her mother's side of the overlapping conversation but guessed the other side, the giant woman complaining of the brutish treatment of her daughter and demanding satisfaction. "Listen," her mother told the woman, "you brat hustle my girl. My Riley too soft." The women issued some kind of challenge and Riley's featherweight mother accepted and stepped out the door. Riley heard the thigh rubbing and stair creaking sounds of the big woman hurrying away and her mother's parting comment in Spanish, roughly translated to, "If you don't like it, come back and I'll stick your head in my toilet bowl." *Toilet,* a benevolent translation. The sharp bang of their door punctuated Riley's early lesson in toughness and the world's predatory ways.

She couldn't confront her interviewer. This was a different world. Funny thing was she had worn her most business-like outfit, a nice skirt, a white blouse, and her medium-heeled shoes. Maybe the skirt was a little tight. Successful women dressed conservatively and she wanted success. If things worked out she would shop. Her other clothes were okay for her short term temp assignments, but there was no future in that. Companies that relied on temps were more pick up artists than partners.

"This certainly is a beautiful campus," Riley said, changing the subject, making small talk, but with a purpose. The way she used the word campus showed she was up with corporate lingo. She had become a connoisseur of words. She had a journal where she recorded her favorites. The green, leather covered book was a gift from her mother and her most prized possession. Even with her tiny printing, it was half-full now. She wanted it to last forever.

"Yes," the Human Resources woman said. "We are proud of it."

AC&C was said to be a place where an impressive temporary could get hired permanently. After that, the sky was the limit. She was ready to give them her best, even willing to adapt. *Adaptation* — modification to fit a new use, new conditions. It was her word of the day, which meant she carried it with her on an index-card and must use it in some form in at least three sentences. Adaptation had been an earlier word of the day, but she chose to repeat it now for its timeliness. It was an important trait of achievers and a sign of maturity. There were limits. She wasn't going to dress like Ms. Mouse of Human Resources.

Little lady prim and proper took Riley's smiling countenance as capitulation. Satisfied, she uncurled her bumpy lips and threw a bone. "You did well on your practice test."

Riley enjoyed the surprise she heard in that. "Oh, thank you," she said, all shyness and appreciation.

She knew she did well. When determined, she always did well. The test consisted of typing, taking shorthand and telephone courtesy. To make it more real and test her interpersonal skills, they had her role-play with an ancient man who wore suspenders plus a belt and two squeaky hearing-aides, a retired executive who became so enamored of her that several times he forgot his role-play name. Taking care to save him embarrassment, Riley stared at his name tag and said, "Mr. Green, you are so astute." At the end of it all, against the rules and through strong coffee breath, Mr. Green whispered to Riley that he would give her the highest score and recommendation.

The HR lady went through some more paperwork, wetting her fingertips on a little orange sponge as she flipped the pages. She studied Riley's résumé and asked about her secretarial school certificate and two-year associate's degree. Riley told how she earned both after she discovered her love for learning, and, did it all while working nights. She didn't say she waitressed in a bar and a bowling alley because the lady seemed unduly interested in the *range* of her work experiences: temping for furniture sellers, auto renters and loan sharks, pawn brokers, fitness clubs and junk yards. They were dues paid, Riley said. She didn't mention how she sometimes wondered if anywhere in this whole wide world, was there a finance company, pawn shop, fitness club or junk yard not run by a sleaze ball.

The HR lady seemed to be stalling, tapping her fingers and playing with the reading glasses that hung around her neck, as if she had a hard choice to make and didn't know what to say next. Later, Riley found out AC&C was desperate for good administrative help. They had the worst time finding people who could follow simple instructions and string two logical sentences together. Finally, her interviewer said, "Well, I think we're going to offer you something. To try you. I'll call the agency this afternoon."

Riley had to contain herself. She was through sleaze balls. Soon she would deal with smart, educated people. Corporate people.

Birthday Boy

father — call from home — genius — man of steel

Harmon spent the rest of Friday imagining opportunities — some ridden to glory, some mishandled to humiliation. That evening he took care to bury this new worry deep in his bag so it couldn't escape and ruin his weekend. It didn't work.

Anxiousness woke him early Saturday, ruining the luxury of a day with no alarm clock. One pursued opportunity along a double-edged sword. Success and failure — you couldn't chase one without the possibility of catching the other. It took a certain amount of fearlessness to deal with that. Harmon admired the fearless people with a big appetite for challenges, people who seized opportunity whatever the odds and went straight at it. His father was such a person.

His father grew up in an orphanage near Buffalo, a child of the great depression. He never knew his own father. His total schooling amounted to four neglectful years. His was a youth of all work and no play. The orphan boys were lent out to local farmers to help pay for their keep. The overseers made sure they got their money's worth. His father told of mistakenly picking up the packed lunch of a farm family's natural son. The feast surprised him: ham sandwich, an apple, two sugar cookies. The lunch meant for him was always the same, two slices of bread spread with a thin glaze of dry and colorless welfare peanut butter. The farmer's son got the lunch intended for Harmon's dad and complained about it. Harmon's innocent father got a cuffing. Yet, seizing the slightest opportunity — a GI Bill sponsored course on auto mechanics following his Army service — his father became a success and had his family, land and house and owed no one a nickel. Stories of his father's unfortunate youth were still dear to Harmon. He thought of the mistaken lunch whenever he watched his father scrape out the remnants of a peanut butter jar, just as he thought of his father's deficient education whenever he saw him read by tracing each word with a fingertip.

Every Saturday he phoned his parents. He placed the call to save them the long distance charge. But today was his birthday and they would call him. They wanted it that way. He waited in his apartment's living-room, recumbent on his recliner, his lap full of paperwork, catching up on the week's memos and mail.

The phone rang at six p.m. sharp, just as he knew it would, his mother as dependable as a two cylinder John Deere tractor. The ringing echoed off the bare walls, just like his footfalls did when he walked on his hardwood floors. There was nothing in the living room except the chair, a floor lamp and a nineteen-inch television set propped on two phone books. In his monkish bedroom was a single bed, just the steel frame and mattress, no headboard or footboard, the bed complimented by an unfinished nightstand and alarm clock. Cardboard moving boxes still served as his dresser.

He answered before the second ring.

"Happy Birthday!"

"Thanks, Mom."

"How are you?"

"I'm good."

Harmon reminded himself to put optimism in his voice. The last thing he wanted was for his mother to worry.

"You're eating regular?"

"Yep."

"Taking some time off? Enjoying yourself?"

"Oh yeah, mom."

He was making up his life, but at least he wasn't as homesick as before. His first months at AC&C had been so bad that he comforted himself with a promise to spend no more than a year in New Jersey. In that crisis he fooled himself into thinking a year would be sufficient to make his father proud and accomplish something of note for his résumé. Get the training AC&C was rightly famous for, then find something close to home—that's what he told himself.

"Okay honey," his mother said. "Well, happy birthday again and here's your father."

He and his mother never talked much. It wasn't that they didn't have a lot between them. They just couldn't get started.

"Happy birthday son," his father said. "Twenty-seven and talented. How's it feel to have the world on a string?" Plenty of optimism in his voice.

"Thanks, Dad. How are you?"

"Good. A late one last night though. Three calls."

"You took all three?"

"Yeah."

"You shouldn't do that Dad. That's too much."

His father was on twenty-four hour call from their upstate New York farmhouse. His main territory was a stretch of State Thruway, west toward Syracuse and east toward Utica, a heavily trafficked truck route with lots of breakdowns.

"What time did you get done, Dad?"

"Late. So, how you doing? They make you Vice President yet?"

"Not yet."

"I see the stock is up but it looks like another round of layoffs."

His father kept a close watch on the business. Every Saturday morning he visited the local library where the librarian compiled the week's AC&C related articles for him. His father read closely and had a better understanding of the company's current problems than many of Harmon's colleagues.

"Yeah dad, more downsizing." At AC&C you didn't say layoffs. That was on the banned word list. In the Marketing Department you never said price increase—it was a *price adjustment.* "Probably bigger than the last round. Nobody's safe. Last week we had an all day meeting about that."

"Boy, you sure do a lot of meeting."

"We do."

His father had asked about that before, in amazement that smart, educated people spent so much time talking about what they *planned* to do.

Harmon thought about that, too, the popularity of meetings. He had a great interest in management science. He studied Peter Drucker's classic books, subscribed to two leading business magazines and faithfully read his complimentary AC&C copy of the Wall Street Journal. He had learned something about meetings—they were a way of avoiding decisions. Just gather a group of corporate staff types in the same room, add an influential boss to encourage posturing and presto, the simplest issue, something any sensible dairy farmer could decide in five minutes, grew into an all day meeting with B-School buzz words flying around like straw dust in a hay-barn—scenarios and synergies, exigencies and contingencies, impacts endogenous and exogenous—all resulting in pages of minutes, an expanding agenda, formation of a task force with representatives from ten different departments and a new schedule of meetings in perpetuity. Everything but a decision.

"When," his father asked, "do you expect the cuts to stop?"

"Never."

"Never?"

His father enjoyed the articles about business strategy and tactics, but not the ones about layoffs. Every story of thousands let go translated in his mind to some father unable to give his kid the best. That had always been his father's passion, to give his boy the best—from his orthopedic baby shoes to his Rawlings *Finest in the Field* baseball glove to his college education; to give his boy the best so he could be the best.

"What I mean dad, is that there's more to come. That's what all our analysis is about now, the up-front cost of downsizing versus the long term savings. It all comes down to cash flow. You know, when does the company break-even."

"You think it's all necessary?"

"It depends. It's complicated."

Harmon knew what the free market advocates said. It was a powerful argument, that the government's verdict to deregulate AC&C was well deserved and long overdue and that the American consumer had been too long saddled with high prices and low technology. Certainly truth in that and a strain that appealed to his intellect. But he was eyewitness to the consequences for long-time employees, those hired, nurtured and embedded in the former ACC's maternalistic culture of lifelong job security. For them, deregulation proved cruel and unusual punishment. Where a smile and cover-your-ass and go-with-the-flow had long reigned, survival of the fittest took hold, driven by competition, its invisible hand promising the best in products, but bringing out the worst in people. When the inevitable job cuts followed he heard defiant bravado, "It's probably the best thing that ever happened to me. For every door that closes another one opens. God never gives you more than you can handle." All from fifty year old managers with jumbo sized mortgages and kids heading to college, managers who needed a good salary and full benefits, but whose unmarketable skills revolved around making slides and attending meetings. Inevitably, fearful worry overwhelmed false bravado. He heard women and men crying in their cubicles. Sometimes he felt a gratuitous anger at the weak for their weakness; sometimes he felt he had more in common with them than the hard chargers. Ultimately, his heart was with the unfortunate and that made him question his own toughness and wonder if he really belonged.

"I keep seeing it in the paper," his father said. "They call it *rightsighting*. That's a new one on me. I never heard that before."

"I think, dad, that they meant rightsizing."

Fancy words tripped his father's tongue. He wasn't a mangler like Joe, but grammar and pronunciation weren't his strong suits. Once, when they were in line at a Ponderosa Steakhouse, his father looked up at the menu and, wanting the buffet, told the girl at the cash register, "I'll take the *buffit*." The girl giggled. Some kids in line did, too. The cash register attendant straightened her face and asked Harmon what he wanted. He wanted a steak and baked potato, had been thinking about a sixteen ounce T-Bone all day, but after due consideration and in a voice louder than necessary, he ordered the same as his father, the *buffit*.

"Rightsizing?" his father asked.

"It's about the cuts dad. About getting down to the right number."

"Why don't they just call it what it is then, you know, letting people go?"

"I don't know dad."

"Maybe they could make that a class, in the business schools. A course on saying what you mean."

Harmon laughed at the improbability of that. "Well dad, I guess it all comes down to the numbers."

"I guess so," his father said. Then his voice went lower, like it did when he thought of something insightful and apropos. "You know what I read once, son."

"What Dad?"

"That if you spend too much time counting numbers, soon only numbers count."

"That's good dad. Where'd you read that?"

"I can't remember, but it stuck with me. But you know, they're a lot smarter than me. I mean, that's why they're running the show. That head guy in charge, that Yates, from everything I read, he's really something. A genius they say. You know they're even talking about him running for president."

AC&C's public relations department had a whole staff for seeding newspapers and business magazines. Most of the articles about Preston P. Yates, the company's hard charging CEO, who had been chosen to lead it in its new competitive environment. The stories were meant to establish Yates's genius as the key factor in why AC&C would make it. The most amazing thing of all, the man's middle name was, literally — *Proffitt*. The journalists loved it. Most of them used the propaganda verbatim.

"But, what do I know?" his father asked.

"You know a lot dad."

His father knew what was most worth knowing and, pronunciation problems or not, Harmon had been proud of his father for as long as he could remember. In second grade, when Miss Inca taught her lesson on interconnectedness, she had each student make a drawing of what their parents did. Harmon's was unintentionally impressionistic, a stickman holding an oversized wrench. Next, his teacher had everyone stand and tell what their parents did. They went in alphabetical order. Most of the students were the children of farmers and after an eloquent girl spoke of feeding the hungry, that line was liberally repeated. Until Thomas Wilson spoke. "My father," Thomas said, "is a doctor. He saves people's lives. He's got plaques on his walls for that. He's got diplomas, lots of them. He's got his picture with the Governor, he's got—" Miss Inca interrupted with, "Thank you Thomas." Harmon wished he didn't come next, but Wolcott followed Wilson. He didn't stand until Miss Inca nodded to him. "My father," Harmon said, "is a truck mechanic." He sat right down. "That's wonderful," Miss Inca said. "We need mechanics. We need—" Thomas Wilson, eight years old, interrupted her with, "No way." He turned to Harmon. On the playground he would have said Wolcott's a lying liar, but in class he just stared hard and said, "Your daddy's no mechanic. Mechanics are made of steel." Harmon still smiled when he thought of that. He loved the image.

"Sounds like you're doing good though," his father said. "If you're the one doing the analysis, that means they got bigger things planned for you."

"Oh yeah," Harmon said. "I'm doing great. How are you feeling dad?"

"Son, it's summertime and you know what that means." His father laughed. "The living's easy."

His father's job was never easy and was too hard for a man pushing sixty, especially in Central New York's brutal winters. Every time Harmon saw a truck stranded alongside the road he thought of his father, just as he did when he smelled axle grease at a gas station, or read some homespun wisdom.

"You know," his father said, "people up here keep asking about you. They say, 'When is Harmon coming home for a visit?' Stanley at the coffee shop, old Bert at the feed store, Miss Harriman at the library. They say, 'We never see that boy anymore. Tell him we miss him.'"

"I know. I miss them, too. But it's tough, trying to get away."

"Do you figure to get back home anytime soon, maybe for a weekend? Before your vacation?"

"I don't know Dad. I hope." His vacation was two months away and he knew he wouldn't make it home before then. "I'm really swamped now."

"Well, keep your focus. That's what's important. Keep your eye on the ball."

"I will."

"You're mother wants to say goodbye."

"Harmon," his mother said, "I hope you're gonna enjoy your birthday?"

"Oh yeah, Mom. I'm going out tonight and tomorrow."

He spoke the literal truth. Right after their call he was going to the diner. Tomorrow, Sunday, he'd eat there again, right before a trip to the laundromat. During the week he made the cafeteria's lunch special his main meal, weekends and holidays he had the diner's early bird special, always alone and always at the same small corner table. In his apartment it was nothing more than shredded wheat and milk in a plastic bowl.

"Good," his mother said. "Have some fun."

"I will Mom."

But he wouldn't. Certain places affected his mood. He could feel it crawl over him, a sad broody spirit while eating at the diner accompanied only by his briefcase, or sitting in one of the laundromat's cheap molded plastic chairs, or at the movies by his lonesome on a Sunday morning. The laundromat, the small table at the diner, movies in cavernous theaters during the discount hours—resorts of the lonely. Something he had never imagined himself being.

"Bye, Harmon."

"Bye, mom."

"Oh, one other thing honey. Did your paper start yet?"

"I got the first batch yesterday. Thank you mom. That's a gift I'm really going to enjoy. Tell dad I said thanks, too."

For Harmon's birthday his mother bought him a subscription to the local newspaper, bunched and mailed off once a week to New Jersey. He enjoyed reading about the local happenings. Something as simple as a wedding notice with the groom not a doctor or the son of doctors, the bride not a professor or the daughter of professors, but rather the groom a *fuel attendant* and the bride a *part time nail technician*—that kind of thing could take him home again.

Riley at AC&C

hired — processing — Mrs. M — the past

She started on a drizzly Monday.

On her walk from the bus stop to Headquarters the rain pit-a-pattered her umbrella. The air smelled of rich, wet earth and the more stalwart birds were out and singing. A light mist came off the man-made pond. She arrived with a full hour to spare. No way would she be late on her first day. Her heart pit-a-pattered, too.

***

During a half-day orientation they took her picture, made her a name tag and had her complete a lot of paperwork. After lunch, she watched a heavy-handed film about behavior in the workplace, then met her boss who gave her a strictly business reception and assigned her a work station. She was part of a clerical pool supporting a group of marketing managers. Her duty: processing words, but first, she had to adjust her chair so her toes could touch the ground.

Her very first assignments revealed a kink in the process. It turned out the managers couldn't write a simple sentence. She read terrible things like: *Utilizing a proactive approach we will dynamically achieve positive differentiation through a multi-cultural marketing strategy that recognizes, embraces and leverages the diversity of our workforce and of our customers to maximize our market position and penetration.* Unable to live with that, even as the innocent processor, she suggested this: *Our customers have differing needs and we will adapt our products and services to meet them.* The author curtly thanked her for the suggestion. Then he suggested she stick to typing and, in case she cared to know, her effort demonstrated she didn't understand the sophistication of the AC&C enterprise and its market environment. Maybe, with time, that would come. He hoped so, for her sake.

But she was aboard. She had doubted it would ever happen, even after she got a letter of confirmation. Now, just walking the busy halls and seeing all the rushing, important people gave her a great sense of having arrived.

***

After that long first day she was tired, but a good tired. On the bus ride home, the sky cleared and everything looked fresh. Walking from her stop to her apartment, she imagined everyone watching her and knowing, just by her manner and dress, that she was a professional woman carrying important corporate material. Her bag was full of information on AC&C, its history, its marketplace and competitors. She requested it all, to show initiative.

When she passed her old apartment she imagined her mother once again hollering her home, first in English and then, if she stalled, in Spanish. Her *madre* wanted her girl home when the streetlights came on and no dilly-dallying. "No deely-dolling," as her mother said it. A full corporate day under her belt, she was busting to tell someone. She knew the right person. She stopped and looked up to an open second floor window and the silver-haired lady who commanded it.

"Hola, Mrs. M."

"Hola," Mrs. M said, turning away from monitoring the neighborhood's goings-on, squinting, having trouble locating Riley. Better focused she said, "Hello honey."

"Hi," Riley said.

Mrs. M and Riley's mother had been long time neighbors and best friends. They had each other's back, when that wasn't easy and when it wasn't just phony street talk. Mrs. M had known Riley's father. Knew him *too much*, she said. In that, she was one up on Riley who didn't know him enough.

"How you doin' sweetheart?" Mrs. M's Spanish accent was no fainter than twenty years ago, most every *i* squeezed into an *e*, but her voice was rough and gravelly now.

"I'm fine," Riley said.

"You want to come in, honey?"

"Thank you, Mrs. M, but I can't."

Riley looked down the street, to signal she had things to do at home. She knew how much Mrs. M enjoyed their talks, but she didn't dare go inside, not if she was to get home with time to study her materials and then take a long triumphal soak in a bubble bath with a scented candle and soft music.

"Ay me Dios!" Mrs. M said. "Such a pretty girl."

One of Riley's earliest memories was of Mrs. M bouncing her on her knee, playfully counting the faint row of freckles that crossed her nose, telling her what a pretty girl she was. As a young girl, Riley thought herself uniquely homely. By her late teens, after a miraculous transformation, she got a lot of compliments on her looks. Mrs. M once told her that Spanish and Irish was a bad mix. *Mal, mal. No natural.* But she said Riley was lucky. She came out perfect. Not joking when she said it.

"Honey," Mrs. M asked, "how is the jobs goin'?"

Despite being shut-in and losing her eyesight and hearing, she always knew what mattered most to the people she cared about. Mrs. M had myopic eyes but a 20/20 heart.

"Good," Riley said.

"What?"

"I'm doing pretty good," Riley said louder. "I had a big day today."

"How come honey?"

Riley stepped closer, directly under Mrs. M's window, so that without shouting she could speak above the neighbor's squeaking fan.

"I started at AC&C." She had delayed the news until now, believing a premature announcement might jinx it.

"ACC," Mrs. M said, her voice rising with wonderment. "Now you really somethin'! What a big place, huh?"

"It sure is."

"You know somethin'?" Mrs. M asked.

"What's that?"

"The only other people I know that work there, they clean the baños."

"Well," Riley said, "I'm only a temporary. For now at least."

"I know you do good. The way you go after things."

"I hope so. I really want to."

"I so proud of you," Mrs. M said. "So smart. College. Success woman now."

"It's not so big a deal," Riley said.

"Oh it is," Mrs. M said. "Such nice clothes. I just wish you madre could see. Oh! ¡Madre Maria! Would she be proud."

Like an arrow through Riley's heart. She changed the subject. "Mrs. M, how are you doing?"

"Mas o menos. Cannot complain."

No complaints from a woman confined in a hot, stuffy, four-hundred square foot apartment, in unremitting pain from rheumatoid arthritis and dependent on an aluminum walker, her eyesight failing from macular degeneration, her stomach and funds eaten away by her medicines. None of it going to get better. But she was *tough*. Simple as it was, Riley liked that word, its guttural single syllable sounded like what it meant. Tough had lots of definitions. Her favorite: substantially made or constructed. That fit Mrs. M.

"You with anyone sweetheart?"

Mrs. M's favorite question. Never far away and always sure to come. Part of the price of her friendship.

"No one special," Riley said.

No one at all more like it. Lots of reasons but none that would impress Mrs. M.

"You must meet nice boys?"

Riley smiled. In the question equal parts concern and exasperation. Mrs. M had strong feelings about how a young woman should live. But the world was different now. Her mother and Mrs. M had no options. It made her shudder when she thought that, just a generation earlier, her life would have been like theirs. But she was rich with options. She didn't need anyone.

"The good ones," Mrs. M said, "take no advantage."

There it was, allusion to the unmentionable, Riley's teenage pregnancy. Her past. Just in time, the tinny whistle of a tea kettle came from behind Mrs. M.

"Your kettle," Riley said. "It's boiling."

"Oh my. One *minuto*, honey. Don't go now."

Mrs. M turned and was gone, the thumping of her walker echoing out the window. Riley felt odd standing there all alone and seemingly without purpose. She rubbed the building's brownstone front, as if touching an old friend. She would steer Mrs. M to another topic. Not that it would change the past.

She got pregnant at seventeen. That's when she quit school for real. She wasn't going to duck waddle through her high school's halls like so many other girls, knocked-up and proud of it. "Now," her mother had said, "you end up like this. That happen when you *estupido* and no shamed." What a fight they had. Her mother's harshness fired by the mixture of great love and great disappointment. "So you pay a price alone. That boy, he even less ready than you for such a thing. He like the makin' only. And now he gone." Gone he was. Just disappeared. Somebody said he joined the Army. Riley couldn't help but think about her father, how the boy and he were peas in a pod. Disappearing peas like the ones the street hustlers used in their shell games. She never mentioned that to her mother. Some things weren't worth it, even to win an argument. The boy abandoned her but her mother didn't. *Familia*, her mother said, "for best or worst." When it came to her mother, Riley never doubted that. But it didn't mean anything goes. "Know one something," her mother said. "For sure you not to be *un Parásito. Mi nieto* to have a strong *madre*." Her black eyes shone brightly when she said it.

"Okay," Mrs. M said, back with her tea. She took a sip. "¡*Maldita sea!*"

"What's wrong?" Riley asked.

"I forgot *mi* sugar. I'm sorry honey. You know how I love *mi* sugar."

"Don't worry," Riley said. "Take your time."

Mrs. M went back into her kitchen.

Four months into her pregnancy, Riley miscarried. "No medical reason that I can see," the doctor said. "These things happen a lot more than most people realize." The doctor wasn't broken hearted. Riley could tell he thought the miscarriage a good thing, or at least not a bad thing, the gods-of-order, or whatever, looking out for society. Or maybe he thought he was God. Riley's confused heart didn't want a baby, but didn't want to lose *her* baby. She had a premonition that someday, losing her baby would feel a lot worse than it did now. She asked the doctor for a favor; tell her mother that the miscarriage wasn't her fault.

The doctor had known her mother forever and he stopped at their apartment. Her mother said she already knew it wasn't Riley's fault, didn't need to hear a doctor say so, and for sure, he should know this was a no pay-for visit. The doctor turned to Riley and asked, "Now what are you going to do with yourself?" He was a nosy, busybody who preached health but stunk of the Camel cigarettes he sucked on in his little alleyway. But it was a good question and he did more than ask it, he gave good advice. He steered Riley to a local neighborhood association and a GED program. She earned a GED and, to her own amazement, found she loved learning, devoid of the high school bullshit. It was the genesis of a new Riley. She especially loved her studying time, just her and her books at the makeshift desk in the corner of her tiny bedroom, her work illuminated by the goose-necked lamp her mother bought her. Her mother would serve her tea and ask if, after four hours, shouldn't she take a break.

"Mamá," Riley said, I want to learn."

"Okay," her mamá said, smiling for seeing something special in her girl. "You want that. You go for that."

She did.

"I'm slow as *melaza* now," Mrs. M said, back again with he[r] sweetened tea. "If I was a donkey, they shoot me. You wanna come in f[o] something sweetheart?"

"I'm fine," Riley said.

"But you look so skinny. What you weigh?"

"I'm good," Riley said.

She weighed one-hundred and fourteen pounds, but she was [s] just five-feet one and a half.

"You such a beautiful girl. But you got to eat."

Mrs. M said that as if Riley were wasting away and it was a[s] she was powerless to fix it; that maybe it was her duty to ta[ke] captive and stuff her with rice and red beans and sweet yucca[.]

"Mrs. M, is there anything you need?" Riley asked. "Somet[hing] do for you? Something I can pick up?"

"Oh, no. Not a thing. What you do is to take care of you self. Get something on them bones."

"Okay," Riley said.

"And," Mrs. M said, "meet a nice boy. Maybe at that ACC. They must have nice boys there, even for a big shot business lady like you."

r

hort,

shame
e Riley

hing I can

PART II

Four months into her pregnancy, Riley miscarried. "No medical reason that I can see," the doctor said. "These things happen a lot more than most people realize." The doctor wasn't broken hearted. Riley could tell he thought the miscarriage a good thing, or at least not a bad thing, the gods-of-order, or whatever, looking out for society. Or maybe he thought he was God. Riley's confused heart didn't want a baby, but didn't want to lose *her* baby. She had a premonition that someday, losing her baby would feel a lot worse than it did now. She asked the doctor for a favor; tell her mother that the miscarriage wasn't her fault.

The doctor had known her mother forever and he stopped at their apartment. Her mother said she already knew it wasn't Riley's fault, didn't need to hear a doctor say so, and for sure, he should know this was a no pay-for visit. The doctor turned to Riley and asked, "Now what are you going to do with yourself?" He was a nosy, busybody who preached health but stunk of the Camel cigarettes he sucked on in his little alleyway. But it was a good question and he did more than ask it, he gave good advice. He steered Riley to a local neighborhood association and a GED program. She earned a GED and, to her own amazement, found she loved learning, devoid of the high school bullshit. It was the genesis of a new Riley. She especially loved her studying time, just her and her books at the makeshift desk in the corner of her tiny bedroom, her work illuminated by the goose-necked lamp her mother bought her. Her mother would serve her tea and ask if, after four hours, shouldn't she take a break.

"Mamá," Riley said, I want to learn."

"Okay," her mamá said, smiling for seeing something special in her girl. "You want that. You go for that."

She did.

"I'm slow as *melaza* now," Mrs. M said, back again with her sweetened tea. "If I was a donkey, they shoot me. You wanna come in for something sweetheart?"

"I'm fine," Riley said.

"But you look so skinny. What you weigh?"

"I'm good," Riley said.

She weighed one-hundred and fourteen pounds, but she was short, just five-feet one and a half.

"You such a beautiful girl. But you got to eat."

Mrs. M said that as if Riley were wasting away and it was a shame she was powerless to fix it; that maybe it was her duty to take Riley captive and stuff her with rice and red beans and sweet yucca.

"Mrs. M, is there anything you need?" Riley asked. "Something I can do for you? Something I can pick up?"

"Oh, no. Not a thing. What you do is to take care of you self. Get something on them bones."

"Okay," Riley said.

"And," Mrs. M said, "meet a nice boy. Maybe at that ACC. They must have nice boys there, even for a big shot business lady like you."

PART II

Opportunity Calling

a summons — dreamer — bliss — reality

The laundromat felt like a sweat room. It had taken until the middle of August, but New Jersey's true summer weather finally descended — a clammy blanket of heat and haze and humidity. Harmon stood outside, but never wandered so far that he couldn't keep an eye on his two loads, through both the washing and drying.

When he returned to his apartment, loneliness greeted him. Loneliness was his private doorman. He tried to keep his thoughts on his vacation, just three weeks away. He would ride along with his father on a road call, playing the helper's part like old times. He would take his mother out to lunch at the hotel, just the two of them so he could treat her to whatever she wanted and a glass of wine, not worrying her about the cost the way his father always did. He would take long walks through the back fields, enjoying Upstate New York's early fall, scaring up rabbits and pheasants, descendants of those he scared up as a boy.

In his bedroom, he found a blinking answering machine. Before he could relieve his curiosity he had to free his hands: in one a fifty gallon plastic trash bag stuffed with t-shirts, underwear, socks, sheets, pillow cases and bath towels; in the other, nine wire hangers and his full complement of dress shirts, six white, two blue and one pink, all removed from the dryer while still damp to prevent wrinkling. He didn't own an iron and he needed one more shirt to accommodate his two-week laundry cycle. For now, he wore a blue shirt twice. He dropped the bag on his bed, hung the shirts in his closet and hit the message button.

Sunday, seven-o-six p.m., the machine's automatous voice said. Then a woman's voice, high-pitched and demanding, *Mr. Yates requires your attendance at the Monday morning meeting of the Leadership Team. The meeting will be held in the CEO's large conference room, directly opposite his office. The meeting will start at seven a.m. sharp. Clear your schedule for the entire morning. Don't be late.*

His breathing stopped, like when his strongman uncle had snuck up from behind and bear-hugged him when he was a kid. The message was clear about who, what, when and where, but not why. Was it a practical joke perpetrated by one of his colleagues, one of the more sadistic ones? An out of the blue summons to a Leadership Team meeting was enough to panic any manager and Harmon presented an easy target. He had a reputation for taking things too seriously. He could picture the guys loafing in the cafeteria, enjoying coffee and their crude imaginings of his terror.

He played the message a second and third time, his ear closer and closer to the answering machine, listening with microscopic concentration. The voice sounded familiar, the biting tone of Mr. Yates's Executive Assistant. He wondered, could this be the big opportunity his boss had mentioned, coming his way two months later? At AC&C one never knew. His nervous excitement stuck and grew.

The Leadership Team was a select group of managers chosen to implement the CEO's great change initiative, a group at the white-hot center of the company's current turmoil. Why would a lowly staff manager be commanded to attend? What could he contribute? How did Mr. Yates or his Executive Assistant even know Harmon Wolcott existed?

***

Later he discovered the circumstances. His boss's boss, the department's designated representative, wasn't available. He had sliced off his left thumb, clean at the knuckle, while trimming hedges. No doubt, his mind was not on his task, probably absorbed in trimming his department's budget instead of his yard's hedgerow. His boss wasn't available either. She was in Manhattan attending a three day workshop: *Arabophobia In The Workplace*. Diversity training was the only AC&C obligation sacred enough to excuse one from a Leadership Team meeting. Most gratifying, his boss had endorsed him as a capable fill in. Her endorsement, along with all his digits being intact and his having completed this year's diversity training, made him next in line.

***

The anticipation of the meeting, only twelve hours away, led to a restless, alarm-clock watching, dream charged night. The most evocative dream was a trip back to the best time of his boyhood, when any call after 8 p.m. meant a truck breakdown, a rescue mission and adventure.

In his dream it was a freezing winter night, the sheriff forbidding all but essential travel. The wind was blowing so hard that the old house's windows rattled in their sashes and the snow swept across the north field and filled the yard. Not unlike a real Central New York winter's night, except the fanciful snow fell in flakes the size of Frisbees and so hard it soon covered the barn. The phone rang and his father didn't answer, just said, "Let's go." Dream or reality, Harmon knew what to do. Like a ready fireman he had his outfit laid out in the spare bedroom: heavy wool socks, cotton pajama bottoms for a layer under his jeans, and two sweatshirts for under his hooded jacket. He kept the socks attached to the pajamas so he could slide into both in one movement. In the unheated hallway, his boots shook themselves awake and marched forward with their buckles jangling, like magical toy soldiers come alive in a kid's movie. Then he and his father were in the truck and driving along the pitch-black, two-lane Thruway where their world shrunk to a few feet of snow filled headlight beams. The fields to either side were an impenetrably black wasteland inhabited by unseen but surely horrific monsters of the type that could survive in such a place. The truck's heater was as bad as in real life and his breath hung in the cab so thick that he formed it into blocks that he arranged with his fingers. It was he and his father against whatever nature and the supernatural could throw against them. Instead of a disabled tractor and trailer, their headlights found a stranded ship with two tall masts and listing thirty degrees. He had recently read an illustrated book on the lost Franklin Expedition and the ship resembled *HMS Terror*, enough to transform him and his father into intrepid rescuers and the truck's driver into a lost arctic explorer. Then the dream ship transformed and had a hood and diesel engine. On real repair missions, his role had been carrying the old canvas bag that held flashlights and flares, plus a wool army blanket and the thinner gloves his father wore for handling tools. Under the hood he held the trouble light and handed his father the right sized wrenches. In dreamland his father worked in a surgical mask and wore white latex gloves, so strange because his father always wanted tools put into his palm with a firm slap, just like a surgeon. His father was the best at getting a truck started, but the ship, truck, wouldn't start until Harmon spotted a loose wire and reattached it.

After he woke, for a few blissful moments, the deep rumbling of the diesel engine stayed with him, as did the satisfaction of his indispensable role in its starting. Then, the reality of his coming meeting hit him.

A Different World

advancement — big shooters — carpetland — gossip

In just seven weeks, Riley advanced from word processor to administrative assistant. There was a shortage of administrative assistants. The job required thinking and initiative. Her word processing supervisor paid her a complement. She said Riley, with her intelligence and energy, was under-utilized. On her new job she did light typing and a range of other administrative duties; a nice change from being tied to a monitor and keyboard. She felt the satisfaction of her hard earned credentials and experience paying off.

***

Her energy made her stand out among the sluggish support staff like a compulsive in Sleepy Hollow. While the long tenured assistants insisted on following every bureaucratically prescribed step, and did so in flamboyantly slow motion, Riley served her clients' ends without undo worry about the means. Normally, something as simple as ordering a ream of paper took several days, but she made regular raids on the supply room, always during the storekeeper's extended lunch hour when the shelves sat unguarded and she could snap up two of whatever her people needed. Managers began fighting over her services and when word spread of a go-getter among the assistants, she got drafted to support the Executive Leadership Team. She was too good to waste on cubicle dwellers.

"We'll start you processing vouchers and making travel and meeting arrangements," the supervisor of executive secretaries said. "We'll see how you handle that."

She handled it well. She took care to check the travel itineraries, making sure they were efficient and comfortable. She shunned intra-company mail and personally delivered the tickets and trip information, always with a smile that, if reciprocated, she followed with questions about the traveler's destination. Geography was a branch of knowledge she needed to brush-up on. How she'd love to attend a conference in Acapulco, Boca Raton or San Diego with the company paying for everything. She'd skip the parties and go exploring. Sometimes she ran to the cafeteria or the on-site dry cleaner or shoemaker — a glorified errand girl in the service of the executives. But every job has its dignity denting parts. Before long, if a regular secretary was on vacation or sick, she was the first choice to fill in.

She called the executives the *big shooters*. She called executive row *carpetland*, because once through the big doors the first thing you noticed was the thicker and softer carpeting. Executive row was unnaturally quiet. With its wood paneled walls and whispering secretaries, it reminded her of a funeral parlor. Leaving the regular office area and entering through the glass doors was like walking off a noisy street and into a library. There was something about the high-strung atmosphere that made the work and the executives seem important. Maybe the big shooters were smart enough to design it that way.

Despite the aura of propriety, the executives didn't mind that some of her outfits were less than businesslike. There was one red skirt which even she thought revealed too much. But, the thinness of her wardrobe and the fact she liked to tweak straitlaced sensibilities made her bring it out of the closet. On red skirt days the executive need for her shorthand services exploded and she went home with writer's cramp and the *big shooters* with eyestrain.

The big shooters were fussy. They were pampered princes of indulgence with a host of idiosyncratic preferences to remember. Mr. P liked his coffee thinned with hot water, one-fifth hot water; remember that—*one-fifth*. Mr. J worried a lot about germs, don't ever touch his phone or put your hands near the rim of his cup. Mr. K only used pencils made of cedar, incense cedar from California, No. 2 soft. The soft lead requirement conjured a joke but she repressed it. Everything must be proper on Executive Row. All correspondence was classified with an ink stamp. An elaborate set of stamps to choose from, escalating from *Proprietary* to *Private and Confidential*. Riley read everything that appeared interesting and the stricter the stamp the more things appeared interesting. Not much of real interest, though, and she came to believe that all the secrecy just hid the banality of the bosses work and protected their big salaries.

There were things that required secrecy: behavioral matters, executive behavior. Things that the company's code-of-conduct couldn't control, even if it had been developed by a Ph.D. consultant at a six figure cost, featured active verbs and got distributed to every employee on laminated cards. Riley discovered this when the big shooters all attended a top secret, two day strategy seminar.

Only the supervising secretary attended, due to the extreme confidentiality of the seminar's subject matter, something about changing the AC&C culture. Back at the office, with no big shooters and no boss, the working secretaries enjoyed the rare opportunity to talk among themselves without worrying about who listened. Newcomer Riley kept busy at her desk, organizing files, pretending the talk didn't interest her.

Most of the dirt was not a surprise, clichés of young and affluent males behaving badly; cliché's, but the living truth. Things like the need to instantly distinguish between the telephone voices of a wife and a girlfriend, and in the harder cases between the wife and ex wives, girlfriends and ex girlfriends.

"Don't mess that up honey," Mr. K's secretary said to Riley, trying to include her. "Mess up anything else, but not that."

"Tell her about Mr. K," another secretary said.

"What can I say? He's just the worst."

"I don't know what he's got. Maybe he's—"

"What he's got is no secret."

"What?"

"Money! You know what he's pulling down here?"

Riley certainly wondered.

The salaries of the regular managers were no secret. Their *suggested* contributions for the annual United Way drive were based on a percentage of their salary and the clerk who canvassed had a complete list. Only if pledges fell short of one-hundred percent compliance did the drive's chairperson get involved. Eventually, every management employee contributed the suggested amount. When necessary, the collection methods were about as subtle as a leg breaking. However, top management salaries were another matter and a tightly guarded secret.

"How's a million plus bonuses sound?"

"No! For Mr. K?"

"Yes."

That was a surprise. Riley knew the big shooters did well, but not that well. She stayed quiet.

"A million? For what? I mean, the man's an idiot."

"He's not an atom-smasher. I'll give you that. But he is a good bullshit artist."

"But a million? For bullshitting? God!" Now the enquiring minded secretary sounded as if she wished she hadn't asked. "I mean, he couldn't run a lemonade stand."

"Listen honey, you don't know the half of it. I mean his perks. You know a limo picks him up and takes him home every day?"

"Maybe they're afraid he'd get lost."

"Yeah. And he's got a personal financial adviser, paid for by the company. And a personal trainer, even though he's still got that little pot. When he moved here, into that mansion he bought out in the hills, the company paid the difference between that and his old place."

"No."

"Yep, and he's always getting bonuses. I know because I have to explain them to him. 'What's this for?' he asks, like I'm supposed to know. Some of those bonus checks, they're for more than we make in a year. I mean all of us, together. I mean you'd like to have just what his country club membership costs. They all got that, that stupid country club. Imagine what goes on there! And the expense accounts. Don't get me started. Please. I don't think they ever pay for a meal or a drink."

"And we have to pay for our lousy coffee club."

A brief lull but Riley wasn't worried. A spirit of iconoclasm had taken hold and there would be more.

"I'll tell you this," Mr. K's secretary said, looking up from her nails, "him and the wife know how to spend, financial advisor or not. Trust me, that they got in common. That's why she sticks with him. I'd like to have just what she spends on clothes." She held up her left hand and wiggled her fingers. "And here."

Riley didn't care how much the jerk made, not for all the money in the world would she ....

"She's got that new car, too, right?"

"Oh yeah, the Mercedes. Everything's heated, the seats and mirrors. Just like his. One time, when I rode to a meeting with him, it was winter and he had that seat warmer thingy on; I thought I was having hot flashes."

The secretary quoted Mrs. K, in her voice and manner a practiced parody of spoiled fussiness. "Well, I don't know. I guess I just got a little tired of the BMWs. You know, sometimes change is good."

"Tell about all the work Mrs. K gets done."

"On the house?"

"No! Not on the house. Who cares about the house. You know, on herself."

"Look, I shouldn't talk about that. I mean, we could all use a little."

"But she's had a lot. Right?"

"Huh, huh. And I know, nip-by-nip and tuck-by-tuck, because I do all the bills and insurance forms."

"You do?"

"I always have. Listen, when you support him it's part of the job."

"You're kidding."

"I'm not kidding." The secretary looked to her file cabinet, where the proof existed.

"You think the wife's gonna do it? Or him? I mean, Mr. K with a calculator? That would be dangerous. He might hurt himself."

"So spill it. What's she had done?"

"I shouldn't—"

"Come on! You can't tease us like that!"

"Well, let's see. What can I tell about?"

"Just go alphabetically."

"Well, she's had the Blepharosy, ugh, the Blepho, Bletho-something. Blepharoplasty…. Maybe I'm not saying it right, but it's close."

"Blephasrsy? What's that?"

"For under the eyes. The bags under her eyes. She got them sucked away. She had it done twice. She didn't like the first job. They didn't suck out enough."

"No! She can't be, what, twenty-eight?"

"She's thirty. But it's not just her. He had it done, too."

"What? The bag sucking thing?"

"Yeah. And he didn't even need it. I mean I told him it looked great, but I couldn't even tell the difference. He turns and says, 'You got to look from the side.' Like he's a movie star or something, you know, like he's got a profile."

"Maybe they got a deal. A two sucks for one thing."

Riley coughed into her hands, to disguise a laugh.

"I didn't know she was thirty."

"Oh, yeah. You know what happened when she turned thirty?"

"What?"

"Oh my, what a day that was! Mr. K planned the day off but had to come in for a critical meeting. What drama. He left her alone on such a traumatic day! The black pearls made up for it, though. She got them the next weekend, in Key West. Thirty-thousand."

"No!"

"Oh, yeah, swiped on the Amex. And the orchids, some kind that only grow in Hawaii. Flown in for her, fresh."

"From Hawaii?"

"Oh, yeah. She just *loves* that kind of orchid. You know she's already had a face lift?"

"No?"

"Yep. Three years ago. A good job, too, but if you look close, right behind her ears, there's this scar, a teensy-weensy pink one. She doesn't cover it up. Probably doesn't even know it's there."

"But you spotted it."

"I did."

"He hasn't had one, has he? I mean a face lift?"

"Not that I know of."

"And you would know."

"I would. But, like I said, he's no slouch. He uses that new stuff to grow hair. He rubs it on his little bald spot. I walked in on that once." The secretary rubbed the crown of her own head to show how Mr. K did it. "And his vitamins and minerals—by the handful. I'm surprised he can keep them all straight. Oh, and his moisturizer. He's putting it on his face all day long. He's afraid of wrinkles."

"What a couple."

"Yeah. Then there's what she did, after the last brat, but no, I *really* can't tell that."

"Oh my God! Something better? You got to tell."

Riley, thinking the same, you've got to tell.

"Well, I couldn't believe it myself."

Mr. K's secretary started giggling, unable to get out what she wanted to say.

"Come on girl!"

"Well. Oh my! I shouldn't have started this," tears now, from laughing, carrying black eye makeup onto her cheeks.

"I think I'm gonna pee myself!"

"Come on honey! Get control."

A tissue provided, only the best, the most absorbent and softest, kept in real oak dispensers on each secretary's desk.

"Oh my. Okay now. What she had was a, a, oh my—"

"Yes?"

The secretary gathered herself, as if preparing to blow out birthday candles. Then, during a pause in her laughing, before it could start again, she got it out. "A Vaginoplasty."

"A what?"

Getting the word out calmed her and she could go on.

"A Vaginoplasty. And I know I'm saying it right because I paid attention and looked it up. A Vagin-o-plasty."

"Oh my God!" one of the other secretaries said. "You mean a love-knot."

"A what?"

"See," Mr. K's secretary said, her full composure and professional voice back for the detail telling, "if a woman wants to tighten up, after having kids, especially after the last one, she can have this procedure done. As I understand it, they just tighten up the muscles. Stitch them up, I guess."

Riley slid further behind her desk and crossed her legs.

"She did that?"

"Yes."

"For him?"

"I guess for him. I mean, yeah, for him. I'm sure, for him."

"Oh my god. Here's what I don't get. After all that he still has the girlfriends?"

"These guys are different. They say it's really about something other than sex. Power, I think. Anyway, that's what the headshrinkers say. It's about power."

That night Riley fell asleep questioning if she were as worldly as she thought. Maybe not. Or maybe she was from a different world.

Monday Morning

a chance — wonders — insignificant

He drove under the big green and white road sign and reclaimed his worry bag. The official start to his day, but his mind had been in full churn before that; dominating his thoughts, the Leadership Team meeting.

The meeting required a lot of thought. It was a chance to shine and, if presented with the opportunity, he would love to make a positive impression. What was it his father always said? *If you don't help yourself, the only helping hand you'll get is when they lower you in the grave.* The stakes were infinitely higher if Mr. Yates actually chaired the meeting. A manager could go a whole career without exposure to such power. One good impression could work wonders. Get your name positively lodged in the CEO's memory and you never knew when it might match an opportunity. The CEO was the ultimate opportunity broker. On the other hand, one bad impression would likely be the only thing Yates would ever know about you and enough to ensure your being forever passed over, or worse. There were plenty of stories of miserable outcasts, unfortunates who rubbed the CEO the wrong way and were now long gone from AC&C or serving as Installation/Repair supervisors in urban New Jersey, posts where they parked their cars behind barbed wire fences and technicians carried walkie-talkies in case of life threatening assaults. Maybe that's why, as he exited the highway and turned onto the headquarters entrance road, he longed again for the close capsulated quarters of his father's truck, where even in the middle of a raging blizzard and surrounded by shadowy monsters, nothing could harm him.

Even with such big things on his mind and after many such arrivals, the magnificence of the sprawling complex still impressed him. Designed by a famous architect at the height of AC&C's monopoly power, when grandeur mattered and cost didn't, the pagoda shaped buildings stood like mysterious temples. Driving up to them was like entering a forbidden city.

His father never got tired of hearing about headquarter wonders. The buildings held over a million square feet of office space and all the amenities befitting the world's largest corporation. The first floor featured a cafeteria, credit union, dry cleaning service, barber and shoemaker shops, a gift and sundry store and a movie rental kiosk. Two nurses and a doctor staffed a state of the art medical suite. Floors two, three and four were regular office space, but the fifth floor was reserved for the top executives. Their offices had private balconies, an adjacent health club and boardroom which had been featured in movies about wealth and power. To avoid mingling with commoners, they had their own separate stairway to the executive dining area. Underneath it all was parking for a thousand cars. For those too important to drive themselves, chauffeurs were lodged in private quarters adjacent to the complex. The CEO could commute to Manhattan and back without anyone driving, he had a private helicopter. Quite a headquarters, indeed.

***

He parked beneath building one, in his regular spot. To park in an unfamiliar spot, on a day like today, that would test fate too much. He sat in his truck for a few minutes and put on his business persona. It felt like part of him now. He thought if you pretended something enough, it became part of you.

He skipped the elevator for the stairway. Climbing stairs was a good tension reliever and he needed relief. A fast climber, he was on the fifth floor in a minute. There was no one else around. It was 6:28 a.m. He caught his breath and silently, self-consciously, walked through executive row, past the wood paneled walls that suited the low light and dignified quiet, past the secretaries' unnaturally neat desks and the offices they guarded. The cloud-like soft carpeting brought back Joe's description of the fifth floor and the ethereal function of its occupants — *the place where the rubber meets the sky*.

The motion sensitive lights came on when he entered the CEO's conference room. A magnificent room with ergonomically perfect chairs arranged precisely around a highly polished wood table. In the middle of the table a black console with buttons and gadgetry for controlling audio and video equipment, at each place, a leather notepad branded with the AC&C logo. He remained standing, moving one of the chairs out and sitting down seemed like too much of a presumption. He lifted one of the notepads and held it to his nose. He loved the smell of genuine leather. If the pads were to keep, he would send his to his father.

He set his briefcase at the table's far end and looked down the long, shiny surface to the CEO's place; Mr. Preston P. Yates's place. Hard to believe the man would sit right there. He was excited for the opportunity to observe the CEO up-close, but also comforted that there would be a table full of senior managers between them — like studying an exotic but dangerous creature from a hunter's blind.

Mr. Yates's chair was different, bigger and plusher and covered in tan leather. The other chairs were made of black, space-age material. Maybe they were more ergonomic but, next to the CEO's, they looked small and insignificant. The way he felt.

Harmon and Riley

they meet—whiff of possibility

As usual, Riley was the first secretary in the office. Something unusual, though, the lights were already on in the CEO's conference room. She wondered if it might be Yates himself. He was known to get in as early as six. He was a hard worker.

Fearless, she snuck up and poked her head in. A young man stood there. He looked befuddled.

"You're either lost or early," she said.

Harmon Wolcott jumped.

"Yikes," Riley said, jumping at his jumping.

"Sorry," Harmon said.

"I'm sorry," Riley said and stepped into the room. "That I scared you."

"It's okay," Harmon said. "I'm not scared."

"You're wound pretty tight, though."

"I guess I am, you know, a little nervous."

"And a little early."

Harmon looked to the wall clock and nodded.

"Why?" Riley asked.

"Why?"

"So early and so nervous?"

"I was called to meet with the Leadership Team."

"Oh my! Called to the Leadership Team."

Iconoclasm in her voice. No shared reverence for the Leadership Team. That surprised Harmon, especially here on the fifth floor.

In her first weeks at AC&C, full of a sense of adventure and the desire to succeed, Riley had repressed her natural inclination for iconoclasm. Inevitably, as her perfectionism ran headlong into the many and manifest imperfections of a huge bureaucracy, the gloves came off. Her mental health demanded it; the place demanded it. She still tried to control it, as her mama would have wanted—to bottle it up when it was inappropriate—like now with a stressed-out young man who appeared innocent.

"I haven't seen you here before," she said. "And I know them all because I'm their designated runner."

"Their what?"

"Runner. I run for the supplies and the drinks and the sandwiches. If the omniscient and omnipotent, but very sedentary, Leadership Team needs something, I run for it."

"Oh," Harmon said, surprised at the burst of vocabulary. "Well, I'm Harmon. Harmon Wolcott. I haven't been here before. I mean at the Leadership Team. I've never even been on the fifth floor."

"Well you're not missing much, at least not as much as you think. But anyhow, I'm Riley. Riley O'Brian. You want a coffee? I'm about to make some."

"No thanks."

"How about a tea? You look like you need something and you look like a hot tea drinker."

"Tea would be great. Thank you."

"I'll be back. You try to relax. Trust me, there's nothing about this crew that deserves you being nervous. Maybe early, but not nervous."

"I just want to do my best," Harmon said.

He watched her walk away. She's really something was his first impression. She was small but intense. She had unusually colored hair, sort of a copper, and bright eyes that challenged you right away and were alert to everything. He wished he had her skin tone, like a permanent tan. He never liked his own pale color. All his farm work required a broad-brimmed hat and long sleeved shirt. His father wasn't as fair but had already had skin cancer removed from his ear and forehead.

Whoa, Riley thought, in the executive kitchen. This boy is serious. Something about him though, something she liked. *I just want to do my best.* His sincerity made her want to help. She was a sucker for sincerity. She didn't sense it very often. A whiff of possibility about him.

She dug through the cabinets, searching for tea bags. She liked his looks. His skin was so fair and his face colored easily, showing his every emotion. He was tall and, in a healthy way, thin. Mrs. M would enjoy another fattening project. At first Mrs. M insisted on Spanish only for Riley, but frustration overrode pride and prejudice, until nice was her sole criteria.

Only two types of tea bags found, it was either English Breakfast or a lemon herbal concoction that she couldn't imagine anyone drinking unless it warded off some plague. She returned with a Styrofoam cup of hot water, the English Breakfast tea-bag, two creamers, two sweeteners, two sugars and a stirrer. She took her man for a sugar guy, but brought the sweeteners just in case. The other secretaries bitched up a storm whenever someone not a paying member of the club got a drop of their coffee or a single tea bag. *I'm not supplying the whole friggin' company ... Let her buy her own ... You know how much he makes?* But one tea bag wouldn't break the bank and there would be no drinks at the meeting. CEO Yates set an example from the top and, as part of his cost cutting initiative, he had issued a decree banishing extravagances such as company paid coffee and tea. He even deputized all employees to call him immediately if they spotted company funded drinks or cookies at a meeting. He would take appropriate action. But, Riley thought this was different.

She set the tea on the conference table.

"Thank you ma'am."

"Ma'am?" she repeated, not posturing, genuinely amazed at hearing such a thing. She looked closer at Harmon and said, "You sure are new to this team."

A bloom of red on his cheeks. He said, ma'am, out of habit. His father always used it and Harmon picked it up from him.

"You're blushing!" she said.

He shook his head no and blushed more. She liked that.

"Well," she said, "I've got to go. But I'll see you again," she winked, "as soon as they need someone to run for something."

She went back to work. Her first task: turning on the lights for the big shooters.

Leadership Meeting

discombobulated — the man — a tantrum — an answer — anointment

Maybe someone on the Leadership Team would need her to run for something. He hoped so. He sipped his tea. Previously unimaginable, now something else competed with the upcoming meeting for his attention. She said her name was O'Brian. A ghostly hint of freckles ran across her nose and her brown eyes were flecked with green, but she didn't look like an O'Brian. She had the slightest accent and it wasn't Irish. The way she talked about the Leadership Team, that was the last thing he expected on Executive Row.

He had called her ma'am. That was dumb. Made himself look stupid. Made himself look a hick. When nervous he said dumb things and this attractive young woman, who had a hint of freckles on her nose, a little accent and paid him attention, she made him nervous. How did she know he was a tea drinker? Something about her big words put him a little more at ease. He was more at ease with intellect than beauty.

Other attendees arrived: Division Managers from Finance, Billing, Systems, Marketing, Human Resources. They all looked as if rudely rousted from bed, nobody foolish enough to come late, but everybody carrying coffee and sipping at it, like hummingbirds at a feeder. Each new entrant stared at Harmon with a, who-is-this-guy look.

Preston P. Yates entered the room at one minute after seven. A sudden change in the managers. Small talk stopped. Faces glowed with the backlight of awe. Slouchers straightened, brought their eyes front and center, raised and readied their pens. The managers were all big shots in their own divisions, but in Mr. Yates's presence, everyone was an underling.

CEO Yates didn't acknowledge the room, he just sat and stared at the door. He was shorter than Harmon thought, of medium height. His gray, pinstriped suit fit perfectly, but up close and in person he looked too thin. It made his Adam's apple protrude and he didn't look as radiant or healthy as when he was on stage or on television. It was probably the toll of his seven day a week, twenty-four hour a day, impossible job. During his meetings he kept his suit jacket on and so did all attendees. His shirt was a white button-down, his tie red with thin silver stripes, the knot tight like Harmon wished he could do. He seemed perfectly comfortable ignoring everyone. He was the most self-assured man Harmon had ever encountered.

The CEO's Executive Assistant came in, pulling a squeaky-wheeled contraption with a large, overstuffed case strapped to it.

"Okay," Yates said, "let's get started."

"Almost ready," the assistant said, unpacking a computer. She was a tall woman, in her heels probably taller than Yates, but thin as a starveling, easily lost in her boss' shadow.

Harmon dared a longer look at the CEO. His father would want details.

Preston P Yates: Chief Executive Officer and member of the Board of Directors, business magazine cover boy with an annual salary of over fifteen-million dollars and stock options currently valued at over one hundred and fifty-million dollars. He was beneficiary of a long list of lucrative but unquantified perquisites. More importantly, he was a man widely believed to be the most powerful executive in America and the driving force behind the plan to revitalize AC&C, all of the corporation's great resources at his personal command, the senior management team just along for the tumultuous ride. And here sat Harmon Wolcott, at the same table, his attendance required.

The assistant finished setting up, walked to the door and closed it. Tough luck for latecomers. Yates always scheduled leadership meetings for seven a.m. Regular business hours he reserved for core business functions: raising revenue and cutting cost. The CEO was a tireless proselytizer for raising revenue and cutting cost. He often stopped unsuspecting staffers in the hallway, getting up close and personal, demanding to know: *What are the only two ways you can add value to this business?* If the startled, intimidated employees couldn't speak for themselves, he answered for them, "Raising revenue and cutting cost."

"Let's get started," Yates said again, looking to his assistant who tapped impatiently at her computer's spacebar, trying to hurry it, as if it didn't appreciate who waited.

Previously, Harmon had only seen the man live at a distance—an imperial presence commanding the stage for his annual address to the CFO organization. From across the conference table, what struck him most was the size of the CEO's head. A current story, maybe even true, said that Yates, suffering chronic neck pain, visited a top New York neurologist who, initially stumped, finally weighed the great head and concluded it was too heavy for its supporting muscles. Perhaps only such a generous cranium could contain the brain necessary to manage the convoluted affairs of the new AC&C.

The assistant still not ready, Yates drummed the table with his fingers, his energy grudgingly throttled, his impatience filling the entire room. Although his tenure as CEO had been brief, just five and a half years, stories already mythologized his insistence on getting what he wanted, when he wanted it. Once, on a Sunday morning, needing a critical data point and unable to open a subordinate's locked office, he bashed the door open with a fire axe. A bottom line, results man.

Her computer now fully awake, her fingers poised over its keyboard, the eager and anxious assistant nodded that she was really ready. Yates required detailed minutes of his every meeting. He was already drafting a memoir of how he fixed the business. The rumored title, *Turnaround: The Gospel According To Preston*.

"I want to ensure you all of one thing," Yates said, no time wasted on introductions. "I mean to get us to a better place and I'm moving fast."

The CEO believed in fast. His proudly proclaimed modus operandi: *ready, fire, aim.* He made a clockwise sweep of the room, his eyes fixing on each manager. He hesitated for just a second at the one strange face. Even that brief connection sent a charge through Harmon, like a jolt from a tractor's spark plug.

"About this journey to a better place. There is something you all need to decide."

Yates bobbed his head up and down, punctuating the gravity of each manager's decision. His full crop of hair was perfectly trimmed and still black, with just a touch of gray infiltrating the temples. According to Harmon's boss, the CEO got his hair trimmed every Tuesday while in his office chair dictating memos, maximizing use of his precious time. Details like that, little things about the man, fascinated Harmon. The boss told another story Harmon never forgot, about her one visit to Yates's magnificent office. It wasn't her description of the room's power evoking splendor that fascinated him, nor the rumored adjoining sleeping quarters with full-sized bathroom, it was what she noticed on the edge of Yates's desk, turned out so all could read it. A humble drug-store birthday card, signed, *Proud of you, Dad*. Yates's birthday had long come and gone.

"Decide this and decide it fast," Yates said. Do you want to come along?"

Fast deciders, the Leadership Team nodded their heads in unison. They looked like a synchronized swim team. Harmon nodded too, even though he could only speculate about the journey.

"If you choose to join me," Yates said, "it will be an exciting, rewarding experience. I will be filling unoccupied space."

The CEO often spoke in philosophical riddles. After his speeches, the staffers liked to gather for a favorite pastime—deciphering what the man really meant. Joe played another game, counting how many times Yates said *I*. The count was hard to keep so he bought a hand held tally counter. The standing record for a half-hour presentation, eighty-two. Joe submitted the counter as a business expense and got reimbursed his $9.95.

"If you choose not to join me," Yates said, "then that is the appropriate choice for you.

A tone of accusation in that. The team wasn't moving fast enough. Knowing looks from the managers. Yates preached either, or; my way or the highway; you're with me or you're history. Always with the same apocalyptic warning — AC&C was in a life and death struggle, with death certain unless his plans were implemented quickly and to the letter. The validity of his forebodings and solutions provoked intense arguments that, in a twist of irony, considering the man so revered efficiency, prolonged many a break and lunch hour. Opinions ranged from Yates the redeemer-genius to Yates the destructor-egoist. Sarcasm was heavily employed in support of the latter. Joe had an often photocopied cartoon on his cubicle wall, it showed an ancient, long-haired prophet explaining to a follower the mandate of circumcision. In Joe's version, Yates was the prophet and after getting his orders the wide-eyed follower asks, *Ok, let me get this straight, you want us to cut the ends of our dicks off?*

"I want you all to know," Yates said, "that this is not the old ACC."

That was the start of the CEO's stump speech. Harmon had heard it before, but felt privileged to witness it firsthand. It was a passionate dissertation about the old ACC and its many sins; how it was a pig swilling at the public trough, fat and happy with the assurance of its guaranteed rate of return; how monopoly and guaranteed return only guaranteed spectacular waste and arrogance. He said this created an insular management team of total incompetence and that AC&C still had too many people nurtured in that wasteland, managers set in their old regulatory ways, thinking they were at the top of the hill and gazing out at retirement and longing for that promised land. All this in AC&C's new competitive environment that required a stark choice; change into a nimble and aggressive competitor, or be dead company walking. A fed-up patriarch enlightening his overly indulged children about the real world and its hard ways, the part of his job Yates labeled for fawning interviewers as missionary work. Hard edged, but so true, Harmon could imagine himself standing and shouting, "Amen."

Near the end of his monologue, Yates told his managers to convey a sense of urgency, to make their people understand they were in a fight for survival, to build some fires under some asses, because, it was as simple as this — AC&C could not continue on its current trajectory.

"Questions or comments?"

The CEO always ended with this, his curtsy to participatory management, perhaps some echo from one of his Ivy League classes. Managers with a lick of sense knew it was time for a softball question, something like, *How can we best help implement your strategy?* If unable to concoct such a trifle, the next best choice was silence. On questions of policy, the CEO spoke *ex cathedra*.

Against this universal understanding and all common sense, the Systems Manager spoke his mind. "Could it be we're moving too fast? The systems can't keep up."

A collective breath holding, everyone looking to the ignorant interjector. Systems types were notoriously slow on the political uptake, masters of bits and bytes, but butchers of situational awareness. This one so clueless he even had a little smile on his face.

"Too fast?" Yates said, his face instantly red and a chromatic match for his tie. "Too fast?" His neck bulged against its custom collar. He looked like a cartoon thermometer about to burst.

"You," Yates said, staring at the systems guy. "You know what you should do?"

The man didn't. Yates told him.

"You and all cocksuckers like you should retire. That's what you should do."

Harmon locked his eyes on a small patch of the fine-grained table top. He didn't know what the others were doing or thinking, maybe they were used to this, but it shocked him, the sudden violence of it.

"Too fast," Yates said? "Maybe for incompetents like you. Huh? Do you hear me?"

Harmon looked up, and when Yates glanced his way, he nodded quickly, to assure the man that he heard him. The assistant's typing continued uninterrupted. Harmon wondered if it were verbatim.

Yates took a deep breath. That must be good. The Systems man stared into his own lap, his smile gone. He appeared on the verge of tears. His quiet obeisance seemed to rekindle Yates who slapped the table and said, "This cannot continue! It will not continue!"

Tenser silence until Yates asked, "Do you know what a philosopher once said?"

No one did.

"If you can't teach someone to fly, you teach him to fall faster!"

Harmon wrote that down, to look it up later. The Systems Manager twisted in his seat.

"I," Yates said, "would rather see this business fail completely, see it disintegrate, than have it hang on like some parasitic sponge, sucking up investors capital." A minute passed until, with his face cooling to less fiery hues and speaking softly to himself, Yates repeated, "Fall faster."

The seasoned Division Manager from Billing sipped his coffee. A sign the worst was over. Harmon dared a sip of his tea.

"What business are we in?" Yates asked.

Not an angry question. Just a matter-of-fact inquiry of the whole room, a simple question calmly posed, as if the last few minutes never happened.

More tension though. Yates often used simple questions and wrong answers to publicly expose muddled thinking. The more sophisticated managers tried to impress by parroting the CEO's own thinking, sufficiently camouflaged to pass for their own. A delicate operation, but with potential rewards.

"Well?" Yates asked.

No one seemed to know the answer. The silence ratcheted up from uncomfortable to unbearable, any answer a high stakes gamble.

The brave Billing manager offered first. "Well," he said, "we are in the telecommunications business."

"Wrong!" Yates said, his answer not nasty but purposefully ebullient, emphasizing his belief that what business AC&C was in remained shamefully misunderstood.

Yates scanned the team for another answer, critical lessons being taught here, if necessary more pride must be spilt.

Throat clearing by another manager. "Umm, we are in," she paused, her answer tentative, almost apologetic, "the communications business. The *total* communications business."

"Closer," Yates said. "But still wrong."

The assistant typed away.

"How about you," Yates asked.

Already sorry for the next unfortunate, Harmon looked up to see who it was. His sympathy evaporated. Yates had addressed him. He was it! He felt disoriented, like he had just come off a giant roller coaster. No time to think, he answered from instinct.

"Sir, we are in the information business."

Yates stared at him. The assistant's fingers hovered above her keyboard, ready to immortalize Harmon's disgrace.

"Absolutely right."

Harmon's leg shook. The best he had hoped for was, "Closer, but still wrong."

"Mister ..." Yates looked to where Harmon's name tag should have been.

He had forgot to wear it. That was another of the CEO's pet peeves; everyone was to wear their photo ID at all times. Yates looked to his assistant. She looked at her computer.

"Wolcott sir. Harmon Wolcott. He's filling in for Mr. Miller."

The assistant smiled at Harmon, as if he could be someone. Harmon felt all the other eyes on him. To his assistant, Yates said, "I want Mr. Wolcott as a member of this Leadership Team. I want him at the next meeting and all subsequent meetings. I want him on Project Armageddon. Get him a Leadership Team nametag and make sure he's at tomorrow's meeting."

"Armageddon?" the assistant asked, half whispering. "That, too?"

"Yes," Yates said. "Armageddon, too."

Harmon felt a sudden weight descend on him, as if someone had placed a lead dental vest on his chest. This was enormous. He could feel envy all around him.

"See," Yates said, pausing, commanding the group's whole attention. "I don't' care about title or level. That kind of thing is for little thinkers. I'm a big thinker and I want big thinkers around me. Out-of-the-box thinkers. Problem solvers. People with insight." As if to say, all of you just witnessed a great and rare happening, the anointing of an enlightened one.

Harmless

plugged in — endurance — snoop — volunteer

Riley's daily aggravations began accompanying her home. A sure sign she had plugged into the corporate world. A different absurdity every day, but always from the same sources: her supervisor's slavish reverence for rules, her colleagues incompetence, her clients arrogance. Plenty of psyche chafing vexations that took a front seat in her consciousness.

***

Her boss needed her right away.

Riley hated being interrupted while doing something well because nobody else would do anything at all, often because nobody else was around; they were all on extended lunches or breaks. Besides being in early, she always worked straight through the day with a quick lunch and no breaks. The norm among her colleagues was a late arrival, followed immediately by a trip for coffee and something sweet, then a day full of gossip, interrupted by more cafeteria trips and occasional work. If they had to hang around a few extra minutes, it was proof of martyrdom.

Whatever her boss wanted, it couldn't be good. Her boss looked for every opportunity to aggravate her, every opportunity to stick it to her with the worst assignments. Truth be told, and Riley took pride in her capacity for self-discovery, she wasn't blameless. She could've done a better job of humoring her boss, heeding her little harmless rules. She could've considered the office was the lady's home turf, more than that, probably her whole life, pitiful as that may be. But those thoughts came late at night, when Riley was alone and at peace, safely tucked away, when she could permit reflection. *Reflection*: the action of turning back or fixing the thoughts on some subject; meditation, serious consideration. During the day she couldn't bring herself to do a simple thing like pretending to walk the straight and narrow. Her stubborn pride made no allowances for that.

So she paid the price; a lot of consequences for the boss to choose from. Like assigning her to support the most anal-retentive managers, or dedicating her to a task force, or having her coordinate the blood drive. A task force, the ultimate weapon. It meant being slave girl to a group of egoists camped in a conference room: make their copies, run for their supplies, wipe their white boards, most of the managers so self-important and lazy that if they could they would have hired someone to breathe for them. But she wasn't going to quit, whatever the aggravations, not before she had reaped the benefits of her initiative. It was a matter of maturity, of accepting short term pain for long term gain. A matter of endurance. Lately, that was her favorite word. *Endure*: undergo, bear, especially without giving way; of a thing: withstand strain, pressure, etc., without being damaged. It would all be worth it. She had already thought about the skills to highlight on her new résumé: communications verbal and written, document management, meeting coordination, scheduling, travel management, presentation development, office administration. She liked the sound of all that.

It turned out her boss needed her to make a name-tag for someone. That was the emergency. How dumb. Not necessarily punishment, the boss liked her to do all the nametags. She liked the way she stenciled them, the care she took to make every letter clear, the result more arty than the printer, but still professional.

Thirteen letters and one space: H-a-r-m-o-n space W-o-l-c-o-t-t. She recognized the name. It was the shy young man she had surprised that morning in the CEO's conference room. Some coincidence. She had even changed her day because of him. Except for Fridays, when she enjoyed the cafeteria's fish dinner, her lunchtime habit was to eat alone, unpacking her brown-bag lunch in some vacant office or conference room, searching a newspaper for unfamiliar words that she could pin to the tip of her tongue for ready practice. But that day she had had lunch in the cafeteria with the other secretaries. Detective work to do.

A subtle snoop, she had cast her bait and waited.

"There was some guy in the conference room when I got in today, at quarter to seven." Matter-of-factly stated, the emphasis not on the guy but on his being there so early.

"You get his name?"

"Yeah, but I forget. He's a new member of the Leadership Team. A real nervous guy. Maybe Walters or something like that. Walker? It started with a W, a young guy, looking like he was lost, like he didn't belong."

"Was it Wolcott?"

The bait struck.

"I believe it was."

The hook sunk.

"That's got to be Harmon." A giggle. "Harmless Harmon."

"Harmless Harmon?"

"That's what the girls call him. Because he's the only one that doesn't hit on them."

"Oh," Riley said.

Her fellow secretaries had more.

"It's a shame 'cause he's cute. I know someone who tried hitting on him."

"What happened?"

"No luck." A laugh. "Harmless."

"Maybe he's shy?"

"Could be. But honey, we don't have time for shy around here. A good looking guy shows up, in a management job, he's gonna get his bones jumped."

"They all say he's a decent guy. Not like most of them. Not a jerk."

"Well, maybe he's, you know—."

"Nope. I tested him."

"Tested him?"

"Yeah. I showed him a little leg. Just a peek."

A bare, shapely leg swung out from under the table, to demonstrate.

"What happened?"

"He looked."

Riley had wanted more, but being too curious might have been conspicuous and it only took a little thing like that for the whole office to start talking. She had gotten enough. That's why she volunteered to deliver the nametag.

Joe's Place

a visit — malcontents — mister mom

"That's it."

Yates ended the extended Leadership Team meeting with that simple statement, then jumped out of his chair and hurried out of the conference room to address some other momentous matter. His chair spun a full circle from the energy of his leaving.

In his absence, the room deflated. The assistant hastily packed her equipment and followed her boss, the cart squeaking behind her. Harmon gave her time to cross the hall and disappear into Yates's office. Then he hurried out the door, before any of the Leadership Team members could corner him.

First the Leadership Team, now Armageddon. Whatever that was, it sounded daunting. Too much happening too fast; he needed someone to bounce all this off of, someone who knew the ropes. He decided to visit Joe. He took the elevator to the first floor where he entered a cubicular labyrinth more complicated than the cornfield maze his back-home neighbors built to attract families to their pumpkin farm.

Two aisles before reaching Joe's place he heard laughter. Sure enough, his feet up on his wastebasket, Joe was holding court, entertaining some malcontents. Harmon couldn't discuss his situation in front of the visitors and he doubted they would give him the courtesy of privacy with his subordinate. Maybe he could wait them out.

Joe's cubicle was a magnet for malcontents, young and old. The seasoned bellyachers agreed with all of his merciless criticisms of AC&C. So why did they stay in such a place? Their most convenient alibis — wives and kids. It was the wife who wouldn't consider moving, the kids whose welfare precluded any risk taking. Among themselves the younger workers spoofed the old-timers and Joe was a favorite butt. Still, they enjoyed him, especially when the craggy old veteran ragged on the company. Joe papered his walls with sarcastic sayings and cartoons. His fortieth anniversary plaque had arrived with the hanging hole on the bottom and he didn't bother to have it replaced. Instead, he hung it upside down in his cubicle's most conspicuous spot, a symbol of the state of the business. Joe dug at itches others didn't dare scratch, at least not in public. He enjoyed the freedom of nothing to lose. He was fully vested in the company's pension and benefit plans and rumored to have accumulated a half-million dollars worth of stock in his savings plan. His conspicuous penny-pinching lent credibility to the number; his lunch, everyday, was a can of tuna with a pack of relish mixed in. The relish and a plastic fork appropriated from the cafeteria.

"Hi Joe," Harmon said.

"Hey superstar."

Joe liked to tease about Harmon's relatively speedy promotion. Joe was an upgrade & transfer from craft, where he spent ten years climbin' poles and pullin' wire. After more than thirty years in management he was still a first level and determined to stay so. His golden rule: avoid any and all exposure to the big shots. One day, Harmon was walking in the main hall with him and the next thing he knew he was talking to himself. Joe had spotted their Division Manager coming and ducked down the first available corridor. "Stick your toe in with the big boys," Joe often said, "and you takes your chances." His self-deprecatory, self-satisfied, self-description: *a has been that never was.*

Joe's teasing was his backhanded way of saying he liked Harmon. He didn't like many of the younger managers. He called them *off the street hires* because they didn't come up from craft with all the dues paid that that implied. But Harmon had humility and deference. He respected the older man's prodigious knowledge. Joe was a veritable register of AC&C codes and procedures. Still, Harmon wouldn't wish Joe on any boss.

"We were just talking about the re-org," Joe said.

"It's only a rumor," Harmon said, hoping to shorten the conversation.

"Yeah," Joe said, "but it'll happen. Because that's the one thing they're good at in this place — reorganizing. They get so much practice."

They did. In the midst of its post-deregulation chaos and never-ending attempts to redefine itself, AC&C was addicted to the magic bullet of reorganization. The announcements came with head-spinning frequency, each and every redrawn organizational chart unveiled like a newly found treasure map with upper management confidently asserting that this time they had got it just right and now all roads would run downhill. Each and every announcement was followed by months when everybody was too busy with political repositioning to waste time on the day to day *mundanities* of running the business and satisfying customers. Harmon's current boss was number eight during his five years at AC&C. Once he had three different bosses on the same day; the first replaced in a standard reorganization, the replacement replaced that same afternoon in an emergency reorganization of the standard reorganization and the re-org of the re-org leaving the first replacement without a job and up in the air, literally, as he was already flying in to headquarters from California.

"So," Joe said, "you got five years in."

"Yeah," Harmon said.

"Before you know it, you'll be celebratin' ten. Then one day, you look in the mirror and soo-prise." Joe drew an imaginary bell in the air. "You're head's got the AC&C shape."

The visitors laughed at that. AC&C heads were employees so long in that institution's peculiar environment that their noggins evolved, figuratively, to the shape of the company's iconic logo.

"Yeah," Joe said, "before you know it, you're wearing the *olden* handcuffs."

Harmon suppressed a laugh at that. Joe meant *golden* handcuffs, AC&C's benefit suite of perquisites that vested and grew based on years of service: vacation and personal days, insurances, savings and pension plans. The over/under was commonly put at ten years. Once a manager passed that mark the price of leaving began to outweigh any youthful wanderlust, real or imagined. There were many analysts whose most carefully prepared and regularly updated spreadsheets analyzed not business propositions but the optimal time to retire.

"Oh yeah," Joe said, holding up his hands like a manacled prisoner, "the *olden* handcuffs."

That posture showed where his pants, overmatched by his stomach, were an inch short of connecting at the waist. A belt held them there, its last two holes ragged, obviously punched by hand, probably by hammer and nail. His trademark sport coat hung over his chair back. It was the same one he wore every day, large enough to almost fit his girth but unaltered to his short arms, the sleeves stretching past his fingertips. The checkered, mangy coat was famous enough to acquire its own nickname—*The Horse Blanket*.

"You see Mister Mom around?" a visitor asked Joe.

"Randy?" Joe said. "He's on vacation. Probably Disneyworld."

For fun, the boys liked to provoke Joe's put-downs of their colleagues. A pump easily primed. Especially for stories of Randy, a.k.a. Mister Mom, an Assistant Staff Manager Joe continually busted on for being overly domesticated.

"How'd he get that name anyway?"

"Mister Mom?" Joe said. "Oh, that's a good one."

Everyone settled in for the story. Practice makes perfect and Joe was a consummate story teller.

"See, we're all in this meeting. A couple years ago. Some waste of time circle-jerk about methods and procedurals. Anyhow, there's a knock on the conference room door and it's Randy, with his kid."

"Randy's got a kid?"

"Yeah. A boy. He was about four, back then. The kid's sick so Randy looks to his old lady who's sittin' in this meetin'—"

"His wife works here?"

"Yeah. Tina. You know, in Costs & Rates."

"Tina in Cost & Rates? Her? Wow!"

"Yeah. Hard to believe, huh?" Joe raised and lowered his eyebrows, lecherously. "So anyhow, the kid's sick."

Harmon could picture it. It wasn't unusual to see kids brought into the office for lack of a caretaker: sick, flu ridden or strep-throated kids crying in a cubicle, hungry kids making dinner of leftover bagels or microwave popcorn, exhausted kids wrapped in a topcoat and sleeping under a desk. At first it surprised Harmon. Now he was harder to surprise.

"So Randy says to his old lady, 'The center called me to come get him, but I can't keep him.' The kid buries his face in Randy's pant leg and everyone turns to Tina. She says, 'What do you want me to do about it?' Everyone turns back to Randy. 'Well I picked him up,' he says. 'But you know my boss.' His boss was a guy we called Rambo, because he was so tough."

"That was Hegarty, wasn't it? The guy everybody called Rambo?"

"Yeah, that was him. A tough sum-bitch, too, but let me finish the story."

"Sorry."

"So, Randy says to Tina, 'My boss sees this, he'll probably fire me.' She shakes her head and says, 'Can't you see I'm in the middle of this meeting?' She waves some slides at him, the stuff she's gonna present. 'I've got deliverables here. You're gonna have to keep him.' So the kid digs deeper into Randy's pant leg. He's bawling now."

"Who, the kid?"

"Yeah, the kid. So Randy says to his old lady, 'I got to keep him?' Tina says, 'Yeah' and then gives him a big, duh!' 'Well,' Randy says, 'you want me to get fired?' Tina ignores him and gets busy flipping through her slides, you know, her deliverables, like Randy's not even in the room. Everybody's real quiet now. I mean you could hear the kid wheezing. Randy says, 'So what if I get fired? Then what do I do?' Now everybody looks back to Tina. 'Well,' she says, looking up and staring at Randy like he's some kind of simpleton, 'then I guess you'll have to learn how to cook and clean.'"

"No."

"Yep."

"So what did Randy do?"

"He took the kid and left."

"Man! That's a good one!"

"Yeah. That's when Randolph became Mister Mom."

***

Harmon never got to discuss his situation with Joe, but he enjoyed his visit. Joe could take his mind off of his worries, even if only for a few minutes.

Riley Delivers

tagged — miracle worker — flirt

Riley found her man. He was sitting at his desk, looking bemused.

"I've got something for you, Mister Wolcott."

"Oh," Harmon said. "Hello."

She waved the plastic covered name tag at him, smiling like a mischievous child. "I've got to tag you."

Harmon said nothing.

He was in shirtsleeves and she looked behind his door and found his suit coat t on a wooden hanger. She walked to his desk, dangling the coat in front by two fingers.

"Please," she said.

He put the coat on and she took him by the lapel and pinned the tag there. He was taller than she thought.

"Pin the tail on the—" she said.

"Thank you," Harmon said, his cheeks flushing.

She moved a little closer. He went back on his heels. He looked as if he'd rather be anywhere else.

"I mean," she said, "I'm not saying you're a donkey."

She adjusted the tag, making a job of getting it just right, pulling him forward a bit, as if she were doing it for a little boy. The more he fidgeted, the more she enjoyed it in a sensual kind of way.

"There you go, mister Leadership Team man."

"Thank you," Harmon said again. No ma'am this time.

"So, how was your meeting?"

"Good."

"That's it? Good? Not engrossing? Not elucidating? Not enlightening?"

"It was interesting. Very interesting."

"Did Yates perform any miracles?"

"I'm not sure—"

"You know, did he make the blind see or did he walk on water and take soil samples? You know, anything like that?"

"Well, no, not that."

"I heard," Riley said, "that he's so busy now that he delegates his miracles. You know one time he ordered his staff to cure a blind man?"

Intuiting his part, Harmon asked, "What happened?"

"They made the guy deaf. Then they worked late and made him lame. That was their stretch objective."

Harmon smiled but couldn't think of anything smart to say. Better to say nothing than make himself look simple again.

"Okay," Riley said. "Just making sure you have your name tag. Can't be a leadership man without a name tag."

"Thank you," Harmon said.

She walked away, looking over her shoulder, waving her fingers at him. "Bye, Mister Wolcott."

He said, "Goodbye." Then added, "Miss O'Brian."

Riley was glad he added her last name. That meant he had been thinking about her.

Harmon Reflects

attraction — three types — a new type — a disciple?

That night, in bed, wide awake, Harmon thought about her. When she pinned the tag on him, her head just under his chin, he had inhaled the fresh, clean smell of her shampoo. He could still smell it.

Her manner and movements were tom-boyish. She didn't wear makeup. She didn't need it. She didn't advertise her beauty. All that made her more attractive. Did she weigh a hundred pounds? Her breasts were small but firm bulges against her sweater. It felt good to feel such attraction. He hadn't thought fast enough to give a hint that he was so attracted to her. Slowness was his curse. He hoped he would dream about her. He had enough to build a good dream on.

His usual pre-sleep ritual was wondering about his new life. He ruminated on it the way anthropologists study old bone fragments. At its center AC&C, the corporation and fictitious person, created not by God but by statute. AC&C, the driver of its flesh and blood employees — whether they were moving up, coming down or shuffling side to side. And what was a corporation? The beneficent economic engine, some said. The greedy, evil entity, others said. Well, it could be both and everything in-between because what it really was, was human beings. That's all — an official, organized conglomeration of human beings, from top to bottom, with all the virtues and flaws of the race. Maybe with some things exaggerated, by the pressures of day to day business.

He needed to get back to his mundane worldly affairs. They required his full attention. He had spent dinner and dessert studying the Armageddon pre-meeting material, a capsulation of the causes of AC&C's foundering. The treatise could be summarized as too much and too many: too much waste and too much overhead, too many management levels and too many decision making steps. At the root of the problem, too many people, illustrated by comparison to industry benchmarks. The focus of Project Armageddon — what to do about it?

AC&C had some slackers, or as Mr. Yates liked to say, too many people not pulling at their oars. Harmon knew that. Some who couldn't pull and some who wouldn't. Was looking the other way fair to those who then had to pull harder? Was it fair to the shareholders who trusted their life savings to management in expectation of its fiduciary trustworthiness and a fair return?

The real purpose of the Armageddon team was not to find solutions, but to implement them. Preston P. Yates had all the solutions. The CEO oozed certitude and Harmon wished he could be as certain about anything as Mr. Yates was about everything. The core principle of Armageddon was this: there were two types of managers, performers and non-performers. The consequences for the non-performers — termination. After years of softening up in a maternalistic monopoly, they were to be turned out into the marketplace, like sheep driven from their pens. Harmon thought a lot about this. Were there lazy managers among his colleagues? Some. Managers who failed to keep their skills current and adapt to a rapidly changing business? Many. What bothered him most was the attitude many in power held about the sacrificed — that if they weren't meant to be shorn, they wouldn't be sheep.

Harmon might be wrong or he might be weak, but he had his own more nuanced view. After a great deal of contemplation, he had concluded AC&C had three main types.

Lifers: Products of the monopoly past. Years ago they and the old *ACC* chose each other. A fair deal. The workers craved security and they got that in the form of an implicit contract — don't cheat on your vouchers and don't cheat with the boss's wife and you have a life-long job. The monopolistic, rate-of-return regulated entity needed overhead to balance steadily increasing revenues, and salaries were the most politically popular class of overhead. Government and industry working together and the arrangement made everybody happy. But now, cast into the newly deregulated world and after a thorough marinating in mediocrity, the old time employees were incapable of adjusting. Their *modus operandi* — minimum effort and maximum attitude. In an ironic rite of self-sacrifice, those traits, along with the great savings from eliminating their seniority based salaries and benefits, made them the first targets in company-wide layoffs.

Sophisticated Survivors: Go-along to get-along people. Stealth slackers, playing the delicate balancing act of appearing committed to the company, but avoiding the worst of the fray by flying under management's radar. The talented among this group had to work hard at not standing out. Their greatest fear was some insightful boss might recognize their ability and suck them deeper into the nastiness. The masters of this type were goldbricking wonders, doing little productive work and yet receiving good appraisals and bonuses.

AC&C-aholics: First to arrive, first to volunteer, last to leave. Their vocabularies sprinkled with AC&C terms and acronyms, their fondest wish a place on the Leadership Team, whatever the cost. Family and friends in life's backseat — their kids' school plays attended by nannies, every household chore and repair done by hired help. Different types than the hard workers back home. Back home it was what got done: acres plowed and planted or fences built or hay harvested. At AC&C bragging rights were for time spent. *I was here to ten last night* one-upped by *I was here to midnight and took work home.* Monomania a badge of honor.

Those were the main types, but Mr. Yates imagined a new, higher type. That intrigued Harmon. The CEO preached the doctrine of *Shareholder Value* and everything his higher type did, all the revenue raised and all the costs cut, was to benefit the shareholder. The shareholder was the company's *raison d'être*: not technological advancement, not the employees, not even the customers. Ultimately, if the shareholders benefited, so would the employees and customers, even the neediest citizen who never thought about AC&C would unknowingly benefit by the wealth it created. And, if the shareholders didn't benefit, nobody could. The message appealed to Harmon, the logic and demonstrability of it all, the easy measurement tool, too, just follow the stock price.

What to call this new type? How about *Guardians of the Shareholders?* Mr. Yates the iconic example. Harmon Wolcott, his humble disciple?

Armageddon

dream team — visionary — consultant — raised stakes

The Armageddon meeting started at 6 p.m. Mr. Preston P. Yates presiding with his twelve disciples: his executive assistant, ten senior managers and Harmon, all handpicked to implement a miracle. The senior managers had coined their own nickname, The Dream Team, for all the talent gathered in one place. Harmon wore his poker face to mask his nervousness.

"I am starting you on the path to revolution," Yates said, kicking things off. Their mission was nothing less than to fundamentally remake the corporation by transforming its culture. "I intend to radically alter AC&C, to change its heart and soul. I am an alchemist. My job is the transmutation of the base into something precious."

Yates the chemist and visionary.

"My appearance this morning will be brief. Just enough to launch and inspire."

The visionary led from the mountain top. He didn't muck around in the day-to-day. Idea generation was his calling, not implementation with its hand dirtying details. In his first act at AC&C, Yates had assembled all the Vice Presidents. A come to Preston meeting, he called it. It was a big assembly; AC&C had more than a hundred vice-presidents. After a wine and cheese reception, Yates spoke of his leadership style. That speech became famous.

"Say that in 1940 the Allied Command came to me with the problem of German U-boats sinking their shipping. I would have thoroughly considered the problem. Then I would have provided the solution. Boil the ocean. Now I know what everyone would have said, all those little thinkers lost in the minutia. It can't be done. It's impossible. How, how, how? Can't and impossible and how, the hobgoblins of little minds. You see, the details, the particulars, I leave to the people who work for me. That's what I pay them for. My job is to imagine and inspire. That's what I'm paid for. They don't pay me to do little things. They don't pay me to pick fly shit out of pepper."

The CEO'S charge to the Armageddon team followed the same theme. "You," he said, "are here because I trust you to do what the little minds say is undoable: to totally transform a business and do it while that business continues to function day-to-day and meet its obligations to its shareholders. A task of complexity akin to disassembling and reassembling a 747 while it's still in flight."

Complex indeed. Such a great undertaking, the changing of an ancient and embedded culture, fascinated Harmon. To be a part of such a transformation excited him. But Yates paid him no attention, as if the previous day's Leadership Team meeting and his insightful answer had never happened. Did he even remember Harmon? Managers spent anxious hours wondering and worrying about such flimsy signals. A smile or frown, a nod of recognition or a blind eye, did they indicate the CEO's feelings about them?

"Hear me good," Yates said. "I want you to know that you are not alone. To help you in this daunting task, and given the absolute need for out of the box thinking, I've decided to employ a group of very special people. I have contracted with Dagwell, Nordhoff and Applewerth, The Transformation Management Group."

A collective deflation. The Dream Team's intimate dance with the CEO suddenly interrupted by a shoulder tapping interloper — another consultant to add to AC&C's long list.

"DNA-TMG," Yates said, "are corporate anthropologists."

From the perplexed looks it was clear no one had ever heard of corporate anthropologists.

"They are experts," Yates said. "At gaining an understanding of a corporation's culture and leading the transformation process. Think of them as your guides. As you climb the mountain, they will be your Sherpas."

In his five years at AC&C Harmon had become familiar with consultants, an infestation of them, many hired to improve morale that surveys showed at an all time low and still falling. A distinct breed, consultants, hired guns brought in to fix what indigenous management couldn't or wouldn't. Experts. Joe had his own definition of what AC&C considered an expert: *Someone from out of town — with slides.*

"I will now introduce someone very special."

Yates looked to his assistant who stepped out of the room and quickly returned with a tall woman dressed in a form-fitting, gray pin-striped business suit. The newcomer stood erect, her golden hair swept back and tied tight to her head, her unblinking eyes so blue that Harmon wondered if she wore tinted contacts. She had a soft leather satchel strapped over her shoulder. She held her head high and looked natural doing it, not stiff but majestic. A well bred look.

"This," Yates said, "is Elizabeth Dagwell, Chairwoman of the DNA-TMG."

The size of the contract, and the chance to add AC&C's still resonant name to their client list, always brought a consultancy's heavy hitters, at least to initial meetings. The chairperson or an executive vice-president would kick things off, followed for a week by senior analysts, their hair specked with grey and their tongues with silver. The group's gravitas established, things were gradually migrated to a group of progressively lighter-weights, until all that appeared were a seemingly endless and interchangeable supply of recent MBA graduates, all from prestigious institutions, all smart and endlessly willing, all overworked and under experienced. As Joe put it in mixed company, "The biggest corporation in the world, being counseled by kids that six months ago were jerking-off in a college dormitory." With all male audiences, Joe had the kids *finger-fucking* themselves in their dormitories. He preferred the second version. It got more laughs.

"You are very fortunate," Yates said, "to have this precious resource for the next eight weeks. Seize the opportunity. Be courageous. Be fearless. Follow wherever the process leads. Allow the process to stretch you."

That was it for the Chief Executive Officer. A baton-passing nod to the DNA-TMG Chairwoman and he left, his assistant hurriedly following, the two of them off to whatever next required his vision and her assistance.

For a moment, Elizabeth of DNA-TMG stood purposefully still. The room required a cooling off period before one alpha followed another. She dressed flawlessly, every crease and curve just right, her whole look understated but for a gold stick pin on her collar, a rendering of the double-stranded helical chain of DNA. Harmon thought it surely a play on Dagwell, Nordhoff and Applewerth. A most sophisticated touch. When she spoke, she exuded power accessorized by sensuality.

"The first thing I want to say is this. It can be done." She repeated herself, emphasizing and pausing after each word: "It—can—be—done." In a more somber tone, "Make no mistake though, transformation is never easy."

She detailed her credentials. BS-NYU, MA-Columbia, PhD-Princeton. Twenty years of experience. The simple math and a surprising conclusion, she was in her mid-forties. She looked younger than that.

"Do you know how I know it can be done?" She paused long enough for the question to ripen, a natural's sense of timing. "Because I have seen it done. I know it works."

Consultants could still seduce Harmon. He had a particular weakness for the paid motivators. All professed a unique and magic formula for redemption and all expressed supreme confidence that their way worked. Each had an impressive list of the saved, the Fortune 500 companies they had transformed. Among the foolproof approaches sold to AC&C: Fake it until you make it—which meant pretending you were good at something even if you weren't. Practice certain habits, the number and manner varying by practitioner but each sure their combination was just right. Go primal and conquer your fears; spend a week in the wilderness with your work group, roping across gullies and free falling into each others' arms, breaking boards with your bare hands and walking over fire with your bare feet. All the approaches had the same lofty purposes: to make each person the best AC&C employee he or she could be, to make each a cost-cutting, revenue raising machine. Most of the programs proved harmless enough, except to departmental budgets. Some humiliated the more faint-hearted and Harmon learned to take vacation days to avoid the worst of these, like the seminar that encouraged associates to squat in front of their co-workers and cluck like chickens before telling everybody their innermost secrets. Some proved downright dangerous. One woman broke her wrist while trying to break a board in half. Only one session killed someone. A finance manager died during a wilderness survival weekend from a heart attack while climbing a rope, the first strenuous physical activity the man had done in thirty years.

"Notice," Elizabeth said, "I didn't say I have done it, because I haven't done it. My clients have done it. We at DNA-TMG merely facilitated. The people charged with creating the change must live the change. People like you, each of you selected by Mister Yates, each of you a proven leader in your own right."

So undeserving of that, Harmon felt an urge to object.

"Now," Elizabeth said, her smile gone and her voice more solemn, "over the next month or two, the hours will be long and the sacrifices great. Your families will suffer. I know that. Throughout my career my own family has suffered. They have suffered greatly."

She looked away for a second, as if needing a moment for reflection. The room stayed respectfully silent. Her family's suffering being imagined.

"But much is asked of those who have much to give. You all are about to start on a journey of transformation, AC&C's transformation and, inevitably, your own. Nothing else you do in your lifetime will compare. In the coming weeks each of you will be in the spotlight, with responsibilities far beyond what you've had before, with burdens lesser people would consider unfair. Sacrifice will be commonplace, because that is how you make a difference. Each of you fully committed to Mister Yates and his vision because he has chosen you, because he believes in you. If you justify that belief, I promise you that nothing else you do will equal what you accomplish here. I know that, whatever the cost, when my final breath comes, I will look back upon my business transformation work as my life's justification."

Now Harmon saw her eyes as more steel grey than marine blue, her formal reserve more cold than cool. She announced a break. He needed it.

***

After the break, the corporate anthropologist took on a different tone, signaling a shift from the inspirational to the practical. She outlined DNA — TMG's process and the necessity of strict adherence to its tenets.

Harmon liked the surety of process, a step by step set of instructions that, followed faithfully, assured success. Like when the tractor wouldn't start and his father said, "Son, it can only be one of two things. It's either not getting gas or it's not getting spark. We find which, we fix it, then it starts." And it always did.

AC&C was more complicated than gas and spark. Elizabeth said they would work in teams and concentrate on the areas most in need of transformation. That meant three teams: Systems, Customer Care, and People — the areas Mr. Yates identified as critical to changing AC&C's culture. Each team would have a champion, chosen from among senior management, someone who felt deeply about that team's particular mission and stood ready to use the power of his or her high office to demolish all obstacles to success. That made sense. At AC&C level meant everything and if Albert Einstein were a Level 1 and the congenital idiot nephew of some VP a Level 2, even on questions of quantum physics Albert would be the one taking orders. Each team would have a leader, chosen from among the Armageddon team, for his or her proven expertise and leadership. Team leader was the key position and required total commitment, for its extraordinary burdens and responsibilities. The leader was the one person responsible for every aspect of a team, the one person to look to when things didn't go right. Another well thought out procedure: if buck-passing earned gold medals, AC&C would be Fort Knox.

Elizabeth turned to her notes to describe the teams and their responsibilities: the Systems team responsible for ensuring people had actionable information, the data they needed, when they needed it, and in the right format; the Customer Care team responsible for ensuring that customers were cared for from first contact, through the sales and ordering process, to implementation and understanding their bills and establishing a lasting relationship; the People team responsible for ensuring that AC&C's human resources, from the executive officers to the newest hires, were fully engaged and productive.

"Now," Elizabeth said, "I have the privilege of announcing the team leaders. After that, each of you will have the opportunity to volunteer for whichever team you prefer. All team members will be volunteers because, and I don't say this lightly, just to be associated with this effort is a privilege."

Harmon didn't see privilege in the collected faces. Their dour looks betrayed something else, a common desire to escape the meeting free of a team leader's extraordinary burdens and responsibilities. Team Leader was a lot to ask and he understood his senior colleagues' fears.

The real drama wasn't in the Systems and Customer Care announcements. Both team leaders were predictable, only one representative from each group in the room. The Systems manager was the replacement for the man who had challenged Yates at the Leadership Team meeting. Both he and the Customer Care woman had established reputations for competence and eighty hour work weeks. The drama was in the People Team choice; there was no clear favorite, no inevitable choice, no established AC&C people person.

"The People Team is critical," Elizabeth said. "So much so, that Mr. Yates has particular interest in it, and just wait until you hear this." She clasped her hands together, her diamond ring sparkling. Something big coming. "Mr. Preston Yates has volunteered to personally champion the People Team. In his own words to, 'work as closely as necessary with the team leader to ensure success.' Now how's that for commitment!"

Murmuring throughout the room. The team awestruck by the previously unimaginable come true; Preston P. Yates descending from his mountain. He must really be interested in the People Team.

Harmon wondered, should he volunteer to serve on the People Team? He must volunteer for one of the teams, that was expected of Leadership Team members and, even if, as was most likely, he served as the team's gofer, it would still be a way to learn more about Mr. Yates.

Elizabeth picked up her notes and read aloud. "As Mr. Yates put it to me, 'The People Team is responsible for ensuring that everyone is pulling an oar.'" She smiled, as if that phrase were fresh to all. "And now, Mr. Yates's personal selection to lead this team."

A long pause, Elizabeth was an artist in the power of suspense. A preternatural quiet came over the meeting; a lot of shifting and nervous glances. People slid down into their seats, as if they might disappear. The air flowing through the overhead ducts sounded like rolling thunder.

"Mr. Yates's personal selection is, Harmon Wolcott."

Riley's Secrets

treat—precious things—what if

"Thank you honey," Mrs. M said. "But you really shouldn't."

"It's okay," Riley said. "I like doing it."

Mrs. M enjoyed McDonald's milkshakes and Riley enjoyed indulging her. Strawberry, Mrs. M's favorite. Riley liked the shakes, too, especially chocolate, but she didn't drink them—too much sugar. A McDonald's visit always tested her willpower. She usually won. She had considerable willpower.

"Let me get you money," Mrs. M said, lifting her walker from the floor, aiming it toward her bedroom.

"Oh no," Riley said. "Please."

"You sure?" Mrs. M said, asking as always despite the certain and never changing answer. The asking was important to her.

They sat in Mrs. M's tiny living room, amidst an improbable number of whatnots crowded onto every flat surface; shelves and tables and windowsills chockfull with treasures collected over half a century. Mrs. M most loved snow bubbles, religious scenes her favorites. Riley bought Mrs. M a new one every Christmas, the shopping for and presenting of it one of her joys.

Riley sat on the rock hard convertible sofa where,, as a kid she had sometimes slept, and Mrs. M spoiled her *best girl in the whole world*. She served her ice cream topped with chocolate syrup and marshmallows and let her watch television until she fell asleep. Mrs. M was one of those women with abundant love, but no child of her own. It had to come out and Riley was the lucky recipient. Mrs. M sat on the fabric covered, straight backed chair that made it easier for her to get up. She was so grateful for such a little thing as a milkshake that Riley drank a cup of tea and ate a cookie she didn't want, giving her host the satisfaction of fair exchange.

"Oh my," Mrs. M said, looking to the gym bag Riley carried home, along with her briefcase. "You still doing that fightin'?"

She meant the boxing Riley did at the local gym.

"It's fun," Riley said.

"When you hurt the nose, I hope you quit."

Strange happenings followed Riley around and hers was one of the strangest broken noses in boxing history. She had started sparring with a sixty-something former middleweight who hung at the gym. Her hardest punches didn't faze the man and he wore the soft, oversized boxing gloves that were called pillow punchers, just tapping at her headgear as if she were a pane of glass, giving her a reason to bob and weave and adjust her timing, making things realistic to put theory into practice. The accident happened when she threw a short right uppercut. The cagey veteran slipped to the side and deflected her punch. It was instinct born of slipping thousands of punches, he couldn't help it anymore than a knee responding to a doctor's hammer, but Riley's parried punch came up inside, her blow catching her square on her own nose, breaking it with a loud crack, like a snapped wishbone. Blood poured over her chin and onto her t-shirt. Her opponent was so horrified that he screamed for help. The whole gym converged and, at the sight of Riley, looked at the middleweight as if he were an animal. "Not me!" he said. Riley spit out her mouthpiece and yelled, "My fault." Then in the gym's new vernacular, "My bad." The unsympathetic owner snapped her nose back in place. All he said to Riley was, "See." That summed up both his being proved right and his continued contempt for the idea of her sparring. In spite of two black eyes and swelling that, for a week gave her a vulnerable and victimized look, her nose healed without a doctor or hospital visit and with just the slightest curve. Everyone said it made her cuter.

"I bet you good at that, too," Mrs. M said. "That fighting. You good at everything."

Riley smiled and picked up a snow bubble from an adjacent table. It was the Manhattan skyline, compressed to include all the important landmarks. She tipped it and watched the white flakes descend over the Empire State and Chrysler Buildings and the Twin Towers.

"Thank you honey," Mrs. M said again, nodding to her milkshake. "I like my shakes, but I love our talks."

Riley enjoyed their talks, too, and more so as she got older. There were things she could talk about with Mrs. M that nobody else would understand. Mrs. M wasn't like most people who professed understanding and sympathy, but upon hearing your miseries couldn't keep the telltale gleam of satisfaction from their eyes. There was a word for that and Riley had it in her journal. *Schadenfreude*: malicious enjoyment of another's misfortune. Amazing how, if you took the trouble, the perfect word existed. *Shod-en-freud-a*. She wouldn't try to pronounce it in public, but when she read it she knew it and how many people could say that?

What she couldn't talk about with Mrs. M, she couldn't talk about with anybody. For a long time that seemed easy, keeping things to herself. Lately it didn't. Things that lay quiet for years bubbled up, like a volcano building toward an eruption.

She looked around the familiar flat, studying, again, the things that made up Mrs. M's treasures. Mrs. M had lived in that same apartment for more than forty years. *Día por día*, she always said. Amazing, how day by day can add up to a life. A new treasure, on the table next to Riley's chair, propped against the base of a lamp, to give it prominence. It was the business card Riley had given Mrs. M, the first person so honored. The same day Riley's boss gave her a little cardboard box tightly packed with five-hundred cards, a sample glued on top, buff paper with a raised AC&C logo, numbers phone and fax, addresses regular and e-mail:

Riley O'Brian
Consultant
Administrative Support

The first week she kept one in her pocket and looked at it every five minutes, all her touching fraying the edges.

"So honey," Mrs. M said, "how is everything at that ACC?"

"Good," Riley said. "I'm still learning. I make some mistakes and they aggravate me some but I keep going. I have endurance. I endure."

Mrs. M pondered that until Riley asked, "Mrs. M?"

"Yes Honey?"

"Could I have a little more tea?"

"Of course."

Mrs. M leaned forward, gathered her ankle-length housecoat and gripped her walker, the first motions in a deliberate and painful process that would eventually get her standing. Riley stopped her and walked to the little kitchenette. From an antique copper kettle, she half filled her cup. She dunked the tea bag but the water turned only a pale yellow. She tested the water with the tip of her little finger. Lukewarm.

"Mrs. M," Riley said, from the kitchen, from where it seemed easier to broach the subject. "Remember when my mother wouldn't let me change my last name?"

"Sure I do. She wanted you to have a father, or at least a father's name."

"Yes," Riley said, "that's why. But, I wonder, what do you think he would have said?"

"You father?"

"Yes."

"Oh, he would want you to have the O'Brian name. Long as that don't cost him nothing. He was here today, he be bragging of you."

Riley came back into the living room and sat on the sofa. She had her own carefully constructed theory about her father, that some overpowering life event had prevented his being a husband and father. That he just didn't care was too hard to take.

"See," Mrs. M said, "I shouldn't say, but facts the facts and he is always a bullshitter."

"Mrs. M?"

"Yes?"

"You think I'd be okay as a mother?"

"What? Why you …" Mrs. M leaned forward and lifted herself half-a-foot off the chair, to give her words more force. "You be the best!"

"You think?"

"The best!" Mrs. M said. Her hands moved in a sweeping motion, to say better than all the mothers in all the world and not a single doubt about it. "I telling you, you be so good."

"You really think so?"

"I sure do. Honey, tell now, there is someone?"

"Oh no, no, it's not that. It's just, you know, sometimes I wonder. You know, how would I have done if things had worked out?"

"Oh honey, you make a wonderful mamá. What so important is you still can. You have time. You find the right one, you know, one of the good ones. He is out there."

"You know something Mrs. M?"

"What honey?"

"My baby, he'd be nine years old now."

Mrs. M didn't say a thing, just nodded, as if confirming the arithmetic.

"I had a dream about my baby the other night. He wanted to take karate classes, but it cost too much. They wanted $5000 a month, in my crazy dream."

"Oh honey."

"You know something?"

"Honey?"

"I don't care what it would've cost. He would've had karate and anything else he wanted."

After her pregnancy ended, she knew what everyone assumed. That she had quit on her baby. Even now, ten long years later, her anger lingered. When she imagined the neighborhood busybodies talking, it made acid bubbles pop in her stomach. A lot of nosey neighbors thought they knew stuff, but they didn't. She started to cry and Mrs. M reached out and motioned her over and Riley came and sat at the foot of her chair. Mrs. M pulled her closer and put her hand on her head and patted her like she did when she was a little girl.

Too Much

sanctuary — panic — deadwood — opportunity to excel

Before the Armageddon meeting ended, Yates's assistant entered and handed Harmon a note. The People Team, his team, would meet the next morning at 9 a.m. in the CEO's conference room. Mr. Yates himself had the room between seven and nine, so it would be the CEO coming out and Harmon going in. Would he take the very same chair?

Things moving fast, just as commanded. More in the note. Harmon directed to develop a preliminary work plan: the People Team's *Statement of Purpose*. The plan due the day after tomorrow, right after Mr. Yates's annual address to the CFO group. Harmon to present it directly to Mr. Yates.

The enormity of it — member of the Leadership and Armageddon Teams, team leader of the People Team — all because he had spit out one lucky answer. His previous challenges, what he had thought life and death now seemed a child's game.

Was it too much? What he most wanted now was a chance to think. So, he retreated to a men's room at the end of an out-of-the-way corridor, his favorite hideaway for its remoteness. Shut-away behind the steel door of the far stall, he felt the temporary respite of sanctuary, a place where no one would come knocking and no phone could ring, the world's confusion and uncertainty locked outside.

Tonight he would call home with the good news. Some bad news, too, his vacation was surely cancelled, but his father would understand; it was about the needs of the business. What he didn't want was for his father to get too excited, to start anticipating awards and promotions. His father wouldn't see the complications. There were pros and cons. Leadership of the people team was a big stage and on a big stage you could screw up big. And, when you screwed up big, everyone knew it. But there would be no glass half full or half empty for his father, only opportunity gushing over the sides. *Son, now you show 'em what you got.*

Alone in his *sanctum sanctorum*, he felt a backwash of panic. He tried but couldn't stop it. What if he got put on the spot? *Tell us more about this information business.* What if Yates expected more great insights from him when the sad truth was he didn't have any? He remembered that the whole idea of the information business was his father's, something he had brought up in one of their talks. What if he said something so stupid that it infuriated Yates to a red faced explosion? He put his head in his hands and tried to calm himself. He felt his familiar self-reproach. He needed, again, to overcome his own weakness.

The bathroom lights clicked off from lack of motion, from too much thinking and not enough action. What would someone think if they came in and found him locked in that stall, the windowless room pitch black?

He walked to his office on an emotional tightrope, teetering between excitement and fear, between aspiring young professional and scared little boy. He passed vacant cubicles and offices, emptied by consolidation and rightsizing and de-hiring. People once sat there, their lives full of critical meetings and memos and deadlines. As he walked through the eerie emptiness, fear won. Impulsively and against all corporate protocol, he took the coward's way out. He decided to call his boss' boss, at his home where he convalesced from his hedge trimming accident. He thought the Senior Division Manager, already nicknamed *Thumbless*, would be insulted, maybe furious, that a lowly Staff Manager had taken his rightful spot on the Leadership and Armageddon Teams and now headed the critical People Team. He thought the man might, justifiably, demand his place back. Maybe, out of magnanimity, he'd offer to keep Harmon on as his assistant.

"That's great," the man said, upon hearing the big news. Undisguised joy in his voice, like a kid on the last day of school. He was ecstatic that he had been passed over. It struck Harmon then, this man was the personification of what Mr. Yates called *deadwood*, one of those who could see retirement from where he sat, probably offering his nighttime prayers for an *offer*: the term given to a boost in pension and benefits designed to encourage early retirements. With his age and years of service he had to be close to the promised land. Maybe he could even smell it.

"I'm not sure," Harmon said, feeling his delicate way, "that I'm ready for this."

"Oh you'll do fine. It'll be great exposure for you. I like to see a young person's talents exposed."

Said with an easy magnanimity. Too easy. So easy Harmon couldn't help some contempt for the sayer. He knew this man had once been badly abused by Mr. Yates for not having some piece of arcane information at his immediate recall. The abuse was public, in the hallway outside the CEO's conference room, the story widely told, how Yates's anger had grown until he poked a finger in the Division Manager's chest and demanded, "Give me one reason I shouldn't fire you right now?" The man couldn't give one, at least not on command, and that only stoked Yates's anger and his poking grew harder until, backing his victim up to the fifth floor's southerly windows, he finally asked, "Give me one fucking reason I shouldn't fire you right now?" The story, perhaps embroidered in the telling, but Joe claimed to know someone who witnessed the whole thing and even saw the red marks on the victim's chest. Now, having seen Yates in action, Harmon no longer doubted the story. Maybe escape from the spotlight of leadership was worth the sacrifice of a thumb.

"Harmon," the Division Manager said, "anything else?" In the background he heard the tinkle of ice dropping into a glass.

"Well," Harmon said, "is there anything you can tell me about Project Armageddon?"

"Armageddon?" The Division Manager sounded surprised at the word. "Well, I've only been in one meeting where it was mentioned. It's one secret that's been kept. That, in itself, is amazing."

"But you've heard of it?"

"Yeah. They say it's Yates's special baby. Harmon, you know your Bible?"

"Some."

"Well you can look it up. See, Armageddon is the last battle at the Day of Judgment. My friend, who's a full VP and in the know, said Yates called it, 'Decisive conflict on a great scale.' Yates likes that kind of stuff. My friend said it actually scared him, how Yates got all wound up at the meeting where he announced it. You know how he is. Or at least you will. Bye the way, Armageddon's in *Revelations*, but I can't give you chapter and verse."

"Okay," Harmon said.

"Everything's good then?"

"Yes. I'm sorry for calling you at home."

"That's okay. Don't worry about it."

"Thanks."

"And Harmon?"

"Yes?"

"You know what I'd do if I was you?"

"What?"

"Think of this as your opportunity to excel."

PART III

People Team

AC&C time — minutes — history

Harmon arrived for the initial People Team meeting with a sense of relief because the doing couldn't be as bad as the anticipating. He had managed teams before, that was part of his job, but this was different; now he would be leading managers of equal and higher rank and in a high risk venture. He had relayed the news to his father the night before. "Now that's opportunity," his father said. "Here we go!" Talking to his father right before bedtime was a bad idea.

He walked past the conference room. It was empty. Mr. Yates must have finished early. He entered and set his briefcase down at the head of the table. The CEO's big leather chair was missing. They probably locked it away between meetings. That was okay, sitting in it would have been too much of a usurpation.

The room's whiteboard hadn't been cleaned. Cryptic notes there, in red and blue marker, enough to hint at personnel issues. HC for what must be head count, lots of numbers with negative signs and scribbling that looked like staffing and attrition. Corporate security wouldn't like an un-wiped board and God forbid if Mr. Yates heard about it. He was fanatical about security and expected his staff to see to it. Harmon wiped the board clean.

Too antsy to sit, he stood and looked over his notes. Most of the marginalia was indecipherable, added during his fitful night when he woke and scribbled ideas in a notebook that shared his bed. Introduce himself and the team's purpose, then have everyone else introduce themselves. That was how he would begin. After that, a brainstorming session of some kind to get off on the right foot. Everyone enjoyed brainstorming; it was like playing at work. His own brain stormed with likely disasters. Everyone would look to him for leadership. Unanswerable questions would be directed his way, posed by people who asked them because they were unanswerable. *What's our strategy?* That was the kind of question he had watched so many project leaders squirm over, middle managers without the easy flowing sophistry of the Vice Presidents or the intimidating presence of Preston P. Yates. No one dared challenge real authority, but today they would have license to challenge Harmon Wolcott, to knock off his pedestal the boy wonder who knew AC&C was in the information business.

***

9:00 a.m. and he was still alone. He had expected that. That was the AC&C culture he knew. *AC&C time,* some called it. The same people who would risk life and limb to avoid being late for one of the CEO's meetings, and who wouldn't step out if their bladders exploded, arrived at colleagues meetings as late as they pleased and came and went based on their circadian rhythms.

At 9:10 the first team member arrived, a blonde woman, wearing the condescending expression of royalty visiting commoners. Caitlin. Harmon knew her mostly by reputation. She had served a year as Executive Assistant to Mister Yates, that high profile service followed by immediate promotion to District Manager. Harmon said hello, but she ignored him and dropped her appointment book and notepad on the table. She got busy testing the chairs until she found one adjusted to her liking and hung a translucent pink sweater over its back. She wasn't a good start. That was another of the strange things Harmon discovered at AC&C, something akin to opposites attract. If you wanted to recruit inefficient people, you started an efficiency team. If you wanted prejudiced people, you started a diversity team. If you wanted nasty people, you started a people team.

At 9:18 a man wearing a guest badge and escorted by a clerk came in. Harmon greeted him. A small, hairy eared guy, smiling as if privy to life's secrets. He was the DNA-TMG representative. His white shoes needed care, a spider web of dark cracks along their tops. His polyester suit immediately reminded Harmon of his father's one and only, bought off the Sears sale rack and on call for life's unavoidable ceremonies. All in all, a serious downgrade from stylish Elizabeth. Not his fault for being late, though, security had to clear him.

9:25 and Harmon pretended to be busy looking through his notes, sneaking glances at the wall clock but revealing no irritation at having to wait for late comers. Any hint of irritation on his part would only highlight the lack of respect for him and his team leader status.

A familiar whistling punctured his pretense. It echoed from the hallway, *Wasted Days and Wasted Nights,* Jurassic Joe's signature tune. Harmon couldn't believe it. Believe it or not, it was true. In strolled a grinning Joe, an outsized coffee mug in his right hand, a newspaper pressed under his left arm. "Hey Joe," Harmon said, trying to appear happy that a colleague had joined him. "Hey superstar," Joe said and saluted with two fingers to his forehead, a lazy salute of disgusted resignation. Harmon's boss, his and Joe's mutual boss, had dumped her most aggravating subordinate on to a special project. An old AC&C trick. When headquarters requested assistance from the remote locations, the arriving *help* resembled a rogue's gallery of misfits, malcontents and incompetents. Joe was fond of saying that the not so distant Statue of Liberty and its famous inscription wasn't really meant to welcome immigrants to New York Harbor, but regional outcasts to AC&C Headquarters Staff. *Give me your tired, your poor ... The wretched masses of your teeming shore ... Send these ... to me.*

That was it. He could sense it. A team of four. Caitlin, one chair removed on his right, the DNA-TMG guy across from her, Joe slouched at the table's far end as if in a different meeting. He had expected more. Not one manager from the Leadership Team had volunteered for the People Team. But four was okay and with no senior managers the team might be easier to manage.

The room got quiet, except for an irritating vibration coming from the overhead fluorescent light. Caitlin closed her appointment book and stared ahead with a pious face, as if to say, "Let's go and I don't know about the rest of you, but my time is valuable". The DNA-TMG guy smiled complacently, as if he had all the time in the world. Joe put his pipe and tobacco pouch on the table and then, with a purposefully loud rattling, shook his newspaper open.

"Okay," Harmon said, "maybe we can begin." He heard the weakness in his voice, a voice unaccustomed to command. The simple comfort of being just a plain team member, the serenity of sitting back and being led, he had never appreciated that before.

"Now," he said, "perhaps the best way to start is by going around the table and introducing ourselves. Maybe with a brief statement as to why we each volunteered for the People Team."

"Who," Caitlin interrupted, "is taking minutes?" She stared straight ahead, rigid and earnest, speaking to but not deigning to look at Harmon. "We've gotta have minutes."

She was right. A bad start, to forget the basics and have Caitlin correct him.

"I've been through this kind of thing before," Caitlin said, piling on. "We must have a detailed record of our proceedings. Especially a list of deliverables. I'm talking about when a deliverable is due and who's responsible for it. A detailed list and constantly updated. If you don't track it, it won't get done."

She was probably repeating word for word what she had heard Mr. Yates say sometime, somewhere. But she was right. Whoever said it first knew AC&C.

"Any volunteers?" Harmon asked.

Silence. A team leader's nightmare.

"Get someone," Caitlin said

"Someone?" Harmon asked.

"A clerk."

Harmon looked to Joe.

"If you want," Joe said, glancing over his paper with practiced indifference. "Yeah. What the hell. Get a clerk." Joe couldn't take AC&C matters too seriously.

"Okay," Harmon said, "I'll step out and see what I can do."

The team's first action was putting the minute taking onto a clerk.

"Good," Joe said. "I need a break. All this coffee. My teeth are floatin'. He looked to Caitlin, a purposeful look, to see if she were listening. Then he added, "I gotta take a spit and a piss."

Caitlin's face pinched at the crudity. Joe grinned. Something in the grin said he and Caitlin had some history and Joe planned on enjoying himself.

Teammates

drudgery — crossed paths

In her short AC&C tenure, Riley had worked on plenty of dumb tasks, assignments that bored her to distraction and rubbed away her romantic notions of corporate enrichment. She had drudged by hand through thousands of customer invoices because the billing systems were screwed up. She had upended chairs and tables and CPUs to find and record serial numbers because the inventory system was screwed up. She had audited the expense and voucher and petty cash records because they were screwed up, too. *Malfunction Junction*, she called her department, with lots of malfunctions and malfunctioners.

This morning she sat in a vacant office at a cold steel desk, flanked by a flatbed cart with three boxes of forms, the Finance group's vacation records. Her hapless task was to go through all that paper, three years of slipshod accounting collected from the group's eight clerks, to make sense of it all and determine how many vacation days each manager had taken, compare that to what they were entitled to and net the difference. The whole vacation tracking system was so screwed up that CEO Preston P. Yates had declared a new policy, no more carrying over, year after year, large chunks of vacation time. Now, one week of carryover was the limit. Use it or lose it. Unused vacation days represented outstanding obligations. Preston P. Yates didn't like outstanding obligations.

***

"Ms. O'Brian," Riley's supervisor said, "your talents are needed elsewhere."

That surprised Riley. She figured the unannounced visit was with the hope of finding her malingering.

"Just drop everything, gather your stuff and follow me."

"Your wish," Riley said, "my command."

What could it be? What could be worse than this? Maybe the toilets had overflowed. The secretaries playfully argued over who had the worst assignments and who supported the most helpless clients: managers unable to refill a stapler, or transfer a call, or send a fax, forget about adding paper to the copying machine or fixing a paper jam. One of the male secretaries had a story that was hard to beat. His VP underwent a hysterectomy and while she recuperated he not only collected her mail and dry cleaning and shopped for her groceries, but for two weeks he reported to her large rambling house where he cleaned the cat's litter box and carried his boss up and down the stairs as required.

Riley followed her supervisor, a woman in her fifties who walked with a bowlegged swagger and who sneakily eyeballed every clerk and secretary with the hope of finding something wrong. Then a surprise. Standing at the supervisor's desk, Harmon Wolcott.

"This is Ms. O'Brian," the boss lady said to Harmon, with a dismissive wave at her underling. "She will provide you and your team with administrative support."

Riley thought that sounded like a task force of some kind, but it couldn't be much worse than the drudgery of auditing vacation records. With this young man involved it might even have compensations.

She stuck her tongue out at the boss. Harmon didn't let on. He didn't introduce himself so the supervisor did it for him. "This is Mr. Wolcott. He is the leader of the People Team, perhaps the most important project in all of AC&C." Still behind her boss, Riley opened her eyes wide and turned her index finger in a circle. *Woopy-do.* Harmon kept his poker face.

The supervisor nodded toward Riley and said to Harmon, "Miss O'Brian is all yours."

"If you can handle her," Riley added.

The supervisor shook her head with subdued disgust and walked away.

"Call me Riley," Ms. O'Brian said to Harmon.

"Okay," Harmon said. He stood still, as if unsure what to do next.

"Well," Riley said, and winked, "lead the way, mister leadership man who heads

the most important project in all of AC&C."

Introductions

hot & cold — a sleight — a team

Harmon held the conference room door for Riley. He couldn't believe his luck, having her as a part of the team. Riley hesitated, suspicious, as if there might be some nefariousness behind Harmon's courtesy. She wasn't used to chivalry. She entered and took the empty seat next to the team leader. Her premonition was right; the People Team was a task force. Even the air had a task force feel to it, hot and dry and thin, as if sapped of oxygen from too much talking. "It's hotter than hell in here," she said.

It was, but she knew what to do. She kicked off her shoes, stood and hiked her skirt. With two graceful strides she stepped onto her chair and then the conference table. Every astonished eye went to her, standing in the middle of the table, her athletic legs commanding attention like a work of marble statuary. Harmon admired her legs but diverted his eyes. Joe widened his. For an instant Harmon thought she was going to dance. She didn't. Instead she squinted at the ceiling tiles, found a small protruding lever and pushed at it. Immediately the air conditioning clicked on and cold air began to fall.

Riley stepped down, wiped off her chair and sat. "There," she said. "An old trick."

"I'm cold," Caitlin said.

"Okay," Harmon said, avoiding eye contact with chilly Caitlin. "As soon as Ms. O'Brian is ready, we'll get started by going around the table and introducing ourselves."

Riley opened her official AC&C pad. She was ready.

After one last glance at his notes, Harmon formally introduced himself and welcomed the People Team. He told how they were part of Mr. Yates's change initiative, responsible for ensuring that AC&C's people, the company's most valuable resource, were fully engaged and productive. He stopped and swallowed, knowing he sounded too robotic, concerned at how the team stared back at him, no hint of inspiration in their faces. But he had saved the best for last, that Mr. Yates considered their mission so important that he was their champion.

Caitlin's face lit with wonderment. Even the DNA-TMG man seemed impressed. But not Joe, he remained slouched with his big belly thrust forward for everyone to admire, his eyes fixed on the ceiling lever Riley had manipulated.

Harmon took a breath, looked to the end of the table, and asked Joe to introduce himself. Joe was still absorbed with the lever, studying it as if it involved magic. The overhead lights reflected off his glasses, lined bifocals that needed cleaning.

"I knew about that," Joe finally said. Then he told how he was volunteered for the *people's* team and that his boss had called it a change *ignitiontive* and selected him because she knew he liked people so much, the latter said with an ironic smile, through a pipe smoker's crooked and stained teeth. He said he'd been at ACC for forty-two years, then gave himself a soft, ceremonial slap for saying ACC instead of AC&C. He ended by saying he had seen a lot of teams come and go and wished this one luck.

Harmon knew what role Joe would play, not a complete slacker, Joe was too intellectually curious for that, but a gadfly who lived for demonstrating management absurdities. That would include a team leader's absurdities. Unfortunately, Joe was good at what he did, a book not to be judged by its raggedy cover, an autodidact who knew the business, top to bottom and side to side, relentlessly negative, but deceptively intelligent. He was an expert on what could not be done and why, always with a handful of sand to throw into the gears of progress, fun to watch for malcontents, but the worst possible nightmare for a team leader. Harmon's only hope was that, as his district mate, Joe might cut him a little slack.

Fred the consultant said he was there to offer advice and counsel but stressed that his intervention must be very, very discreet. If necessary, he would provide a little nudge, which he pronounced as *nooge*. He held his hands in front of his chest and pushed them out very slowly, demonstrating his delicate touch. His was a minimal art.

Caitlin rolled her eyes. Fred's insouciance seemed to anger her. The air conditioning clicked back on and she draped her thin sweater about her shoulders, shivering conspicuously. Instead of an introduction, she started a speech about people and how much they counted and how much she believed in Mr. Yates's vision, all sprinkled with a heavy dose of buzz words — *be part of the solution not the problem, every day is a new day, we can make the difference, seize the moment* — until Harmon politely interrupted and asked that she please introduce herself. A hard look came back. He could feel her disdain. It scared him. She emitted a strange sound, an involuntary snort, then forced a smile and explained why she didn't bother with a formal introduction; everyone at AC&C knew her and she was always trying to respect people's time. That was part of her work ethic. Part of who she was.

"I don't know you," Riley said. "And I doubt if Freddy there does either." Another snort. This time Caitlin's hand went to her nose, to try and stifle it. She shifted her head side to side, trying to loosen her neck. Harmon thought if she were the old steam boiler that heated the family farmhouse the pressure release valve would've popped like the time his mother shut off all the upstairs radiators.

"Well then, my name is Caitlin and I'm here at Mr. Yates's request."

Purposefully brief and to the point. Harmon scolded himself. Before the meeting had started, and despite trying to treat everyone with kid gloves, he had managed to antagonize a person who not only never forgot a slight, real or perceived, but who had a direct connection to Preston P. Yates. She had the man's ear so to speak, maybe more than his ear, though Harmon doubted those rumors because AC&C gossip always assumed the worst and most sordid and there was the impossibility of imagining Mr. Yates in rut over anything other than an attractive balance sheet.

He started to move on with the meeting until a loud throat clearing interrupted him. He looked to Riley who waved her hand, then peeked from behind it and raised her eyebrows. *See me, I'm here too.*

"I'm sorry," Harmon said.

"And I'm Riley O'Brian," Riley said, turning to the team. "I'm here at your request to help with administrative functions."

"Thanks," Harmon said. He lowered his head to Riley. "Sorry for missing you." He meant it. His anxiousness caused him to be rude. He had forgotten basic politeness. Not good.

"It's okay," Riley said. "I've suffered worse."

***

So this was the People Team. Caitlin, Joe, Fred of DNA-TMG and Riley O'Brian. All led by Harmon. A team of five and, already apparent, a challenge more than enough for any team leader.

Down to Work

a question — points — brainstorming — a plan — lubrication — a pipe

Time for work.

Joe raised his hand, the devil in his smile, enough to give Harmon an immediate feeling of dread.

"I would like to know," Joe asked, "what's our mission and how will we know if we accomplish it?"

Oh boy, Harmon thought. Here we go. So much for cutting a colleague some slack. "Joe," Harmon said, "the mission is that I must have a statement of purpose done by this evening. I have to present it to Mr. Yates tomorrow, right after his annual address."

"That's not a mission statement," Joe said. "That's an assignment. That's homework. Your homework."

"Okay," chastened Harmon agreed. "But, actually, I was kidding. Seriously, we're the People Team. So our mission is our people."

"Excuse me," Joe said, "but that statement is meaningless. It's a, whadaya call it? A *toe-ology.*"

"A what?" Caitlin asked.

Nobody answered. Riley jotted a note to herself.

"Well Joe," Harmon said, "I'm not sure—"

"Well you better be sure," Joe said. "Sure to have a good mission statement and *quantumfiable* objectives and a measurement system that *defiles* success. Either that or what you can count on from Yates is a good ass reaming."

Caitlin squeezed her face and turned away, for the crassness of it. Joe looked at her and nodded his head, for the plain truth of it.

Silence again. For Harmon, unbearable, as if the whole world waited for him to put the team on track. Caitlin stared straight ahead, stone-faced. Joe scratched his armpit. Fred of DNA-TMG smiled. All well and good for them. They could afford the luxury of contemplation. Harmon was the one that would stand in front of Mr. Yates tomorrow, on the spot and alone. He needed something now.

"I've got an idea," Riley said.

Everyone looked to her, a clerk stepping out of her prescribed caste. Not the AC&C way.

"Joe," Riley said. "How about you make a specific suggestion. I'll record it. I'm sure it'll be a good start and then we can adjust as needed."

"A *sumgestion*?" Joe said.

"Yeah," Riley said. "Take a shot at what the mission is, or should be. I'm gonna keep track. I'm gonna give two points for positive suggestions. I'll take a point away for anything negative."

Harmon feared trouble he couldn't handle. He wasn't a psychologist or a conflict mediator and as much as Joe could dish it out, he didn't like to take it. He didn't need two strong characters butting heads like Rocky Mountain sheep. To his amazement, Joe smiled, and said to Riley, "You're keeping points, huh? I like that. But what does the winner get?" A hint of lechery in the question.

"That depends," Riley said.

"On what?"

"On how good the *sumgestions* are."

Riley smiled and made a point of raising her pen over her pad, anxious to record. Something irresistible about her smile, the way it rearranged the freckles on her nose.

"So," Riley said, "fire away."

Joe's insurrection morphed to compliance. The old lion tamed, at least for the moment. Harmon hadn't seen that before. And Joe delivered, concentrating, his thinking cap on, AC&C getting its money's worth for a change. He said that AC&C's People are assets, just like everything else the business utilizes. The mission was to *maximight* the return on those assets.

Not bad at all and compatible with Yates's world view. Even Caitlin nodded in begrudging assent. Riley congratulated Joe, said she knew something good was brewing when she saw smoke coming from his ears. Joe lapped it up. Inspired by their minute-taker, the team was off and working, next deciding to make a list of the things keeping AC&C from maximizing the return on its people assets. After that, they would brainstorm possible solutions. It sounded just like what a people team should do.

***

After a slow start, ideas flowed as if from a fire hose. Joe and Caitlin dominated the conversation; Joe focused on business efficiencies, Caitlin on people issues. Riley kept the list. Harmon checked to see if she kept up. She did. She was fast. She made a list of Obstacles:

-lack of respect from upper management
-long hours, discrimination (sexism, racism, ageism, ethnicism, homophobia, prejudice against body type)
-poor pay and benefits
-good-old-boy networks

-lack of support for families
-lack of day-care
-lack of communication
-lack of praise, lack of constructive criticism, lack of courtesy, lack of respect
-being left out
-poor tracking systems, poor billing systems, poor fitness facilities
-long walks from the parking lot
-cold drafts, hot air, stale air
-mice that lived in the air-ducts and came out at night to eat unprotected snacks and diet powders
-non-ergonomic chairs
-excessively critical appraisals, non-critical appraisals, no appraisals
-promotions denied, promotions undeserved, social division by management level, the favored few, good-old-girl networks

When the problems started to repeat, Harmon suggested moving to solutions:

-better communication from upper management
-a weekly all-hands conference call
-a monthly newsletter
-management support for a balance of work and family
-no working past midnight
-allowing only positive remarks in ranking and rating sessions
-revising appraisals to include only positive categories—from trying his/her best to outstanding role model
-thank-you grams for people who do something nice, cash or merchandise awards for people who do something nice, prize raffles for the thank-you gram winners
-better fitness facilities, stress relief classes, information on vitamins and minerals for counteracting stress
-universal use of his/her rather than he, alternate use of he and she, use of the neutral their rather than he or he/she
-a rainbow colored sticker to be placed on the office of every manager who wishes to make a direct statement of his/her/their support for a workplace friendly to all people regardless of race, color, creed, gender, sexual orientation, age, ability or disability
-more upper management mingling with the workers including senior managers using the regular cafeteria once a week instead of the separate Executive Dining Lounge, a lunch and learn series of presentations about different cultures, encouraging people of different backgrounds to sit together in the cafeteria, forcing people of different backgrounds to sit together in the cafeteria

-more team building trips, suggestion boxes in every district, an all-hands candle lighting ceremony to bring everyone together spiritually

Enthusiasm in the room, especially from Caitlin. "Problems and solutions," she said. "I mean, we're supposed to be problem solvers so this is good. Like we used to say about the system and the solution."

Harmon felt a twinge of optimism. Then came a warning, from Caitlin. They would need an overall strategic focus for Mr. Yates. He would demand that. The man was so sharp. He'd want a strategy statement and a tactical plan. That was how his rarefied mind worked, like the time he taught her the difference between strategy and tactics. A strategy was like a plan to starve the enemy, a broad way of thinking; a tactical plan was more narrow, something in support of the strategy, like bombing the enemy's supply lines. The man was brilliant. And he would want everything properly quantified. To him everything else was mute.

Riley looked up, first with a quizzical look, then a sly smile. "Isn't the word moot?"

"You know," word-perfect Joe said, "I think it is. It's moot. Ain't it? Yeah, the word's moot." Joe's eyes bugged out a little, as they did when he was enjoying himself.

"Listen," Caitlin said, a patch of red spreading on each cheek. "I'm not going to put up with any nonsense."

"Okay, okay," Harmon said. "Everybody calm down. We're going to be spending a lot of time together. We have to get along." He tapped the table for emphasis. "We have to respect each other." He meant it. He couldn't afford Caitlin complaining to Mr. Yates, but it was more than that. He didn't like anyone getting picked on. "Why don't we do this," he said. "We have a great start here. Let's work with Caitlin's idea. Let's brainstorm a strategic mission statement and work plan. We can always come back and refine it."

"You're the leader, superstar," Joe said. "You the man."

"Just to see what we come up with," Harmon said. "You know, to keep us flowing."

"I'm flowin," Joe said, making a swimming motion with his short arms. "Are we still getting points?"

"Absolutely," Riley said.

"Let's get to work then," Caitlin said. Her face still squeezed with indignation. "You know, like professionals. Let's seize the moment and make a difference. Let's focus and come up with something that really positively impacts our people."

Focus proved elusive until impatience overtook Riley and she said, "I know one thing this place could use."

"And what would that be?" Caitlin asked.

"Some truth telling."

"Just what do you mean by that?" Caitlin asked.

"I mean," Riley said, "and I don't know if this meets the criteria for a real strategy, but people got to feel safe telling the truth. You know, about the business."

"And they don't feel that way today?" Harmon asked.

"Hell no," Riley said.

To Harmon's shock, Caitlin didn't disagree. Instead, she moved her head back and forth, between yes and no, as if there could be something to it. "Of course," she quickly added, "it's more complicated than that."

"Of course," Riley said.

"Whadaya expect?" Joe said. "Everyone's ascared of losing their jobs. With all the layoffs, you think they're gonna say what management don't want to hear? These people aren't crazy? They're not martyrs. They're not *parajohns* of courage."

"What?" Caitlin and Riley said, simultaneously.

"People," Joe went on, "they figure they tell the truth, they're gonna get mounted."

"God!" Caitlin said.

"Yeah," Joe said. "People being comfortable telling the truth, that would be your change, you know, what Yates is always preaching, your *pair-of-dimes* shift."

A moment of reflection, followed by head bobbing and a sense that they had hit on something. "Much more to it though," Caitlin said. They needed to demonstrate to Mr. Yates that there is a problem, and that meant the problem must be quantified. Quantumifcation, Joe said, was always the tough part. Quantumifcation seemed to stump everyone, until Fred of DNA-TMG spoke. "I have an idea," he said.

The dead arisen.

"Go ahead," Harmon said. "Please."

"Yes. Here's my suggestion. You, the People Team, propose a survey of AC&C associates to determine if there exists a cultural bias against truth telling."

"A what?" Joe asked.

"A survey," Fred said.

"I know about surveys," Joe said. "What's the other thing you said; the cultured thing?"

"A cultural bias," Fred said. His face now animated by consultancy instincts. "A cultural bias against truth telling would explain a fear of ramifications that puts a damper on an associate's willingness to speak the truth. If a scientific survey confirms this, you make a presentation to Mr. Yates and the Leadership Team, identifying the problem and detailing a recommended solution."

"A presentation?" Harmon asked.

"Yes," Fred said. "A muscular *PowerPoint* slide show, supported by a detailed written recommendation. Professional, from the executive summary to an implementation plan to an appendix of suggested follow-up reports."

Caitlin liked it. Riley awarded four points to Freddy who sat up straighter, his nooge given, DNA-TMG's fee earned.

"Better than nothing," Joe said. "I mean we need something, without this we got ..." He made a big O with his thumb and forefinger.

"How about this?" Caitlin said. "For our overall strategic approach, we ask management to commit to making AC&C a safe environment for people to say whatever is on their minds."

"Let's go with it," Joe said, already tapping his pipe on his palm in anticipation of a break. "Besides, if we don't come up with something, we could sit here all day." He glanced toward Caitlin to make sure she was listening. Then he added, "Yeah, we could sit here all day, you know, stuck between a sweat and a shit."

"God!" Caitlin shook her head in disgust.

Joe grinned.

"I need a break," Caitlin said, got up and walked out.

Harmon watched her leave, then said, "I hope she's okay. She seems uptight."

"Ya know why," Joe asked and then answered his own question. "Not enough sex."

"What?" Riley said.

"Yeah," Joe said. "With sex she'd be looser, you know, more, ugh, lubricated."

"I think we all need a break," Harmon said. He didn't want further discussion of Joe's observation. "Let's take ten minutes."

"I think you got what you need," Joe said. "You know, for tomorrow."

"I do?"

"Yep. You take everything we said, add some bullshit and stir. Boil it down to a slide and bada-bing, you're good to go."

"What about this survey?" Harmon asked. "Do you think we can do that? Isn't that complicated?"

"You shake and bake it," Joe said.

"What?"

"You know. Ask some people their opinion. If it doesn't come out just right, you make it work."

"Make it work?"

"Yeah. Like we always do, you know, torture the numbers till they surrender."

"I don't know," Harmon said, "I don't think—"

"Listen," Joe said. "You gotta have something for tomorrow. Is that right?"

"Yes."

"Well like I said, you can go this way or we can sit here all day between a—"

"Okay," Harmon interrupted. "It sounds like I have something to work on."

"You're good to go," Joe said, already moving out of his chair. "I'm done."

"You'll be back, right?" Riley asked.

"Why?" Joe asked.

"Well, first, to develop our work plan, but second, because then you don't have to go back to your regular job?"

"That," Joe said, "is a good answer. I'll be back. But, right now, I need a pipe."

Break

break—butt—apology—something to look forward to

Break time.

Joe took his pipe and tobacco and headed off for the parking garage. Fred wandered into the hallway, like a pleasantly lost tourist. Riley looked over her notes. Harmon took a walk.

He stopped by the windows and the fifth floor view of *Golden Boy*. A bird's eye view and a different perspective from behind the great statue. Even from there, every part shiny, not a spot of verdigris. How often did they clean it?

"It's something, isn't it?"

He turned to see Riley, standing next to him, also admiring the statue.

"Yes," he said. "It sure is."

She seemed smaller, standing next to him in the high ceilinged hallway. She was pretty. He couldn't help but keep noticing it, even in the tension of the People Team meeting. He wondered why he hadn't appreciated her beauty more the first time he saw her.

She moved closer to him. The combination of her closeness and prettiness made him anxious. He turned back to the statue. The gold leafing flashed in the sunlight.

"You know what I call him?" Riley asked.

"What's that?"

"Golden butt."

Harmon laughed at that, his eyes going to the statue's pronounced, muscular backside.

"He's got a great butt," Riley said.

Harmon stayed quiet. A landscaping crew was raking around the statue's base. One of the men stopped, leaned over and pulled a weed from between the paving stones.

"What do you think that thing cost?" Riley asked.

"I don't know. A lot."

A magnificent monument to monopolistic excess, Mr. Yates had called the Headquarter complex. There were even rumors he was trying to sell Golden Boy.

"Well," Riley said, "at least it's pretty."

"Yes it is."

"How long's the break."

"Ten or fifteen minutes," Harmon said.

"You wish," Riley said.

"Yeah," Harmon said, with resignation.

The break would creep closer to a half-hour. Not what he wanted, but he felt the need to go with the flow.

"So," Riley said, "you're running the show?"

"I guess."

"You guess?"

"Yeah."

"You're the team leader? Right?"

"Yes, I am."

"Well then there's no guessing about it. I don't envy you though."

"Why's that?"

"It's some crew you got here."

"What do you mean?"

"Well, you've got blonde-ambition. You've got a forty-year veteran bullshit artist. You've got a consultant with a stuck-on grin. And you've got me. I'd say that's a tough crew to work with."

He had to nod to that.

"So, how'd you get to be team leader?"

"I'm not sure myself. It just sort of happened. I haven't done this before."

"Well, I think you could be good at it. I can tell."

"You can?"

"I can."

He wanted to say more but couldn't think of anything. They stayed quiet for a moment. Until Riley said, "I'm sorry for causing trouble."

"Trouble?"

"Yeah. Caitlin and the mute and moot thing. I didn't mean to make things tougher for you. I just couldn't help it."

"Well," Harmon said, "we seem to be on track now."

"Yeah. I'll try to keep it buttoned up. I get a little worked up over words. It probably sounds crazy, but I got a thing for words."

"That's not crazy. It's, ugh, neat."

"Neat?"

"Yeah. You know, making sure about the right word. But Caitlin might be—"

"Sensitive?" Riley suggested.

"Yeah. But not because of what Joe says."

Riley laughed at that. "Well," she said, "I'll do my best."

"I'm sorry," Harmon said. "About Joe. He can be a little crude."

"Don't worry about that," Riley said. "Joe's a babe in the woods compared to some of the characters I've dealt with."

Harmon believed that. "We should get back," he said.

"Okay. You're the boss. The team leader."

He liked the idea of having her on the team. He liked that he would see her first thing every morning. She was something to look forward to.

Statement of Purpose

words — a slide — a choice — food

After the thirty-five minute break, the team dedicated itself to the Yates presentation. One slide was all Harmon needed. One was all Yates allowed. The man was too busy for more.

The afternoon was it, all the time they had. Saving grace in that, without that deadline, the debate might have lasted a week. Parkinson's Law was the natural order at AC&C: work regularly expanded to fill the time available for its completion. It wasn't uncommon for staffers to spend twenty straight hours in the office, on dozens of tense phone calls with Yates's staff, the back and forth about matters such as the color scheme of a slide presentation.

Harmon and the other two team leaders had ten minutes each for their presentations. Not a second more and sure to be mercilessly timed by Yates's assistant. The Statement of Purpose must be succinct, just the one slide, but there was no limit on the amount of supporting material, the suggested verbiage and supporting facts that Harmon could study in preparation and refer to in presentation. The team worked hard on that. Twice, Caitlin asked Riley to leave the room, due to the proprietary nature of the discussion, the information too sensitive for the ears of a temporary.

After fatigue set in and Caitlin and Joe got and gave enough for individual vindication, the team finished the slide.

People Team
Statement of Purpose

Our people represent our future. They are our most vital and important resource. In our new highly competitive business environment our people represent our positive differentiators.

To optimize our people and their talents and contributions we must leverage our strategy around encouraging everybody to perform at maximal levels.

Communication, the productive interchange of information, is a key facilitator and determinator of our success.

Fear of truth telling is the greatest obstacle to honest and open communication. Any and all obstacles and impediments to a free and open exchange of information and opinions must be eradicated.

We must create a free and vibrant culture with a bias for truth telling and respect for individuals regardless of their gender, race, color, creed, sexual orientation or level of management so our human resources are challenged, fulfilled and stretched while their individual fortes are utilized to maximize shareholder value.

There are substantial benefits from improving communication — tactical, strategic and financial.

After Riley typed it, Harmon began to like it. Amazing how words look so much better when printed in *Courier New 12* and properly spaced. The team congratulated themselves. Caitlin went to her office, to catch up on all her other responsibilities, though she was dedicated to the team, the other demands on her time didn't stop. Fred left to report back to the DNA-TMG brain trust. Joe went home. Harmon thanked a silent Riley.

She hung around until Harmon asked, "So, what do you think?"

"About the slide?"

"Yes, the slide."

"For a full day's work by the whole team?"

"You don't like it?" Harmon said.

"It's pitiful."

"Pitiful?"

"Weasel-worded bullshit."

"That's not very constructive."

"You want constructive?"

"Well yes. I mean I would appreciate any constructive advice."

She handed him another page. "Short and sweet," she said. "Everything else in the backup."

People Team
Statement of Purpose

People are our most valuable assets.
We must maximize our return on these assets.
Honest communication, top down and bottom up, is key.
Fear is the greatest obstacle to honest communication.
We need an environment where all our people feel safe communicating.
There are substantial benefits from improved communication.

Like an envious writer, knowing better when he read it, Harmon tried to convince himself of something other than the plain truth. Her slide was better.

"I have to see Mr. Yates first thing in the morning. I don't have time to consult with the rest of the team."

Riley hunched her shoulders. "Go with whichever you think best."

Harmon held the two competing slides, one in each hand, as if he might weigh them to make his choice. He considered the stakes and put the team's work aside.

"Thanks," he said.

"You're welcome."

"If possible, I need your help. I need to make sure my verbiage works with your slide."

"You mean now?"

He nodded. His presentation was twelve hours away.

"Okay," she said. "I should be getting to the gym, but I know the spot you're in. So, let's do it."

"I really appreciate it. I hope I can make it up to you."

"Well, what you could do is get me something to eat. If I don't eat I'll get the shakes. I'm not much good with the shakes."

"The cafeteria—"

"Is closed."

Harmon looked down the hall.

"Oh no," Riley said. "Not one of those sandwiches from that machine. I need real food."

Dinner

diner — Machiavelli — kindredship — a touch

He had no appetite and without her prompting he would have stayed at his desk. Sometimes he got the shakes, too, when he became so absorbed in his work that he forgot to eat. Sometimes he shook so bad that he had to lay down. No, it was *lie* down! Riley had already made him sensitive to such particulars, afraid to make a grammatical mistake in her presence.

He had suggested the diner, not because it was cheap or he was cheap, but because it gave him the best chance to feel comfortable. Familiar surroundings and all that. Riley said she liked diners.

***

She had never been in a pickup truck before and the high cab surprised her. "This should come with a ladder," she said. But she had no trouble climbing in, even with her briefcase and gym bag in tow. When she brought her leg up Harmon saw a tattoo on her left ankle, a small one that looked like two flags, each about the size of a postage stamp. A nice tattoo on a nice ankle.

In the intimacy of the truck's small cab, he felt self conscious. It was different, away from the office and just the two of them. For the first time in years, since he was a kid driving old field cars out back, he didn't synchronize clutch and shifter and ground a gear.

***

They stepped through the glass doors and into the diner's heavy air conditioning. It was crowded. Harmon usually got there earlier. The big Greek owner looked surprised — he always greeted a solo Harmon. He recovered and took his time considering Riley, his eyes making a slow vertical trip up and down her frame. Elevator eyes. Finished, he shook Harmon's hand, as if congratulating him. The big damp hand swallowed Harmon's. The owner usually just waved him to his favorite table, but now he led the way, like he did for other couples.

Riley studied the thick menu. Harmon didn't. He lacked the will for another decision and the meat loaf was always safe. The waitress was his favorite. A small woman from Guatemala, she had an easy smile and the color and characteristics of her Mayan ancestors, high cheekbones and straight black hair that fell to her waist in a single braid. Harmon thought the ribbon that held the braid in place, with its green and black colors, had something to do with her native village. He had been disappointed the day he saw a young man in a gaudy car pick her up from work.

"Busy tonight?" he asked.

The waitress smiled again and moved her head side to side. *Más o menos.*

He liked to exchange thoughts about work with the waitress. Both took pride in being hard workers. His father always said the best way to stand out was to work harder than everybody else. Probably what the waitress's father told her, the sentiment independent of language or geography.

The waitress took their orders, Riley's given and confirmed in fast and fluent Spanish. The waitress also seemed surprised at Riley's presence, or maybe that was his imagination.

The ordering settled, he took Riley's slide out of his briefcase and the two of them set to work. Riley suggested they first formulate the best words to fit the statements, then try to anticipate Yates's questions and prepare answers. She came prepared with index cards where she could print the key points to emphasize, the likely questions and best answers — take-aways for Harmon to study. She had a very logical mind. Now, even more so than with the team, she spoke with confidence and authority. Harmon wondered where it came from. He knew Caitlin already resented Riley's presumptuous break from her assigned support role. He was ingrained enough in the system to understand the resentment, but he didn't have the luxury of form, he needed help.

***

They ate while they worked, Riley with gusto, as comfortable as could be and Harmon with care; food and its enjoyment weren't important now. The important thing was he didn't look crude.

About his presentation, she stressed the need for brevity and sticking to the point. She had never worked directly with CEO Yates, but had exposure to the other big shooters and big shooters were all the same. Harmon should think of them as spoiled teenagers with attention-deficit disorder. If someone could get them to sit still and listen and make a reasoned decision from facts, then that person should get a trophy and would have earned it. Keep things simple, too, just because someone was an executive didn't mean he was sharp. Always remember that perception trumped reality. She guessed that wasn't his style, but he better get used to it. She sounded like a Jersey City Machiavelli.

He wanted to stick to business, but Riley didn't. Not a haphazard mix of business and personal, a certain method to it, as if she would trade her insights for his secrets. About him, she was endlessly curious. Was his father in management too? Had he brothers and sisters? What was his mother like? Who was boss, his father or mother? Whom did he take after? Her focus on his people and where he came from, every new piece of information led to another question. At first, he struggled against it but after a while he gave in and hoped there was a limit to her curiosity.

"What do you do for fun?"

One of her tougher questions. *I like to walk through the snowy fields back home and ponder life* didn't seem a good answer. *Nothing* even worse. I like to read was the best he could do. He thought again, how he was envious of men who could talk with women.

"What do you have your sights set on?"

For that, he had a ready answer. "I'd like to have more responsibility, so I can contribute more."

She cocked her head and looked at him. She looked like an inquisitive puppy but she said, "That sounds like Human Resources bullshit."

He flushed.

"I want that, too," she said, "on my career planning sheet. Right along with my burning desire to benefit the shareholder." She laughed. "Now, what I really want, at work, is to make myself valuable. I want the company to need me more than I need them. And if AC&C doesn't need me, I want to learn enough that someone else will. I want to show them I know what I'm doing."

"Okay."

"How about you. What does Harmon really want?"

"I want to show them that, too."

"They must think it already, or you wouldn't be the People Team leader. You know," she smiled, "it's the most important project at AC&C. But I'm serious, they must know how good you are."

Part of Harmon believed that. The more logical part. "For me," he said, "it's more than at work."

"Okay?" Riley said, more a question than an answer, because about this she wanted more.

"Well, I'd like to show my father ... I'd like to show him I know what I'm doing, just like you said, through my achievements."

He said it because he wanted her to know that about him. He was suddenly in a truth telling mode. Her reaction gratified him. He could see it in her face, a heightened attention and glow of approval. What he said had gone to her heart.

"That's so interesting," she said. "Because, see, my mother's gone, but I still want to show her. I still owe her that."

He felt himself flush because it meant the two of them were alike in an important and fundamental way, that they were kindred spirits. He asked and she told him about her mother. For the first time he sensed in her loneliness, pain and vulnerability. Up to now he had only seen her free and tough sides. He feared his silence might seem like insensitivity but he didn't say anything because he wasn't good at that. Her questions made him feel exposed, but he still didn't want the conversation to end.

***

On the ride to her bus stop, needing a topic to cool down with, he asked, "So what do you do at the gym."

"I box," she said and patted her gym bag.

She was an endless source of surprises.

"I started just to stay in shape but found I liked it."

"What do you like about it?"

"You know what the primary rule is?"

"I don't think so."

"Clear and simple. *Defend yourself at all times.* Isn't that a rule to live by?"

"It is at AC&C."

They had a mutual laugh at that.

Genuinely interested, he asked more about her boxing. She liked everything about it, she said, even the hard pull of the street-front door, the creaky steps and flaky walls that led to the gym's second floor home. It all lifted her spirits. She even liked the smells. A true boxing gym wasn't a cosmopolitan kind of place. It wasn't a sweat-proof makeup, outfit showing off, aerobics studio. No spinning classes. It was a blood and guts gym. Liniment and sweat. Enter the cavernous main room and you smelled concentrated corporality. An instant antidote to a day spent with over-cologned and over-perfumed paper pushers.

Her enthusiasm peaked when she told of the surprising technicality behind the sweet science. Like how to throw a proper left hook that she learned by listening, from a discreet distance, when the crabby old trainer gave hands-on lessons to his favored few. She told and she showed, lowering her shoulder belt to turn and demonstrate in the pickup's cramped cab.

It was all in the details. Plant the right foot, bob to the left and twist the left toe, like you're stepping on a cigarette. Keep the left elbow level to the floor—right hand up at your chin, always protect the chin. Don't twist too much or you'll lose your balance. Unwind to the right, legs and hips and keep your chin down! Twist your left toe to the right, putting that cigarette out. Uncoil like a mean snake with mean snake intentions. Now let go with the left hand like you want your fist to go through the target. Then back to the start and quickly, don't leave yourself open.

She stopped suddenly, as if embarrassed by her passion. "Sorry," she said. "I like talking about it."

"I like hearing about it," Harmon said.

His slide and backup material was in his briefcase and he owed her, big time. He wanted to drive her home. It was the least he could do. Also, it was a half-hour to Jersey City and when did the last bus run? What he really wanted was the extra time with her. But all she wanted was to be dropped off at her bus stop. Before she got out, she took his hand and squeezed it. "You're going to do great tomorrow," she said.

All the way home and all evening he relived their evening, the details going round and round in his head, with special attention to that touch.

A Good Day

respect — substance — ragamuffin — devotion

She caught the bus with a minute to spare. Another good development in what had been a good day. She felt sure she had surprised Harmon with her business insights, both during the day with the team and later as they worked together. She enjoyed their dinner and thought he did, too. Was there more to come? If so, it was better than just a good day, maybe it was a special day.

On the bus ride her thoughts stayed with Harmon. She knew she liked him from the first. That morning in the big conference room, before the Leadership Team meeting, his nervousness meant he wanted to succeed. And the way he appreciated that cup of tea, there was respect in that. Her mother had always been big on *respecto*. Little things showed it and little things meant a lot. The way managers treated the clerical help, you could tell a lot from that, you could tell whether they had consideration in them.

Substance attracted her. Where did you go to find that? Substance was an anachronism. *Anachronism:* something or someone out of harmony with the time. That's what she was looking for, a man out of harmony with the time. *Substance:* substantial or solid quality in a thing; solidity; seriousness or steadiness of a person's character. Tell me about your achievements and ask me about mine. Maybe yours are mostly hopes and dreams, well so are mine. Tell me about the achievers you admire. Tell me what you really want and what's standing in your way and what you plan to do about it. She would love to talk more about that with Harmon.

***

She took her time walking the three blocks from the bus stop to her apartment. Even with the sun behind the taller buildings, it was still hot. The clatter of talk and radios and televisions spilled out of open windows; a Jersey City mix of English and Spanish and Portuguese, these days some languages she didn't recognize. Polyglottal potluck. Some bare chested boys bummed about on a project stoop, all of them well acquainted with a tattooist. She kept her eyes straight ahead, as if she didn't see them.

No crazy paint for Riley. That had been one of her mother's many rules, later vindicated by her own close observance of smart, successful people. She did have her one little tattoo, procured after her mother's death and placed discreetly above her ankle—crossed flags, the blue and red quarters of the Dominican-Republic on the left and the stars and stripes of America on the right—acquired as an homage to her mother, her mother's home and adopted lands. Also, because it was pretty.

She took care to step over the sidewalk's cracks, the same ones she avoided as a little girl. *Step on a crack, break your mother's back.* The ritual always put her in a reminiscing mood. She had played many a youthful hopscotch game on these concrete sidewalks and when she looked down, she still expected to see her white and red chalked squares.

Her mother wouldn't have been happy about the tattoo. The flags significance wouldn't have helped, Riley knew just how her mother would have reacted—with angry fulmination about trashy people and the trashy ways they called attention to their trashy selves. This followed by a weeklong silent treatment. The thought made her smile. Just a few minutes from now she would enjoy a nice long soak. She would rest her foot on the side of her cast-iron, claw-footed tub, her ankle turned so she could meditate on the flags and all the things her mother was right about. Her act of attrition.

In front of her building, from beside the stoop, a gray and white cat greeted her.

"Hola Ragamuffin," Riley said.

The cat rubbed against her leg. A mangy, half-tailed cat, she belonged to no one but was celebrated on the block for her long life and the dutiful way she nurtured and defended her many offspring.

"How's my ragamuff?"

The cat answered in a faint, scratchy meow, less greeting than demand.

"Okay, okay," Riley said and sat on the bottom step. She knew what was wanted. First, she scratched behind the cat's ears and then under her chin. The ragamuffin lifted her head and closed her eyes. Riley took the chin and held it tightly and with her free thumb gently cleaned the gunk from the corners of the closed eyes. When she was done, the cat vigorously shook its head and then crawled onto her lap, leaving a trail of fur along her slacks. Riley enjoyed pleasuring the old queen, even when it delayed her soak and meant additional dry cleaning. A devoted mother deserved attending.

Whipping Boy

smarts & pride—Socrates—lesson taught—next up

The next morning Harmon woke wishing he didn't have to attend Mr. Yates's eight a.m. address to the CFO. He needed that time to study more, pounding his presentation harder into memory. But not attending the CEO's annual talk was out of the question. Such a sacrilege would outrage Harmon's boss.

He had worked late into the night, adrenalized by the eventful day. He wished he could concentrate on Riley. He would do that after his presentation, when he could give her the full attention she deserved.

Sometimes he thought his presentation was good and felt anxious to give it, but the more he imagined the real thing, standing there in the big office, Mr. Yates and his intimidating intelligence and concentration focused on him, the more he questioned if he could do it. And he questioned how he got to this place where a few hours from now he must stand in front of AC&C's Chief Executive Officer and present him a plan to improve his company. He envisaged disasters—Mr. Yates's dubious scowl, his own stuttering incoherence—all leading to who knows what explosion.

Thoughts of Riley intruded. She wouldn't be denied. She was so smart that it was her slide he would present today, after a team of professionals spent a whole day preparing a different one. She was dangerous, too, the way she courted confrontation with Caitlin and didn't hesitate to tangle with Joe. As much as Harmon avoided confrontation, she seemed to enjoy it. He wondered if she was thinking about him.

He needed a perfect presentation. There was no standard formula for satisfying Mr. Yates. No one, not even his executive assistant, could consistently please him, and pleasing him was the assistant's sole purpose in life. Yates's unpredictability made it especially difficult for AC&C's legion of ass-kissers. They were used to bosses who were tyrannical, but predictable. They could work with that combination, sycophancy their good guide, just grasp the most current mythology and heartily endorse it. Flexibility a must—the zeitgeist was ever changing—one must be ready to support growth or retraction, centralization or decentralization, a loose decision model or a tight one. They all had their day, fell from favor and eventually reoccurred. On the AC&C staff, one needed philosophical pliability, the right proportion of smarts to pride and principle—heavy on the smarts and light on the principle. It made

Harmon think of a story his father had heard and liked to tell, about a desperate man interviewing for a coveted teacher's position during the depth of the Depression. At the end of the interview, the job hanging in the balance, a tough looking old-boy on the rural school board stared down his nose and asked the interviewee, "Do ya'll teach the earth is round or flat?" The interviewee thought a moment and answered, "Sir, I can teach it round and I can teach it flat."

Mr. Yates presented a complicated problem. He was the river's source, AC&C's myth maker, so one could be caught without advance warning when yesterday's wisdom became today's folly. With a single slip of the lip, a fair-haired favorite could become an outcast.

***

In the main auditorium, Harmon had no trouble finding his group. His boss always sat in the center section, as close to the front as possible. She insisted her people do the same. That morning they sat in the third row, the front two reserved for greater rank.

The Chief Financial Officer opened the meeting, reminding attendees of their great good fortune; Mr. Yates again taking time out of his schedule just for them. The CFO kept glancing off-stage as he spoke. Yates never came early to such functions, that would be a waste of his time and one could not exaggerate the preciousness of his time. In the midst of some platitudinous filler, the CFO suddenly stopped, brightened and stood straighter.

"Ladies and gentleman, fellow Finance managers, it is now my privilege to introduce our Chairman and Chief Executive Officer, Mr. Preston P. Yates!"

Yates entered from stage left and walked quickly to the podium. He remained silent for the long applause, staring over the assembly as if he had all the time in the world. When he started, it was with the basics.

"Why does a corporation exist?"

Harmon knew the answer and he wanted Mr. Yates to know that he knew, wanted it so bad that he had an urge to stand and shout, *to benefit the shareholder!*

"What," Yates continued, "makes someone put their treasured capital in the trust of strangers?"

Harmon liked the way Mr. Yates used questions and answers to prove his points. It reminded him of the Philosophy 101 class he had so enjoyed. Unlike Socrates, though, the CEO usually answered his own questions.

"These investors, are they so philanthropical that their love for their fellow man drives them to risk their fortunes? Or, are they technophiles thrilled by the thought of some new gadget? Could they be patriots looking to add to the glory of their homeland?" The straw men floated until Yates punctured them with the answers. "No, no and no!

"Because the investor invests for a much simpler reason. The reason: a fair return. This is how the real world works. It is how it has always worked, from the earliest entrepreneurs taking the great risk of shipping goods across the wine-dark sea so they might command a greater return, to the seventeenth and eighteenth century's antecedents of our great corporations, to the industrial revolutionaries of the nineteenth century. It is how the real world will always work, even for the future colonizers of other worlds. Because that is how it must be."

Preston P. Yates: classicist, philosopher, historian, futurist.

"The more intriguing question, the question that never ceases to fascinate me, is why anyone, especially any one of you, thinks things should be different here at AC&C. Yes, I've heard the whining about change. Ever since I arrived here I've heard it. Too much. Too fast. Well tell me, what makes anyone think that AC&C is Sleepy Hollow, that it is the land that time forgot, that it is immune to change or that it should be? I don't think we should be immune to change. Do you?"

A murmured no while the associates looked at each other circumspectly, as if each was sure of his or her self, but not his or her neighbor.

"I'm not going to linger on this. That wouldn't be a productive use of my time. So, succinctly, for all you doubters and deniers, and I know you are still out there, I will address each of you one last time by saying this: grab your left ear with your right hand, then grab your right ear with your left hand and pull your head out of your ass."

Loud laughter at that.

"Now once your are more, ahh, clear-headed, do this. Look at the person to your right and then at the person to your left. Soon one of those people will be gone. Gone! Unless there is a marked improvement in our performance. And not in some fanciful future. Soon means the immediate future."

No laughter at that.

"It's not because I like that future. I don't get some thrill out of this painful process. It is because the market demands it. AC&C's very survival demands it. We must, I repeat, we *must* get control of our cost structure."

The tension now tangible. Yates's thoughts on cost control could cause the AC&C world to wobble in its orbit.

"Why do I say this at this time and in this place and this openly and honestly? Because you in Finance are critical to the mission. You in Finance must understand the need to cut costs and live that creed every day. If you don't understand and support and execute this policy who will? The folks in Marketing and Sales?"

Tension relieving laughter at this, at the very thought of marketing and sales types worrying about costs.

"If not you in Finance, then who will be my cost cutters?

Silence. It could not be anyone else.

"You know the question I like to ask, especially of our friends in Marketing?" Yates turned and smiled at his CFO who smiled back and nodded his head because he knew. "The question I ask, as part of my re-education work, is this: what's more valuable to our business today, right now, raising revenues, or cutting costs?"

The question left to hang a moment, to ripen.

"This question tends to confuse our friends in Marketing, but it is a question that I shouldn't even have to ask here in Finance."

Vigorous head shaking from all those sitting on the stage.

"Let me see now," Yates said and looked purposefully into the audience. He stopped and stared at someone, off to his right. "Ah, there he is, my young friend, Mr. Cluen."

Many in the auditorium knew what was coming. It excited them. They were about to witness someone worse off than themselves. Brian Cluen, AC&C nickname *Clueless Cluen*, was rumored to be the CEO's relative, a remote cousin or such. He was definitely the CEO's whipping boy and, as Joe said, the man needed a whipping boy.

Yates motioned for Cluen to stand. He was a thin, prematurely bald young man of average height. The false smile on his face made him look half petrified and half simple. His role as Yates's designated fool might have generated more sympathy, if not for his own obnoxiousness to peers and subordinates.

"Mr. Cluen," Yates asked, "do you remember the first time I asked you that question; what's more valuable to our business, raising revenue or cutting costs?"

"Yes," Cluen said.

"And do you remember my telling you that there are only two choices and by dumb luck you had a fifty percent chance of being right?"

"Yes," Cluen said.

"So Mister Cluen, tell us now, how did you answer?"

Even odds or not, everyone in the room knew he had answered wrong. His niche at AC&C, and he fit it well, was to be always wrong; a living example of wrongness.

"I said the revenue," Cluen admitted, lowering his head with self-reproach.

"Yes you did," Yates said. "So I guess that's what they're teaching these days at Harvard's southern cousin."

He meant Cluen's Pennsylvania based alma mater. A particularly harsh blow as Cluen was inordinately proud of his exclusive business school, making sure to reference it in meetings and lunch conversations, just in case folks didn't notice his insignia tie. Rumor said that Yates had paid the full fare for Cluen's education. Mean-hearted and kind-hearted, Yates's Jekyll and Hide reputation was another thing that captivated Harmon.

"And," Yates said, raising his voice. "Mister Cluen was wrong. Bad wrong! In this case, a prime example of what's most wrong here at AC&C." Yates turned and faced the whole crowd again to make his larger point. "We're drowning in unnecessary cost. And you see, what they didn't teach my young friend, for all their obscene tuition, was the benefit of cost cutting. But then," Yates pursed his lips and shook his head, "what would an institution that charges $50,000 a year know about cost control?"

Appreciation and laughter at that.

"Now what's our gross margin?" Yates turned and looked again to his CFO. "Ted?"

"Twenty-eight percent."

"That's right," Yates said. He looked back to Cluen. "What's twenty-eight percent of a dollar?"

After a humbling delay Cluen said, "Twenty-eight cents?" An uncertain, interrogative tone to his voice, as if, even after all that time and money spent on his learning, he was unsure about the simple math.

"Good analysis," Yates said, to more laughter. "So, our new dollar of revenue is worth twenty-eight cents, before taxes. Now I ask, what is a dollar of eliminated cost worth, before taxes?" Yates again looked to his CFO.

"The full dollar," the CFO said, playing his highly compensated part.

"The full dollar," Yates said and then repeated, "the full dollar. So Mr. Cluen, would you rather have twenty-eight cents or a dollar? Take your time and think now, use all that education squeezed between your ears."

"The full dollar," Cluen answered, sheepishly, his head down and his shoulders sloping so that he looked like a prisoner of war paraded in front of a hostile crowd.

"Very good!" Yates said. "You have learned."

***

AC&C's people were thankful for the presence of Brian Cluen, like prairie homesteaders were thankful for their lightning rods. Harmon felt special sympathy with the young man. He had something in common with him.

He was up next.

Waiting

on deck—cowardly heart

By the meeting's end, all of Finance had pledged allegiance to cost cutting. Before heading off to meet his fate, Harmon sought out his boss to give her the opportunity of offering last minute advice. It was the respectful thing to do. Always put the shareholder first, she advised. He couldn't go wrong if he did that. He should leave her a message as soon as he finished.

***

He walked to Executive Row. He hoped to see Riley at her desk, but she wasn't there. He was first to Yates's office, ahead of the Systems and Customer Care team leaders, who would also be presenting. He already had a sandpaper throat. When he made presentations, the dryness, combined with not stopping to swallow, could lead to an embarrassing croak that exposed his nervousness to the entire world. He committed himself again to swallowing before reading each bullet point. Simple, in theory.

He stayed outside of Yates's office until the Systems team leader entered, followed closely by the Customer Care leader. He joined them in the waiting room and the secretary offered coffee. Everyone refused and retreated to nervous silence. Harmon stared at Mr. Yates's closed door. Behind it, the control and command of AC&C.

The waiting room was like a gentleman's study. It had two sofas for humble petitioners. Glass end-tables held business magazines that were carefully stacked so only the titles shown. Subdued art hung on the walls and palm trees stood in the corners. Everything perfectly placed.

No sign of Yates. His secretary said it might be a while and offered coffee again. This time the Customer Care lady accepted. Harmon was full of nervous wonder at what the other two had prepared, fearing it was good, better than his, momentarily wishing one of them would screw-up enough that, by comparison, he had to look good, then trying to take that back, fearing that just thinking such a thing could cause God to withdraw all support. He needed God's help.

Ten-thirty and the CEO's door remained closed. On his fifth or sixth review of his slide Harmon had a brief surge of confidence. By the tenth review that confidence was gone and replaced by despair driven disbelief: that he could have approved such an unprofessional thing, that a temporary clerk had actually produced his slide, that he had chosen that clerk's words penned in a few minutes over the full day's work of four professionals. His supporting comments were, he decided, banalities at best, inanities at worst. He wished he had the team version. In that moment, in that waiting room, sophisticated sounding language seemed more fitting. What if he just left, got on the interstate heading north and didn't slow down until surrounded by corn fields? How he looked forward to those corn fields on his long drives. They meant he was almost home. Not a serious thought, but a temporarily balm, like the thought that in a hundred-years' time he would be dead and not a single person would care about what happened that day.

"This is nerve wracking," the Customer Care team leader said, breaking the ice.

"Have you done this before?" Harmon asked. "I mean presented to Mr. Yates?"

"Once," she said.

The Systems Team leader punched away at his calculator, oblivious to his environment and his colleagues.

"How did it go?" Harmon asked.

"Not good. Yates said that Customer Care couldn't manage a whorehouse on a battleship."

"Geez," Harmon said, the women's failure all the more frightening as she had an air of competence about her.

"It could have been worse, though. I was new in the job and he was a little easier on me. I just agreed with everything he said, like I was amazed, too, at how screwed up Customer Care was."

"Was it?"

"Oh yeah. Still is."

"So now," Harmon said, sympathetically, "you're in charge of the Customer Care Team."

"Yes. And you have the People Team?"

"Yes."

"That's a tough one."

"Why do you say that?"

"I'm just going by what I hear."

"What do you hear?"

"That Yates thinks people are the lynchpin to fixing this place. I heard he thinks our biggest problem is that we have too many people and the wrong people. 'People piteously equipped for the challenge.' That's how I heard he put it."

***

Ten-forty and still no summons. Harmon and the Customer Care lady went back to silence, like pilgrims at a place of worship. He had intermittent flashes of rationality, as though his brain miraculously rewired for logic and confidence. In that state he thought what was the big deal and what was the worst that could happen? He could have a life without AC&C. He was a good person and that's what really mattered. Who was Mr. Yates to judge him? But soon he was back to the stomach churning, chest tightening certainty that his life depended on the coming presentation, convinced, again, that he was totally insane for foregoing all the team's work and going with Riley O'Brian's off-the-cuff substitute, wondering why he hadn't found some simple job back home, maybe in the County Clerk's office. He could picture himself at a neat little desk processing fishing and hunting licenses. He even saw the calendar on the County Clerk's wall, featuring some tranquil scene: a straw-hatted boy fishing a meandering stream with a cane pole, evoking slow moving, peaceful days unmindful of the dog-eat-dog world. Something more suited to his cowardly heart.

Tight

a message — bad scared

Riley left her back row seat at the all-hands meeting hoping to catch Harmon before he went into Yates's office. She wanted to be the last one to wish him luck. But her supervisor snagged her. She had volunteered her for post meeting clean-up duty.

***

Finally back at her desk, she checked her messages. From Yates's secretary: "Your boy's here. Call me."

Yates's secretary was one of Riley's buddies ever since they spent a day together in a computer class and discovered their common Jersey City roots. Riley's first friend in a high place.

She called the secretary back. "Has he gone in yet?"

"Nope, he's still waiting. There's three of them waiting. The man's here, but he's on a call with the Governor's office. It's running way late."

"How's he look?"

"Harmon?"

"Yeah, Harmon."

"Truth?"

"Yeah, the truth."

"He looks scared."

"How scared?"

"Bad."

"Bad?"

"Yeah, bad."

"How bad?"

"Shitless."

"Thanks for that."

"Just being honest."

"Well I figured he'd be tight. Let me know when it's over."

Center Stage

big birds — learn or leave — automaton — you're it

"He'll see you now."

Ten after eleven. Over an hour's wait. Harmon would not have objected to a longer wait, perhaps infinity.

He stood up too fast and got light headed. He balanced himself and followed his colleagues. Everyone entered the office as if walking on black ice; the office so big that it was a hike from the door to the CEO's huge desk. Mr. Yates sat behind the desk. He seemed elevated above the rest of the room. He was busy writing. He didn't look up as they entered, nor did he offer a greeting. The great head remained lowered in concentration.

Soft lighting in the office. The desk of rich wood. Cherry? To the side a closed door, beyond it, Harmon guessed, Yates's private suite — bedroom and bathroom. At the room's far end was a small conference table and a wall screen for presentations. Family photos on the desk looked like they were taken by a professional. Yates and a woman and two young girls, the woman blonde and pretty, the girls miniatures of her. Harmon never thought of Mr. Yates with kids. A picture of an older couple, Harmon guessed they were Yates's parents, the man distinguished looking. He looked for the birthday card. It wasn't there.

In Social Styles training they taught him to carefully study a person's office adornments. Such things told a lot about personality. In Yates's office were an abundance of eagles. On the walls and shelves and tables, eagles of every size and rendering: eagle plaques, medallions and statues. On a pedestal was a beautiful wood carving of a bald eagle, above it a large framed picture of an eagle flying in the midst of a severe lightning storm, printed underneath a dissertation on courage, the highlighted phrase: *During big storms only the great birds come out.*

"Okay," Yates finally said, looking up and looking aggravated, as if whatever he had just dealt with hadn't gone well and he begrudged this new intrusion. His assistant gestured to the conference table and the CEO walked to his seat, the others following dutifully.

"What do we have?" Yates asked. No one said anything and he looked to his assistant. "Let's go."

"We'll do it alphabetically," she said. "Customer Care, People, Systems. One slide each. Eight minutes."

Not ten minutes as originally scheduled. Petitioners seldom got the time originally allotted for them, every minute of Mr. Yates's day mattered and there was always some time squeezing emergency.

"Customer Care, you're up."

Harmon breathed. An eight minute reprieve. Anything could happen in eight minutes: a fire alarm, a government decree outlawing AC&C, a catastrophic meteor strike obliterating civilization.

"Mr. Yates," the Customer Care team leader began; her tone different from her waiting room conversation, her voice deeper and firmer. "First I want to thank you for this opportunity."

That was good, Harmon thought. The way she worked off of *opportunity*, using one of Yates's favorite words, feeding it back to him. Yates seemed to like it, too, at least he nodded. The Systems guy, amazingly, was back to playing with his calculator.

The Customer Care presentation didn't live up to its opening. The team leader made it about a third of the way down her slide, delving into metrics for measuring customer satisfaction: *Average-Talk-Time (ATT), After-Call-Work-Time (ACW), Average Handle Time (AHT), First Call Resolution Average (FCRA), Abandon Rate (AR), Cost Per Call (CPC).* Yates listened longer than Harmon expected, but with waning patience, until he raised his hand, like a traffic cop.

"Stop!"

The Customer Care woman stopped.

"More of the same," Yates said.

"Well—" the Customer Care woman's voice suddenly less firm and confident.

"No, no, no," Yates cut her off. A hint of red in his face. "This is not what I'm looking for. I don't want more of the same. What I want is insight, thinking outside the box insight. That's what leads to change. That's what leads to paradigm shifts. That's what these teams are supposed to deliver."

"Okay," the Customer Care lady started again.

"Not okay!" Yates said, his face redder now. Something about her okay he didn't like. He looked at the presenter and then at Harmon, as if he were equally at fault. Harmon stopped breathing.

"I don't want the same old, same old," Yates said. "Why can't you people learn? If you can't deliver insight ..." He pointed to the door. "If you can't deliver that then leave. If you can't learn, leave!"

Harmon looked at his feet. He'd have been happy to leave, his own lack of worth clear to him. Maybe Mr. Yates would be disgusted enough to cancel the whole meeting. That would be a break. Yates sat still for a moment, until he breathed deeply and pressed his thumbs against his temples.

"Harmon," the Executive Assistant said. "Perhaps we should hear from the People Team now."

The Customer Care leader pulled her slide from the projector and sat down. Harmon's throat constricted. He stood up and took his place but, per Riley's advice, didn't put his slide on the projector. He was an automaton now and he would do everything exactly as planned or do nothing at all. That was his only hope.

"Mr. Yates," he said, "the People Team has a challenge for you." He heard that opening line, as if it came from a distant stranger. A bold stranger to challenge Mr. Yates. It was Riley's idea; she said it would ensure his attention. A suggestion Harmon knew he should jettison except now he had zero ability to extemporize. At that moment Riley's brash confidence seemed more like the easy bravado of someone who starts a fight and then holds your coat.

"Mr. Yates, the People Team believes, as you do, that we need fundamental change. We believe in your paradigm shift and we, as a team, believe the time is now." Said too fast? *Slow down. Swallow.*

"We believe AC&C's very survival depends on this and we want to be at the center of this great opportunity and we're going to ask your support. That is the challenge I will address at the end of my presentation." Riley justified the audaciousness of challenging Mr. Yates on the latest AC&C management fashion, that higher levels were meant to support the lower levels. The flipping of the terminology and re-drawing of organization charts were meant to highlight this new paradigm. But including Mr. Yates in the revolution, that was revolutionary itself.

He put his slide on the projector. His hand shook like an old man's and he pulled it back so everybody wouldn't notice. The slide wasn't squared up; it tilted to the right. He moved it and then it tilted left. He tried to center it once more and then looked to the screen. With a blank sheet he covered all but the Statement of Purpose's first assertion.

People are our most valuable assets.

"Mr. Yates, the People Team knows you believe this, but we must drive this belief top-down and bottom-up through the whole organization. Every AC&C employee must believe this, so every human asset is contributing to our success. This principle must become an integral part of our culture."

Swallow and slow down. Should he have said every employee must be pulling at his/her oar? He really liked his next line and thought Mr. Yates would, too. He swallowed and breathed and said it slowly. "This principle must become part of our muscle memory." Did Mr. Yates smile? He thought so. He paused, but the CEO remained silent.

He uncovered the next line.

We must maximize our return on these assets.

"How do we do this? First, we must put our people in a position to succeed." Still he had the feeling of unreality, like he was watching a movie that had somehow sucked him into it. *Swallow.* "We, the corporate staff should perform like a great point guard." His own words here, he knew Yates's love of sports analogies, especially basketball related, *slam dunk* and *full court press* among his favorites. "We must not be a burden on the backs of our field people. They are our scorers and we must give them the ball when and where they can make the most of it."

Mr. Yates still silent, but his face a little brighter. A good glow? Interest instead of anger? Harmon hoped.

Honest communication, top down and bottom up, is key.

"We'll say more about this as, with your approval, the People Team takes a deeper dive into our specific recommendations." *Deep dives* were popular on the staff, a phrase and concept Mr. Yates championed.

Fear is the greatest obstacle to honest communication.

"I'm sure this is controversial, but it is the firm sense of the whole People Team that AC&C has an embedded culture of not encouraging open and honest communication."

Surely Yates would interrupt here and, per Riley's instruction, Harmon would immediately place the legacy stamp on AC&C's communications failings. Yates didn't interrupt. Was that good? *Double Swallow.* Harmon had argued for only one change on Riley's slide and in her suggested backup points, more equivocation here, a direct statement that the communications problem was not Mr. Yates's doing. In their backup verbiage the team had a whole section dedicated to equivocation, amounting to an apology in case they were misunderstood as even hinting that Mr. Yates was less than perfect. At the diner, Riley argued against it as transparent ass kissing and the kind Yates wouldn't like. She argued it was better to first get the CEO's attention and then handle any objections in Q & A. It was Riley's plan and words now, for better or worse.

We need an environment where people feel safe communicating.

"The People Team wants to stress the urgency of this. We feel that with all our other challenges, this is more important than ever."

No one could disagree with that. Now a deep breath and the last line.

There are substantial benefits from improved communications.

Harmon let Mr. Yates dwell on that for a few seconds. Then he said, "Sir, the People Team believes this is the critical piece of our recommendation. So critical that we didn't want to present a shallow view of it. It is our intention, with your support of course, to provide an in-depth analysis of the benefits of improved communications, framed in reference to increased revenue and reduced costs. Quantification is the key."

He thought Mr. Yates would like that about quantification. As the management gurus said, emphasize your weakness as if it were your strength. Joe said it differently, "If you can't dazzle them with data, baffle them with bullshit." Again, he expected Mr. Yates to interject. Again, he didn't.

"That sir," Harmon said, "is our intention." He substituted intention for challenge because he felt comfortable enough for that extemporization and he thought he had overdone challenge. The whole thought of challenging Mr. Yates, whether it fit the new paradigm or not, could be carried too far. The real challenge was that an in-depth analysis cost money and new costs weren't something Mr. Yates wanted to hear about. New costs were normally a non-starter.

He had finished in his allotted time. Now he waited. Part of him didn't care if he got what Joe called a good ass reaming. The relief of having finished the presentation felt sufficient.

"Mr. Wolcott," Yates finally said, his face still neutral, like that of a good poker player. "I applaud your forthrightness."

"Thank you," Harmon said.

He was conscious of the attention of his Customer Care and Systems Team colleagues. He guessed what they were thinking. *Easy to make big-balled statements about change when you were talking people things, then you could say anything you wanted, it's all bullshit anyway, all soft stuff. Try shifting paradigms on something like Customer Call Centers or Information Systems, something real and measurable to the nth degree.* They could think what they wanted, right now it was every man for himself.

"Now Mr. Wolcott," Yates said. "I have one question."

"Yes sir?"

"Mr. Wolcott, How do you *know* that this lack, no, that this *lack* and *fear* of honest communication exists at AC&C?"

"The right question," Harmon said.

He said that because he and Riley had rehearsed for just this eventuality, actually hoping for that question, but he immediately regretted his choice of words. His wording made it sound as if he were putting himself in a position to judge Mr. Yates's questions. He didn't want to imply that.

Yates didn't seem to care. He asked, "So what is the right answer."

"Sir," Harmon emphasized the honorific, "the People Team would like to answer that question. But not just by opinions or guesses. We would like your authorization to conduct a survey to determine if AC&C's communications are as stifled as we hypothesize. Then, if that hypothesis proves correct, we will suggest a path to change, a plan to shift the paradigm."

"A survey?"

"Yes sir. To determine employee attitudes and concerns about the communications environment at AC&C."

Yates silent for a moment. Gears turning in the great head, most unusual when he addressed such an underling. "You're putting a lot of weight on this survey," Yates finally said.

"Yes sir."

"It better be well constructed and accurate."

"Yes sir."

Oh boy, Harmon thought. This is just what he feared, Yates zeroing in on the weakest point of his proposal and firmly committing the People Team to what probably couldn't be done.

"What," Yates asked, "will this survey cost?"

"We believe we can roll most of the cost into the current DNA-TMG budget."

Another question anticipated by the prescient Riley and the ready answer provided for. Yates seemed to like the answer.

"DNA-TMG is on board with the survey? They think we can get an accurate measurement of employee opinion on this matter?"

"Yes sir. DNA-TMG has been fully involved in developing our recommendation."

"Okay," Yates said. "You have my support. But I want one more thing."

Harmon nodded. He was impressed with Yates's ability to cut to the heart of things and make a decision. Yates was a decider. Harmon knew whatever was coming next would be important.

"I want the quantification of projected costs and benefits detailed in a five year view and presented as cash flows discounted and accumulated to a net present value utilizing our current minimum acceptable rate of return. And I want it in Best, Worst, and Most Likely views."

Just as Caitlin predicted. Score a big one for Caitlin.

"Do you understand that?"

"Yes sir," Harmon said.

Some exaggeration in that and maybe Mr. Yates sensed it. But instead of probing the weakness, he took the time to spell out in detail how he wanted the quantification done including the finer points of *CDCF*— Cumulated Discounted Cash Flow. Harmon was shocked by this treatment. He sensed Mr. Yates enjoyed it, teaching the eager young student before him, almost in a fatherly way. He knew that meant he had done well. Dare he think of himself as Mr. Yates's protégé?

When the CEO finished the lesson he said, "And quantification is not enough."

Harmon nodded again. What more? He would have agreed to anything right then.

"See," Yates said, "you must stand behind your analysis. You must commit to it." He pointed a stubby finger at Harmon, to punctuate the *you*. "See Mr. Wolcott, that's how I do business. I want one person with total responsibility."

"Yes sir," Harmon said.

What else could he say? Now something more to go with his pride. The kernels of fear and self-doubt, always present in him, popped.

He was it.

PART IV

Ass Enough?

success — what if — little boy

Yates's assistant ushered the managers out. The Systems Team leader didn't get his chance. The nitty-gritty of systems was never to the CEO's liking and it was his assistant's job to know when he reached his limit; her job more about a man's moods than a company's modes.

"Nice job," the EA said to Harmon, in the waiting room. Without a word to the others, she turned and went back into Yates's office.

Harmon felt like the winner in a gladiatorial contest staged for a sadistic emperor. "I was lucky," he said to the other team leaders and immediately thought his humility sounded stupid. The Systems Team leader pocketed his calculator and gazed about with puzzlement. The eloquent and concise Customer Care Team leader said, "I hate this shit."

Harmon hurried away, the bounce in his step fueled by the potent mixture of success and fear. He had delivered a presentation successful beyond his highest hopes and he had reaped the reward.

He skipped the elevators and took a little-used stairway down to the second floor and his privy hideaway where, in the locked stall, he hid and thought. Mister Yates was impressed with his presentation. He knew that. Might this be the life for him after all, playing with the big boys and winning? He began to imagine such a life. Now that he truly had responsibility for the most important project at AC&C, the consequences of success and failure escalated correspondingly. His judge and jury? Mr. Preston P. Yates.

The consequences of failure were clear, nothing less than total humiliation. The consequences of success were more complicated. Success would lead to a lot of what ifs. Yates's executive assistant was at the end of her two year rotation and ready for promotion. A scary coincidence. What if the CEO took a real liking to Harmon and wanted him as his next assistant? Was he up to that? The position was the surest road to promotion, but an EA worked eighty hours a week and every minute of his or her life was hostage to Mr. Yates's wants and needs. The current EA dedicated her top right desk drawer to headache and stomachache remedies. She generated widespread contempt. The nature of the EA position assumed sycophancy in exchange for an almost certain promotion, but as chief adulator, the current resident parroted Yates's buzzwords and mannerisms and when the CEO strutted about the halls with a silk scarf around his neck, she followed two steps behind sporting an identical scarf. Some found the sight humorous, most found it nauseating. Joe summed things up best, "If Yates said a mosquito could pull a plow, she'd hitch it up."

So Harmon flipped his no-win coin, failure and worry on one side, success and worry on the other. Success even scarier? The thrill of his presentation peeled away like a cheap veneer. No one in the whole world could help or understand. His father, at that very moment, would be sitting in their living room in his old reclining chair, beat-up slippers on, reading the newspaper with a finger under each word, sounding out the harder ones. His mother would be cleaning the house and making sure his father's coffee stayed warm. Both oblivious to their boy's troubles.

Time to be a man. Time to think practically. Consider his options. Look at the positives as well as the negatives. Respect had shown in Mr. Yates's eyes, a moment of recognition that he wasn't dealing with a moron. He should take pride in that. Mr. Yates was the most grudging giver of respect.

So now came the test. Did he have the stomach for what followed? The summer when he was twelve he had worked for a farmer named Albright, to earn money for an off-road motorcycle. He wanted that dirt bike more than anything. His mother hated the motorcycle idea but his father said earn the money and you can have it. The farmer tried him at harvesting hay, Harmon and the farmer's broad-shouldered son walking behind a tractor that pulled a flatbed trailer, their jobs picking up the dew soaked bales by their hay-bands and tossing them onto the trailer. Each bale weighed nearly as much as Harmon. Giving it everything he had, pulling with his arms and pushing with his legs, he managed two or three before one set him on his backside. "Well," the farmer said, not without compassion, "we better let you drive. You ain't got quite enough ass on you yet."

Before he left the bathroom, he rolled his right shirtsleeve up and turned his arm. There, on his elbow, ran a squiggly pink scar, a souvenir from that hay-harvesting, from hitting his elbow against the trailer. He studied the scar and wondered if he still was, and always would be, a little boy without enough ass on him.

Help

advice — sarcasm

There was one person who could help. Back in his office, he kept the door open and watched for her. She had been right about everything. She had prepared him for Mr. Yates like a skilled master, her every instinct spot on, from what he should say, to Yates's likely reaction, to how he should react to the reaction.

***

"It couldn't have been too bad. You're still here."

There she was, her head poked into his doorway, eyes wide open and eyebrows raised.

"It went pretty good," he said.

"Pretty *well*," she said.

He shook his head, too weary for a usage lesson. "Don't start. I need your help."

"Buy me a coffee."

***

He felt conspicuous, coupled with her on the elevator ride to the cafeteria. There was room, just two other people in the elevator, but she stood close to him and her hand brushed against his. Was it accidental? For a moment he thought she was going to hold his hand. He imagined the strangers focused on them and as self-conscious as that made him, he liked it, that people might imagine this young woman with him for more than business.

The cafeteria was about a quarter full with the early lunch crowd. He bought her black coffee and himself breakfast tea. Riley secured the far corner table, the one he preferred. He liked to sit with his back to the wall, the whole cavernous room in front of him, outside the plate glass windows a view of the main entrance and its water fountains and flag poles.

"So," she said, "tell me all about it."

He started but she stopped him. "Slow down. Make me feel like I was there."

She listened, her lips squeezed tight, her eyes alert. In this light just a hint of green in her mostly brown eyes. He told her of the long wait. He told of Yates's abuse of the Customer Care woman and how the CEO's face showed surprise at his presentation, especially the opening when he delivered her surprise line, *Mr. Yates, the People Team has a challenge for you*. In the interest of completeness and accuracy, he told her Mr. Yates seemed impressed.

"At least the man recognizes intelligence."

"It went pretty, ahh, well," Harmon said.

"It sounds like it went better than that."

"Mr. Yates seemed satisfied," Harmon said.

"Maybe he's more perceptive than I thought," Riley said. "I mean, can you imagine the morons he deals with all day, every day, knowing all the while he's paying them big money? That might make anyone an a-hole. But maybe he knows intelligence when he meets it."

"But it wasn't my intelligence," Harmon said.

"What?"

"I used everything you said. Word for word."

"You know," Riley said, "I got most of those ideas from you."

"From me?"

"Yep. Those were mostly things you said first, but then you let the team talk you out of."

"What?"

"You do that."

"Do what?"

"Let people bully you out of your own ideas. Good ideas, too."

"What do you mean?"

"Like when we were working the Statement of Purpose slide. Every time you came up with something good, basic common sense but good, the others had to disagree."

Harmon squinted. He hadn't been aware of that. What else about himself wasn't he aware of?

"Then they redid what you said and turned it into weasel-worded bullshit. Or, as Caitlin says, they *recast* it. And you let them get away with it."

She wrinkled her nose. Harmon straightened in his chair, like a scolded child.

"You let them strong-arm you, you know, big-ass you."

"I didn't notice that," he said.

"That's because you're used to it. You're too nice. Too, ahh, accommodating. Yeah, that's the word. *Accommodating:* agreeable, acceptable, obliging and willing. You give other people too much credit and don't give yourself enough."

Harmon felt hurt and complimented at the same time. The compliment made him change the subject.

"I don't know where to go from here," he said. "There's so much to do. So much that can go wrong."

"What can go wrong?"

"Oh God," Harmon said, as if the amount of things that could go wrong was inestimable.

"Like what?"

"Now Mr. Yates has expectations. I mean, he even said, once, near the end, that this seemed to be in good hands. I heard him say that to his assistant. I think he meant my hands!"

"O my," Riley said, her eyes widening in mock horror. "A compliment from Yates. What could be worse than that?"

"Nice," Harmon said, about her sarcasm. "But what if the survey gets all screwed up? It could even turn out the opposite of what we said. Then what?"

"What?" Riley shook her head. "The survey's a foregone conclusion. It's a *fait accompli.*"

"What do you mean?"

"*Fait accompli:* a thing done and irreversible before those affected learn of it."

"I know what the word means," Harmon said. "I mean I know in general, not like you. I don't memorize precise definitions. But what do you mean it's a foregone conclusion?"

"Do you think the people around here will say this is a place where they feel safe speaking their minds? That communication is good? That anything is good? Huh? You know what I call these people?"

She waited for his answer so Harmon asked, "What?"

"Habitual bitchers. That's what I call them."

"But we have to do a good survey. I mean it has to be right."

"We'll make sure you get your survey."

Harmon took comfort in the *we.* A word he didn't hear enough.

"How can you be so sure?"

"I'll make it happen. But we have to be careful."

"Careful?"

"You can't have a clerk in charge of the earthshakingly important survey, and a temporary clerk at that. So how about this. Put Joe with me and call it a Survey Committee. Even make Joe the chairman or chairperson. Just make sure you keep Caitlin away from me, give her something else, I don't know, maybe chairperson of the Yates Ass-Kissing Committee. That's a full time job for her anyway."

He didn't dignify that remark. He ignored it like a team leader should.

"Why do you think it's such a sure thing, the survey?"

"Because I could walk around here with a pad and pencil, ask ten people a few questions and in an hour have everything you need. But this being the land of constant complication we'll need a team and a process that takes at least a month and spends a pot of money and produces lots of slides. Pretty, color slides. That's the only way the big boys will listen. I know that. Whatever. What counts is that at the end of the day you have what you need."

"I don't know," Harmon said. "I want to do this right."

"Define right."

"Accurate. True."

She stayed silent for a moment, studying him like a sculptor deciding if her work required another chisel stroke. "Listen Harmon," she finally said. "I have a question for you."

"What?"

"Do you want the truth?"

"About what?"

"About how things work around here. About how people get ahead."

"I think I know that."

"You do? Then why don't you tell me."

"You're gonna say it's corny. You're gonna dismiss it. You know you do that sometimes?"

"I do," Riley said, in forthright admission. "But tell me anyway."

The cafeteria was filling. He lowered his voice and told her of his four types theory: AC&C Lifers, Sophisticated Survivors, AC&C-aholics, Guardians of the Shareholders. He had pride in the theory. Even in telling her, he thought it held up.

"Interesting," she said, when he finished. "You really have thought about this."

"Thanks."

"And it's number four that wins, right? The Shareholder's Guardian represents what, the culmination of corporate man's evolution?

"I believe so," Harmon said, ignoring the sarcasm. She was good at sarcasm and he decided his best antidote was sticking to what he believed, maybe even exaggerating it a little.

"You work hard," he said. You do your best. The goal is for everyone to win: shareholder, employees, customers. The goal is a win-win-win situation."

Riley extended her lips and blew the hair off her forehead.

Harmon waited. Her forthrightness usually made allowances for no one, but she seemed to be trying.

"Harmon?"

"Yes?"

"That is corny."

"I knew you'd think so."

"But forget all that. I mean, you do want to do this?"

"What do you mean?"

"You want to succeed? To be the team-leader hero of the People Team?"

"Yes. I mean I want to succeed. That's important to me."

"Okay."

Riley rearranged the salt and pepper shakers then looked out the window, towards the water fountain, as if for inspiration.

"Now, let's take your analysis. Your idea of hard work is nice. And I'm sure it's true, in some circumstances and some places. I admire it and I admire you for believing it. I really do."

He doubted that and must have shown it because she smiled and crossed her heart.

"Sacrilege, too," he said.

"All I'm saying is it's not true here and now," she said.

"I know it's not exactly —"

"No exactly about it. It's not close."

"Not close?" he said.

"Do you want the real truth?"

"Okay. Tell me."

A group took the next table. Riley looked them over. She said, "Let's take a walk."

How Things Work

walking & talking—her depths

"Think you can handle my power walk?" she asked.

Harmon thought he could.

Every day, on her lunch hour, when her work load allowed, she took a walk away from her incessantly ringing phone and away from an endless stream of demands. She had her own way, a carefully mapped path inside AC&C's seven interconnected buildings. A route specifically chosen for the least populated areas and the most challenging stairways. Thirty-five minutes, at her fast pace, covered the whole thing. Her walks more than aerobic, each an opportunity for reflection and, sometimes, revelation.

***

First, a staircase that ascended from the basement level to the fifth floor. She always started there, six full flights that got the heart pumping. Harmon thought he was in pretty good shape, but by the fifth flight he was short of breath and his thighs burned.

"The first thing you need to know," Riley said, over her shoulder, not breathing hard at all, "is that everyone's looking out for themselves. That's lesson *numero uno.*"

He didn't comment, trying to disguise his lack of breath.

"And," she said, "you can apply that to all four of your types, from AC&C heads to your saintly Guardians of the Shareholders. It doesn't matter, from the peons to the big shooters. The big shooters got where they are because they're better at it. They know how to play the game better."

He couldn't deny that. People did look out for themselves. There was a line his father liked: *If you don't look out for yourself the only helping hand you'll get is when they lower you in the grave.* His father got that from a movie, a western. His father liked westerns. But it wasn't as cut and dry as that. Was it?

Riley stood on the fifth floor's landing when Harmon still had half a flight left. She looked impatient, moving her legs up and down, walking in place. She was used to waiting for people to catch up, but she never got good at it. In the hallway it took a while for Harmon's breath to come back.

"You know why there're so many complications around here?" she asked.

"It's a complicated business," he said. "Even Mr. Yates says so."

"It's complicated all right, big time, because complications justify jobs and salaries and big complications justify big jobs and big salaries."

"Okay."

"Think about this," she said. "Who gets ahead here? Is it the hump grinding it out and trying to do the right thing, you know, the slob who works harder than everyone else?"

"I think so," he said. "On the whole at least. But I wouldn't call them humps and slobs."

"Good enough. Let's call them associates. But you think that's who gets ahead?" She tilted her head in a gesture of exaggerated disbelief. Nothing new for her, such a look, but she seemed more aggressive on their walk, as if this was her territory.

"Do you know," she asked, "the story about that guy, the one that came up with the idea for a better way of printing customer bills? Saved a lot on paper and postage, saved AC&C something like ten million dollars a year, maybe more. Maybe it was a hundred million. It's hard to keep track of the zeros around here."

"I heard about that," Harmon said. "Everybody did."

"A big deal, right?"

"They wrote it up big."

"Lot of benefit to the shareholder, right?"

"I'm sure."

"That guy, I think his name was George. George something." Riley strained to think of the surname, not wanting to go on without it. "It'll come to me. For now, let's call him George the genius. He's a pale little guy, like he never gets the sun. Probably hides in his cubicle all day. But nice. A nice man. Some kind of idiot savant they say, the savant part about AC&C's billing process. His whole life is the AC&C billing process. God!" She shuddered, as if suddenly chilled at just the imagining of such a thing.

"Well," she said, "I didn't do it, but I saw the paperwork for his reward. Do you know what it was? What they gave the miracle worker with the great idea?"

"No," Harmon said. "They didn't make that public. What did he get?"

"An American Express gift certificate for a lousy hundred bucks. That and a briefcase with the AC&C logo glued on. A fake leather, plastic, piece of shit briefcase. So shiny you could see your face in it."

"That doesn't seem right."

"And when he got it they had us all stand around and clap and Georgy boy kept bowing down and thanking everyone. I didn't know whether I wanted to hug him or kick him."

"Jeez."

"You know why it happened that way?"

"Why?"

"Because George the genius is not one of the favored few. He doesn't know how to play the game."

She let that sink in, then asked, "Do you know what Caitlin got for her bonus?"

"How could I?" But he did wonder. Everybody wondered what other people got for their bonuses.

"I know what she got."

She stayed silent and made him ask, "How much?"

"$28,565."

Now his look one of disbelief.

"Who do you think," she asked, "did her payroll sheets?"

"You?"

"Yours truly. And it was $28,565, exactly, to the penny. Bonus award on top of all her salary. All for ass-kissing. She is good at it, Ms. Caitlin. The ass-kissing that is."

"Come on now."

"You don't think that's fair? You think I'm too hard on her?"

He did and she said no more.

A turn down a side hallway to stairway number two. Going down was much easier but she was so fast he had to hold on to the handrail. The stairway so seldom used that a string of dust coated the rail and his hand pushed and gathered it, like a miniature snow plow. On the bottom floor she turned tour guide. This part of the basement housed the great edifice's infrastructure: the heating, venting and air-conditioning plant, electrical facilities, loading and receiving docks. Areas most employees never saw but that she knew all about.

"So," Harmon asked, "you know how to play the game?"

"A lot better than some."

And meaning, Harmon thought, a lot better than *you* do.

"So how do you play?"

"To play this game," she said, "in the circumstance you're in now, you have to know what Yates wants. Not the bullshit about shareholder value and all that, but what the man really wants."

"And you know that?"

"I do. By the way, there's the carpentry shop." She nodded to a large, square, partitioned room, its big steel door closed. "I bet you didn't even know there was a carpentry shop down here."

Who did know that deep in Building One's basement there was a whole room dedicated solely to carpentry?

"That's where they made the suggestion box we hung in our break room. A waste of good wood."

"Maybe," he said, "you should drop in some of your suggestions?"

"Oh yeah," she said. "They'd love 'em."

"You know what's behind that?" She pointed to another steel door and a smaller room.

"No."

"A locksmith shop."

"A locksmith?"

"Yep."

Now that was the job. Your own private area where people knocked before entering; your own special function that not a single boss knew a thing about; your job so easily described and measured and appreciated. Some employee locks his key in his office and you open the door and get an instant and sincere thank you. The locksmith, probably the most independent and happiest person in the whole complex.

"So," she said, "the game. See, first of all and especially for you, for someone that's, you know, Mr. Leadership and Mr. Team Leader, you have to know this. Yates is the only one who counts. Forget about everybody else. You've got to figure out what Yates wants and give it to him. The rest of them, even the other bosses, you just grin at 'em."

"What?"

"Just what I said."

She grinned an exaggerated grin to demonstrate, showing her white and even teeth. She had beautiful teeth.

"Brace yourself now."

He thought she meant for the next stairway, just ahead, past the receiving dock. But that wasn't it. Before she started her race up the stairs, maybe so he had time to think about it on his slow climb, she said, "You've got to learn how to grin-fuck them."

She waited for him in the fifth floor hallway, stretching her very fit calves while looking out the windows. He stopped, pretending to stretch, but catching his breath.

"Okay," she said, when they got moving again. "What I just said. It comes down to this. Say someone, your boss or a colleague, wants something from you. Something that takes time and effort. What do you do?"

"Do it." It was all he had breath for.

"No!" She said.

"No?"

"Absolutely not! Now, this is important, you never say no to your boss or any big shooter, you don't even say maybe or it depends. What you do is nod yes and grin. You can even write their requests down if that makes them or you feel better. Then forget all about it and go back to concentrating on whatever it is you're doing for Yates."

"I don't—"

"See if this makes it easier. Yates is the business. He and his satisfaction are all that counts. Don't even think AC&C. Don't even think shareholders. Don't even think about the other bosses. Think only Preston P. Yates, Inc."

Her point made and no adornment.

He had a question. "What if I want to do just what you say. How do I even know for sure what Mr. Yates wants?

"That's the easy part."

"Easy?"

"Easy."

"Okay," he asked, "if pleasing Mr. Yates is so easy, how come nobody seems able to do it?"

"Don't ever underestimate," she said, "how dumb AC&C staffers are."

She stayed silent through the central atrium. You couldn't trust the acoustics there, your voice bounced around. From the top floor they looked down on the indoor water fountain and the escalators that ran to the third floor.

"Did you ever notice," she said, back in a remote hallway, "how Yates thinks of himself as God? The way he holds himself above everyone and talks of saving AC&C and about miraculous transformation?"

"He does do that."

"That tells you all you need to know about his agenda. It's simple, what he wants."

"Okay."

"To aggrandize himself. *Aggrandize:* to increase, magnify, intensify; to cause to appear greater than the reality."

"That's it?"

"Yep. I'll give you an example. A quick one. I know you like examples."

He did.

"Take Yates's personal staff. From everything you know, would cutting the size of his staff be good for the business, you know, if you did one of your infallible cost and benefit analyses?"

"I guess," he said, mostly because he knew that's what she wanted.

"You guess! The whole group is useless. No room for debate on that."

She seemed angry.

"They're all high paid, too. Yates calls other staff people cost causers but bloats his own."

"Okay. Why?"

"Because a god needs worshippers. And a big man needs a big staff." She laughed at that, for the unintentional double entendre. Harmon didn't say anything and she asked, "So what do you do? What do you tell him about his personal staff?"

"What?"

"You tell him he deserves, needs, warrants a *bigger* staff."

She turned a sharp corner and pulled a door open.

"Another stairway?" he asked.

"Just one more," she said. "Six flights down to the basement and then we come back up three. That'll put us right at your office."

News to him. He was lost.

The six flights descended to a dead end, a bare concrete floor and an alarmed door. On the floor a little fur spot, all that was left of a mouse, there for who knows how long, its final resting place a spot so remote the sweepers never visited.

Riley stopped and bowed to the mouse. "I know that's weird," she said.

"I do some weird things, too," Harmon said.

Three flights up to his floor. He was sweating now. On the climb she said, "You know I like to exaggerate some."

"No!"

"A little. Not so much as you think. I know it's not that easy, pleasing Yates. But what is?"

"You know it also seems a little, ahh—"

"Wrong or devious?"

"Something like that."

"Well, Mr. Wolcott, welcome to the real world. You're playing with the big guys now and you either play hard or you quit and take the back stairway to the parking garage and hop on the Interstate North."

He didn't say anything.

"*Comprendes*?" she asked. As if a second language might help.

"*Si*," he said.

The second floor hallway was busy. When they reached his office Riley looked at her watch. Her lunch was over.

"Okay," he asked, standing inside his door for some privacy, "if I, if we, do it just like you say—and let's say the survey supports our hypothesis—then what are we going to do? How do we change the corporate culture?"

She looked at him as if he were simple, as if she were frustrated with his slowness. She stepped into his office.

"Listen," she said, in almost a whisper. "Changing the corporate culture is all bullshit. A fantasy. You put together some program or the other and call it transformation. That's why the People Team is what you *want* to lead. Not something like Systems or Customer Care where somebody just might be able to measure what you do. That's one thing you got going for you. Why do you think Yates decided to champion the People Team? Huh? It's because he can declare victory. He just says the culture's changed and ipso facto presto—it's changed. The great champion takes credit and who's to say he's wrong?"

"Okay," he said, weakly.

"Listen," she said, "when I say it's not that easy, there's more and you're not going to like it."

As if he liked what came before.

"Are you ready?"

As he ever would be.

"Now, to do it right, to really stand out, you have to disagree with Yates, at least once."

"Disagree?"

"Yes. Because the man's not stupid. He knows an ass-kisser when he sees one. He may be the world's leading expert on ass-kissers and he may like it, but he doesn't respect it. He gets too much of it."

"I don't know?" he said. To take this advice, to disagree with Preston P. Yates, that seemed dangerous.

"I know this is tough," she said. "The disagreement thing is scary. It has to be done carefully. Very carefully. Never disagree on something Yates is hot about. Never in front of people. Never make him look bad. Always be aware of who you are dealing with. Think of some king or Roman Emperor with the power of life and death over you. The trick is this: the right disagreement, the purposeful disagreement, it separates you from the herd, inoculates you against the common ass-kisser virus, makes Yates believe you sincerely agree with him the other ninety-nine percent of the time. See, ninety-nine percent means you really believe he's a god or at least a demigod. That's what the man wants."

"He wants *me* to agree with him?"

"Yes, he does. He needs it, too. But only if he believes you are different, not your common, ordinary ass-kisser. So you have to know what you're doing. Every morning, on your ride here, think about it."

As much as he had previously wondered at her, he hadn't known she was capable of all this. She turned to leave but he had a last question for her, a practical one.

"What if we come up with something that Mr. Yates likes and can make him look good. Wouldn't he hold me responsible for implementing it?"

"Implementation?" she said. "Don't worry about that."

"Don't worry about it? You know this place, how it's impossible to implement anything, at least the right way, how everything gets screwed up."

"Forget about that," she said.

"Forget about it?"

"Yep. Because there's one thing certain to happen before implementation."

"What?"

"A major re-organization."

Reflection

overwhelmed — socks

She overwhelmed him. He felt like a student come from an indoctrination by a maestro half genius and half seductress. Where had she come from? Why had she entered his life at this time, just when he most needed her? How'd she get so smart? How'd she get so cynical? He winced when he thought of her cynicism and what life experience must be behind it. You would probably have to go way back to understand.

Her lesson in the ways of the world and AC&C was fascinating but troubling. He needed to think about it, this Riley O'Brian version of the truth where everything was so black and white, like all the things he must do to please Mr. Yates. He wanted to refute it, point by point, even if only in his internal musings. He thought he might, given enough time.

What to do now? Should he run from her as fast and far as possible or should he hitch his wagon to her improbable and combustible star, a star that apparently only he could see shining so brightly. His head told him cast his fate with the team. Safety in the team. Safety in the herd. How about this: use Riley's insights but keep her as much in the background as possible? Would that be dishonest? Not according to Riley's own anything goes approach. What was it she said, told him to write it down? *The strong take away from the weak; the smart take away from the strong.* That was it. He had asked her then, how it felt to be smarter than everyone else. A sincere question. He thought she blushed. The only time he saw that. She didn't answer, but he really wanted to know.

Now his stomach hurt. He wondered if he was starting an ulcer. He was young for that but he knew people at AC&C, his age and younger, that had them. One had a bleeding ulcer so bad he needed a transfusion.

In his car on his ride home he loosened his belt. He didn't need to loosen his pants, they were loose enough. If his mother saw him now, the first thing she would say was, "You're too thin!" His father might not notice.

***

After a fitful night he woke from a dream in which he had arrived at a meeting with Mr. Yates only to discover he had forgotten his socks and had to drive all the way to his little hometown supermarket to buy some and all they had were white.

So strange, the way our fears unwrap themselves.

People Team Report

good news — stuck — a nudge — missed opportunity

Harmon reported back to the People Team; the team so anxious to hear about his presentation that the meeting started on time. He was tired from his poor night's sleep, but calmer now. His goblins were nocturnal beasts that retreated in the daytime.

"Let me begin by saying that we have Mr. Yates's support." He paused long enough to keep the team expectant. He was learning the ways of leadership. "Mr. Yates said we have his full support and confidence."

The team was duly impressed and attentive, sitting up straight in their chairs, except for Joe. Joe had a body made for a slouch. Maybe, by now, it was permanently molded that way. But he was listening, because he screwed his face into a look of all-knowing cynicism. That wasn't all bad since Joe's look soured in inverse proportion to a project's success.

Harmon told the team they should be proud of their work. Then he summarized the Yates meeting. He didn't show the slide he had used, the *Riley Slide* as he had come to think of it, and he massaged his replay to better fit the team's original work. Riley silently complicit.

The People Team liked it all, especially the part about the CEO being happy that they weren't there begging for direction and how the other teams didn't like that. Despite their internecine conflicts, petty or profound, the one thing the team could always agree on was their superiority to the other teams. They took for granted that they were a group of unusually strong and talented individuals. Their conversations about their offspring confirmed this. In total, the team members had seven kids: Caitlin two, Fred two, Joe three; all the children extremely gifted, all in advanced classes, their impressive IQs quoted to the exact digit as if measured by a precision instrument. All in contradiction of what statistics taught about normal distribution.

Harmon laid out their new task that was a final presentation which must be a comprehensive statement of their findings, qualitative and quantitative, detailing the projects incremental benefits over the next five years and, using Corporate Finance's approved Discount Rate, netting all the financials down to a Net Present Value shown three different ways: worst, most likely and best case scenarios. All this presented directly to Mr. Yates for his final approval. "God!" Caitlin said, in amazement at Yates's thoroughness, maybe in description of the man himself.

***

After a break, it sunk in that it all depended on the survey.

"So then," Joe said, "there's still one fly swimmin' in the soup."

"You're sure he's swimming?" Riley asked.

"Oh yeah. He's doin' the backstroke."

"What's the problem?" Harmon said.

"What," the great fly detector asked, "does any of us know about conducting a survey?"

Everyone looked to Harmon, as if he should know.

"Well," he said, "we're all business professionals here. I think, with the proper help, say a course or manual, we can—"

"What?" Joe interrupted. "You think we just read *Surveys for Dumbbells* and away you go? Do you know the complicities of conducting a reliable survey? A scientific survey that's *sadistically* reliable? Do you know what's required for the results to be meaningful? I mean, first you've got to *idemnify* a *significance* target group and then—"

"Joe," Harmon said, "I don't know all the complications. I admit that. But I can tell that you do."

Joe wrapped his pipe against his palm.

Riley had given good advice about Joe. Include him as much as possible, she said. He must have some stake in the project. If he didn't, no matter how well things were done, he would criticize. Harmon thought about Joe's own words about the one great advantage of having Mr. Yates as their champion, "Better to have him inside the tent pissin' out, than outside pissin' in."

"So," Harmon said, glancing at Riley, "I suggest a committee to take on the survey. Let's say, to start with, Joe and Riley."

The possibility of work heading his way further animated Joe. "So tell me," he said. "Where are the resources coming from?"

"Resources?" Harmon said. "We have the resources right here. Don't we?"

"Listen," Joe said. "Not just anybody can do this. It has to be thought out to get a *resentful* sample and don't do that right and your data is useless and say you have that right then you got to avoid sample *basis* and I can tell you that's not easy. A lot of survey's are useless because of *basis* in the sample. Then you need a *tabalatin'* process that assures proper *quantumfication* of the data. Without that, your survey is probably gonna be *rearended* useless."

"Rearended?" Harmon asked, legitimately confused.

"Rendered," Riley said.

"God!" Caitlin said."

"Keep going," Riley said, "I'm getting it all."

"You are?" Caitlin asked.

"There's a lot I can keep going about," Joe said. "I mean without the proper *intrepridation* of the data—"

"Well," Harmon interrupted, "people do conduct surveys all the time. I mean we do them here at AC&C. Right?"

"Just my point," Joe said. "Think of the way things run around here. A lot of that's based on shitted-up surveys."

"Shitted-up?" Riley asked. "Is that another survey term?"

"We have to do it," Caitlin said. "We told Mr. Yates we would."

Deadlocked silence until, in desperation and with no one else to turn to, Harmon looked to the DNA-TMG man.

"Fred, is there anything you can tell us about developing and conducting a survey?"

"Oh," Fred replied. "Very complicated. Tricky. Very tricky."

"That's it?" Caitlin asked. "That's our high priced professional consultation? That surveys are tricky?"

"Fred," Harmon said, "can you be a little more specific?"

"Well, it is so complicated that we, at DNA-TMG, have a special department just for it."

"You have a special department?"

"Yes."

"Can they can help us?" Harmon asked.

"Oh, for sure. Yes, for sure they can help. They conduct surveys. Lots of them. I can make a call."

"That sounds good," Joe said quickly. Joe was always enthusiastic about work flowing away from him.

"A call?" Caitlin said and snorted.

Harmon could predict, know, when a bad snort was coming. This one so loud Caitlin lifted her hand to her nose in self-consciousness.

"You can make a call?" Caitlin said. "Why in the hell didn't you say something before? Like while we were going around in circles about this?"

"I don't want to interfere with good dialog," the consultant said. "That's part of facilitation. Not interfering with healthy dialog."

"What?" Caitlin said again, her voice rising in amazement.

"You did a good job," Joe said. "Of not interferin'."

"God!" Caitlin said.

"Okay," Harmon said. "The important thing is we've got a source of support. We need to get on with this. A committee of Joe and Riley, that's how we'll proceed, but coordinating our efforts with Fred and the DNA-TMG Group, using all the brains we have and all that we can borrow. We need the survey numbers."

Silent agreement. The team following its leader.

"Okay," Harmon said. "This is good. We've made a lot of progress here. I think we're moving in the right direction. Fred will make his call and then we're off and running."

***

The night before, Harmon had rallied his courage toward asking Riley to join him again at the diner or at someplace nicer, and not just for business. He never got the chance. She got up and left the conference room quickly and by the time he dealt with a Caitlin question and gathered his papers and came out, Riley had changed into sneakers and stood at the elevator doors with her gym bag in her hand and hopping from foot to foot, anxious to go. It was a disappointment and a relief. His heart beat hard at just the prospect of asking her.

Noticer

plans—old man—who you are—where you're from

Late Friday afternoon and another week in the books. AC&C associates had their weekend plans: dates, trips to the Jersey Shore, quality time with the family. Life's pleasures courtesy of AC&C salaries.

On Friday the diner featured a fish dinner. Back home a fish fry was more than a meal. It was a tradition. Every Friday, at four p.m., to beat the *crowd*, two or three farm families, the Wolcott's drove to town and the Deerhead Inn where they served the best fish fry in the county, sided with coleslaw and German potato salad.

As a little boy, Harmon would wander about the ancient Inn and explore its eerie nooks and crannies. Some of the corners were dark as a cave. On the walls were ghostly oil paintings of forests and mountain waterfalls. On the floor and shelves were stuffed animals: a huge bear standing on its hind legs, a snarling bobcat, colorful pheasants. If he had been good that week and conscientious about homework and chores, his father allowed him dessert. He was always good and always made the same choice, strawberry shortcake when strawberries were in season, strawberry ice cream when they weren't.

***

The diner's polished interior lacked the mystery of the Deerhead Inn and the fish fry was not nearly as good, but beggars couldn't be choosers. He walked to his booth. The friendly busboy brought a glass of water and his favorite waitress took his order.

Could there be a person more mismatched to him than Riley O'Brian? He laughed aloud more than once thinking of the way she ignited Caitlin with her *mute* and *moot* remark. He was still amazed at her expert corralling of Joe. He worried about her lack of restraint, the way she enjoyed winding Caitlin's watch and her uncompromising attitude when she thought she was right, which, as far as he could tell, was always. All that was dangerous and he was responsible for everything the team did. But there was a strength about her. She was the kind of person that, in a hard situation, you wanted on your side. One thing he had learned about life: you could be certain to find hard situations.

He would call home tonight and tell his father more about the project. No whining, though. His father couldn't relate to the bureaucratic and political machinations. Why should he? His dad was a dig in and do it type. He wouldn't mention Riley O'Brian, not to his father or mother. His mother would get too excited at the mention of a woman in his life. His mother wanted nothing more than for him to meet a nice girl. What would his father think about Riley? He was sure his father would like her, once he got to know her and her dig in and do it attitude. He knew his mother would like Riley, too, as long as Riley liked her boy.

An old man entered the diner. He stopped just inside the doors and repackaged one of the complimentary newspapers. He hunched some and moved slowly. He wore a beat-up railroader's hat. No need for the owner or host to seat him, he had his own spot. He came at the same time and never missed a night, indifferent to days of the week or holidays or weather. Something sad, Harmon thought, about such inviolable schedules, kept by lonely people in diners and bars and cafes all around the world.

The old man walked straight to his booth, the one across from Harmon. "Howdy son," he said.

"Hello sir," Harmon said.

With a shaky hand on the table, the man stood still a moment, steadying himself, making a strange sound, sort of a humming. He started to sit but could only control his descent half way when, in a sudden free fall, he collapsed into the seat. The leather made a loud squishing sound. The semi-controlled fall didn't surprise Harmon, he was used to it.

The man wore a faded flannel shirt with the sleeves rolled up. The shirt itself too much for the hot day, but a heavy thermal undershirt was underneath it, stained yellow around the neck. He opened his newspaper. Taciturnity fit his stoic look, but it wouldn't last. Harmon wanted to concentrate on his work, going over the day's events and planning tomorrow's, but he knew once his neighbor found an article that sparked his interest he would talk with the enthusiasm of the lonely.

He had imagined the old man's life: never married and inured to solitude; his meager income, probably a railroad pension, just sufficient for his meager wants; his house a little clapboard place bought half a century earlier for a few thousand dollars and all paid for; the rooms undecorated save for railroad signs and photographs of greet steam locomotives and old log train stations with hard-eyed crews posed for the cameras. Everything unchanged for years.

"It's all different now." An article found, the man's interest sparked.

Based on experience, Harmon guessed the article was about the dog-eat-dog nature of the world. He didn't offer encouragement. Tonight he needed to concentrate.

The waitress brought Harmon's dinner: fried fish, French fries, and coleslaw on the side. "*Bueno?*" she asked. She knew Harmon liked to use his minimal Spanish with her. "*Bueno*," Hermann answered. His food looked good. She also knew Harmon didn't like bread and liked his salad with the main course. On her other arm she had a basket of bread and muffins for the old man. He always took bread and muffins home, wrapped in paper napkins.

The old man ordered what he always ordered, the meat loaf dinner and coffee. The waitress charged him the senior price, but made sure he got the full portion. She worried he was too thin. "I say prayers for him," she told Harmon.

Harmon ate while looking at his notes. Should he have a talk with Joe? As team leader he had responsibility for the working environment; he knew Joe's comment about Caitlin and sex was out of bounds.

The waitress brought the old man's dinner and checked on Harmon with her usual good cheer.

"You know something?" the old man asked, staring at the waitress as she walked away. "You know what I notice?"

"What's that?" Harmon asked.

"These kids, the waitresses and busboys, they're always happy."

"Yes," Harmon agreed, "they seem so."

"And it's not put on," the old man said. "It's real. I see 'em, the little girls, laughing, helping each other. There's something special about that. God bless 'em."

Harmon had thought about that, too, the inherent dignity of the diner's crew. If the waitresses met in an aisle or coming through the kitchen door, they used their free hands to hug each other. Harmon loved to see that. It warmed his heart.

"See," the old man continued, "here's the thing. These kids are poor. Right? Dirt poor. Not a pot to piss in or a window to throw it out. What do they them pay here?"

"I'm not sure," Harmon said.

"They're a couple thousand miles from home. Most of them don't even know their English too good. A lot of people, I see it all the time, don't treat them so good, snapping fingers at them, that kind of horseshit. But they're still nice. Happy, too."

"You have a point," Harmon said.

"The people they wait on, a good amount of them," the old man looked out the window to the parking lot, "they drive here in fancy cars from fancy houses and they're the crabby, miserable sons-of-bitches. Now why is that?"

"I don't know."

"I mean they got money and things these kids just dream about. Houses, swimming pools, cars, giant TV's; all of it they can't live without."

"It's a good point you make," Harmon said.

"You know what it is?" the old man asked.

"What's that?"

"Know what it is?"

"What?" Harmon asked again.

"These kids know who they are. They know where they come from."

"You think that's it?"

"I do. They know who they are and they carry that with them everywhere they go, even for thousands of miles. It don't matter, different country, different language, different people. It don't matter. They carry it with them."

The waitress came to check on the old man's dinner.

"Honey," he said to her.

"Sir?"

"How come you're so happy?"

"Sir?" The waitress said, confused.

"How come you're always happy?" The old man smiled and moved his head up and down and smiled more, trying to pantomime happy.

The waitress got it. "*Feliz*?" she said. "Happy? I try to be."

"Always happy," the old man said. "Why?"

The waitress thought a moment. She looked to Harmon, as if he might have the answer. Finally she said, "Why not?"

"Now," the old man said, "that's good in any language."

***

The railroad man saw more than you thought; he saw more than most people. Most people wouldn't think him anything special. They'd probably see him as interchangeable with any other old man. But he saw things. He was a good *noticer*. Harmon had a sad thought. Would his friend die alone in his lonely house? Would the police find him there after someone finally missed him, maybe after he didn't show up at the diner for a few days? Would Harmon and the waitress be the only people to miss him?

For desert, he ordered the strawberry shortcake to get such things off his mind. The shortcake wasn't like he got back home. Sometimes you settled.

Growth

mornings together — maturation — a touch

Harmon and Riley's morning meetings became a routine. Always in the cafeteria's quiet corner and starting an hour before their colleagues arrived. Without experts exogenous or endogenous, the unlikely duo determined the People Team's direction.

Riley's appearance, with a coffee in her hand and her leather satchel strapped over her shoulder, always brought Harmon a flicker of exhilaration. How wonderfully strange that one person could change everything.

***

"Listen to me," Riley said, spreading a paper thin layer of low-fat cream cheese on her wheat toast, watching calories that never stuck anyway. "If this survey is going to get prepared, while we're still young, you'd better put a charge under the DNA-TMG guy, old Freddy boy."

"He said he would take care of it."

"Yeah, but we're still waiting for a meeting. It's the only thing holding us back. Freddy boy has the slows."

"I'll talk to him."

"I know you don't like it, but someone has to be the whip-cracker. On the People Team that's got to be you, making sure what needs to get done, gets done. You don't do that and this team thing won't work."

"It's hard." He was going to say give me a little time, but there was one thing Riley had in common with Mr. Yates, you could feel her impatience.

"Hard?" she said.

"Yes it is. Managing the team, keeping everyone going in the right direction."

"Yeah Harmon. That is hard. But I've seen you do it."

"When?"

"When you get mad. Or as mad as you get."

"When did I get mad?"

"Like when you told everyone enough foolishness. Remember, you said that to everyone, me included. We got back to work and no one bitched because you were strong."

"I was?"

"You were."

Harmon nodded dubiously.

"You know," Riley said, "I'll be there as much as you need me."

She put a hand on his arm. A touch of affection. Harmon got up and stepped to the cafeteria's convenience center. He needed another napkin.

How Hard Can It Be

statisticians — intervals — seduction

Harmon did put a charge under Fred, a gentle charge, more puff than blast, just enough to make sure he set up the meeting with his survey specialists. Harmon and Fred were to attend with Riley along, ostensibly to take notes. He was careful to invite Caitlin, but purposefully acknowledging how incredibly busy she was. She was busy, super busy, and she couldn't make it. Joe was more than content to be kept informed.

***

"A very tricky business," Fred reminded Harmon and Riley on the way to the meeting.

Two DNA-TMG survey experts came. The younger man introduced himself as the chief statistician; the older man his assistant. The chief wore a sport coat that made Harmon wonder if it had been discarded by Joe; an awful dark brown polyester. The subordinate dressed worse. His neck was too scrawny for his oversized shirt and his tie knot too big; tie and shirt and coat were all in disagreement. They were walking clichés. It was as if someone had ordered statisticians from central casting.

"We're both statisticians," the subordinate said, his voice defensive, as if it he might not be getting his due.

"I guessed that," Riley said. She whispered to Harmon, "These two probably went into statistics because accounting was too exciting."

"We're thankful for your support," Harmon said. "My first question is, what do you need from us to do the best possible survey?"

"What we need," the chief said, "is a requirements document."

A very detailed document: who the People Team wanted to survey, what they wanted to find out, what margin of error they could accept. The DNA-TMG Analysis Group had a standard format for all this and once they received the required information, their mysterious work could begin.

Harmon liked all that, matter of fact professionals who knew what they needed and what to do with it when they got it. They had thought out processes. They were comfortable working their side of the fence. He felt envious, like when thinking of the locksmith in his hidden shop.

"How long will it take?" Harmon asked.

That's always the question, the chief statistician said. It all depended on when the People Team completed the requirements document.

Usually it was twelve weeks after that. That was the standard interval. In the statistician's voice an obvious veneration for standard intervals.

Riley looked to Harmon. After a long moment of silence, she spoke up. "We need it much sooner."

Harmon nodded.

Both analysts shook their heads no, the subordinate more vigorously. Riley smiled at them. Only the chief smiled back. Riley pouted a little in his direction. How soon did they need it, the chief asked. Four weeks, Riley said, start to finish.

"Impossible!" the assistant said. "Four weeks was plain crazy." His outburst quieted the room. His supervisor finally said it could take that long just for the People Team to supply the requirements and his team to develop the questions.

"I can get you the requirements by close of business tomorrow," Riley said. "All on your standard forms."

"What?" Harmon said.

"COB tomorrow," Riley said.

"Oh no," Fred said, coming awake, almost swallowing his smile. "A requirements document is very complicated. Very—"

"Tricky," Riley interrupted. "I'm sure, but nevertheless, I'll get it to you tomorrow. *COB.*"

"Well," Harmon said, "I don't know. I mean we've got to bring the team up to speed and—"

"Forget the team," Riley said. "We get messing with the team, the interval will be infinity."

Objections all around that Riley met with a simple question: how hard could it be? They knew who they wanted to survey and they knew what they wanted to find out. She looked at Harmon, *don't we?*

"Okay," Harmon said. "Yes. We do. But it's not just that. I mean I'm sure we know what we want. But I think it's more complicated than that." He looked at Fred.

"Oh yes," Fred said. "Certainly. Certainly."

"Look," Riley said. "We require information about AC&C's internal communications. We want to ask questions like: What do you think about communication between management and employees, 10 being excellent and 1 being terrible. Some plain English questions that get right to the point. I can work some up."

"You have expertise in that area?" the assistant asked.

"I will have," Riley said.

"You will have?"

"Yeah. By COB tomorrow."

The statisticians speechless at this dilettantish interloper invading their deliberate and measured profession.

"She's a fast learner," Harmon said.

Riley pressed the chief, even gave him her special smile. If she could get the requirements document to him tomorrow, when could he turn the survey around? Wilting under her pressure and charisma, the chief proposed eight weeks.

"Oh no!" the assistant statistician said.

His boss held his hand up to quiet him. Harmon had grudging admiration for the assistant, at least he was resistant to Riley's wiles. And he was sure the man was mightily overworked. His eyes were an odd mix of yellow and red soreness from too many hours staring at figures. The kind of overworked, computer-fatigued eyes that Joe once described as looking like, *two piss-holes in the snow.*

"Eight weeks," Harmon said. "That's generous."

"Yes, thank you," Riley said. "But let's start with eight, but not put a firm date on it right now." She spoke to the chief statistician. "Let me work with you. We'll see what we can do."

The chief smiled uncertainly. Harmon recognized it for what it was, complete capitulation.

"Okay?" Harmon said.

"Okay," the Chief answered.

Riley offered to sit with him, right then, if he had a few minutes, to go over his format for the requirements. "If we wait," she said, "and start mailing stuff and matching calendars, we'll lose two weeks."

The Chief opened his briefcase and took out some forms.

Harmon felt confident in a record setting turnaround for the survey. He also felt a little sorry for the Chief-Statistician, both his standard interval and his will so easily subverted.

Safe to Say

teamwork — rubric — professionals

As promised, Riley completed the requirements document that evening, first studying the forms while soaking in her tub, where she did her best thinking, protecting the documents in a gallon sized Zip-Lock bag. She completed everything at her little desk, the same one she'd had since she was a kid. She added a handwritten invitation for the Chief Statistician to call her anytime for clarification.

He needed a lot of clarification. He became her telephone buddy.

***

With the survey in DNA-TMG's hands and weeks to await the results, the People Team had time to kill. They were good at it. Some days they even worked late, days filled with long and spirited debates over the best way to improve AC&C's communications, the assumption already made that things were broken and the survey would confirm it. A *preconcerted* notion, critical Joe called it. Riley interpreted his meaning as *preconceived* but later, out of her native curiosity, she consulted the dictionary and found preconcerted was okay or at least close. *Preconcerted*: previously arranged or agreed on. Said on purpose or Joe's one in a million dumb luck? In any regard, a new word for her notebook.

The debates primarily animated Riley and Caitlin; a clash of two disparate world views. Harmon played the conciliator. Joe sat with one foot propped on an empty chair, playing with his comb or pocket knife or pipe, interjecting when one of his hot-buttons got pushed. Heavy-lidded Fred fought a continuous battle to stay awake.

Agreement on some things, mostly those not worth arguing about, like the need for a monthly newsletter. At Caitlin's suggestion two corporate communications people were brought in to help with that. "Always reach out," Caitlin said. "Show you are utilizing all of AC&C's resources. Cast a wide net. Mr. Yates likes that." "There goes the cost to benefit *ration*," Joe said

What would be the newsletter's title? That debate good for a couple days. Perhaps *The Messenger?* Or *The Voice?* How about *The Beacon?* A split on whether it should be paper or electronic, finally settled by agreeing to both. How about a weekly conference call relating the latest AC&C news? Maybe featuring a Q&A with a guest *SME*: subject matter expert. Perhaps a monthly video staged like the network evening news.

Maybe Mr. Yates himself would make an appearance. Caitlin could use her personal access to approach him about that. There should be an 800 number for all associates to call, a hotline to dispel harmful rumors. How about more suggestion boxes, one hung in every department, in conspicuous places? The team liked that and Harmon asked Riley to make another stop by the carpentry shop.

Caitlin worried terribly about proprietary information leaking but the most spirited debate centered on the title for the final report: *The People Team's Official Report To The CEO* sounded classy and authoritative, like a congressional investigation. *AC&C's Communications Crisis* sounded like a call to action. *The Communications Gap or What You Don't Know Can Bite You* had short-lived support.

"Are we sure we're seeing the big picture," Harmon asked. He sensed they weren't. That's why he asked. He was comfortable enough now to want more. "Let's keep our focus on what Mr. Yates wants," Harmon said, with a glance at Riley. "His paradigm shift, that's should be our standard. To meet that challenge it seems we need something bigger."

"He'll want something big," Caitlin agreed. "A game changer."

"I'm thinking," Harmon said, "that what we need is something that when he hears what we plan to do, you know, the title, it hits home immediately with a message of what our communications efforts are about."

A pregnant silence except for Fred, caught somewhere between a wheeze and a snore.

"I think I got it," Riley said.

"What?"

"A rubric. That's what we need. That's what we're talking about."

"What?" Caitlin said.

"A *rubric*," Riley said. "It's a heading that both names a program and gives a brief summary of what it deals with." She tapped her word journal, wherein was the written definition, if required.

Harmon interested, Joe contemplative, Caitlin reflexively skeptical.

"Riley," Harmon said, "please explain what you mean. You know, in a little more detail."

"Okay," Riley said. "If we have a rubric, one that evokes the purpose of our efforts, then any time someone hears it they'll automatically think of our program."

"So," Harmon said, "it leverages us."

"It leverages us," Riley repeated.

"Sure," Joe said. "It's a basic *propagation* technique."

"We need to discuss this," Caitlin said.

Discuss it they did, for four days, until Harmon finally set a deadline of one more day, do or die. It was late on that day, running up against that deadline, when they found their rubric.

"Think about this," Harmon said, trying to rev up the team. "Just what is it we are trying to get across? I mean what is the common thread running through everything we want to do: the newsletter and conference calls and suggestion boxes? What is our universal message? We understand that and I think we can get our rubric."

"I guess I'm not a rubric kind of guy," Joe said, as he played with a short piece of clothesline he now brought with him every day and used to practice his knots.

Caitlin suggested they study what other big corporations did, to get their messages across. They considered: *Quality Is Job One* and *Be All You Can Be* and *The System Is The Solution* and many more. Interesting analogies, Caitlin said. Riley wrote examples on a scrap of paper that she showed to Harmon. Harmon put his forefinger to his lips, thankful for Riley's newfound discretion and encouraging its continuance. Things going so well now, Harmon's own missionary work was paying dividends. Through the weeks he had learned to better relate to Caitlin, to better understand her. A little praise worked wonders and she was praiseworthy. She worked hard and she took pride in her work. And maybe her life wasn't that easy. He heard stories. Like the one about her domineering husband requiring she maintain her weight to his liking and how he banned potato chips from the house and when he came home he checked her fingertips for traces of vegetable oil. You never knew what people endured. An important thing he had learned at AC&C: when you got to know somebody, when you at least tried, maybe you still didn't like them but you could better understand why they did what they did. If you couldn't, maybe you just lacked imagination.

"How about," Caitlin said, tensing with concentration, "something more philosophical, something like: the truth matters?"

"How about," Joe said, "the truth hurts."

"Okay," Harmon said, "okay."

"How about you," Caitlin said to Riley. "You must have something to say?"

Riley had been scribbling. She stopped and repeated after Caitlin, "Something to say... something to say." Then she scribbled some more, held up her pad and triumphantly declared, "Here's our rubric."

On the paper: *Safe to Say*.

"That's it?" Caitlin said.

"That's it," Riley said. "*Safe to Say*."

Quiet for a moment, until Riley continued. "It covers everything we want to get at with our newsletter and conference calls and suggestion boxes. What we're trying to get across is that at AC&C there is, or will be, an environment that supports open honest communication and a free exchange of ideas. That it's a place where it is safe to speak your mind. We want a brief, catchy slogan that says that. A rubric to get that across: *Safe To Say*."

Harmon liked it but didn't want to be the first to endorse it. Joe said he liked it well enough and Fred nodded to that. "Hmmm," Caitlin said. A hearty endorsement. "I like it, too," Harmon said. "I really do."

"Well," Caitlin said. "It shows what we can do when we work together like professionals."

Dreams

rainstorming — dreaming — teasing

The debate turned to how to make AC&C a *Safe to Say* place. The discussions were stimulating and fun: daily brainstorming without the pressures and responsibilities of a regular job. It was good being dedicated to a think tank with smart people, the exchanging of ideas sort of like an intellectual pinball game. At times camaraderie threatened to engulf the People Team, and Harmon was leading the whole thing. It filled him with amazement, that he was the team leader and enjoying it. Dreams do come true. During the best moments he had only one regret; he wished his father was there in the conference room, able to see his son leading with a steady hand.

***

Thoughts of Riley dominated Harmon's mind. But there was a great chasm between thought and action. He considered telling her about his dreams, the ones about her. "I dreamed about you last night," he would say. A strategic move. A way to express his feelings with a reduced risk of rejection. "Oh you did?" she'd reply, with sensual coyness, quick on the uptake, as usual. She was good at that kind of thing, teasing him and making him blush.

He knew what she was up to, when she teased him, and he knew she enjoyed it, but none of that made it easier for him. Her flirting made him uncomfortable in real time but excited him later, when he relived it. *And just what did you dream,* she might ask. I can't tell you, he would say, because it's too embarrassing. It could be just the way to show her what he felt for her without making a fool of himself. But the time was never right and it would be so easy for her to take it all wrong. He knew he wouldn't do it.

One morning she had noticed the photo that he kept on the left corner of his desk: a log cabin set beneath a white-capped mountain, the cabin's chimney puffing smoke into a brilliant blue sky. Something he had brought from back home, clipped from the feed store's calendar. A talisman to evoke calmness. "Tell me about that," she said, always interested in the details of his life. So he shared his pipe dream. Nothing so original, building a cabin in the Adirondacks where he would live simply and get back to basics, maybe grow vegetables and learn to know beans, like a modern Thoreau. *Wolcott's Walden.* "I'll quit and come with you," Riley said. He wouldn't put that past her, the quitting and doing whatever she felt like part.

I'll quit and come with you. Just like her to say that. Why was she single with no mention of a boyfriend? A young woman as pretty as Riley? It was crazy and her rebellious ways still made him nervous, but now he couldn't stop thoughts about the two of them and a secluded mountain cabin. Foolish thoughts. She was just teasing.

Survey

results — ammunition — helper

"Today we have a very special guest. Mr. Swanson is here from the Statistical Analysis Section of DNA-TMG. He has our survey results."

Harmon made the announcement to his team with all due solemnity. It was a big day. He exchanged respectful nods with Mr. Swanson, a middle aged man who wore tortoiseshell glasses and dressed professionally: a button-down white shirt with a striped tie and a blue sports coat. The chief statistician and his assistant were there, too, but fully deferring to Swanson, their public face. At first the assistant didn't sit at the conference table, but took a chair against the wall. Riley moved him to the table.

"Mr. Swanson," Harmon continued, "will present the results to us. But first, I want to thank his team for the professional and expeditious manner in which they conducted the survey. They completed everything in record time."

Riley and the Chief Statistician exchanged smiles. Harmon sat down and Mr. Swanson moved to the overhead projector. He thanked everyone and said how happy he was to be with them.

Swanson took a stack of bound reports from his briefcase and passed them around the table. He pulled out his slides and flipped the projector's on/off switch. It didn't work.

Riley got up and tipped the machine over. "The bulb, she said. "But there's usually a spare underneath." She made the switch and the machine lit.

Swanson started. *AC&C Survey Results* appeared on the wall screen then a new page: *Response Rate*. Under that title a bar chart with two colored columns. The tall blue column touched the eighty percent marker. The short red one at twenty percent. "A very good response," Swenson said. "Approximately eighty percent. Most extraordinary actually; we were hoping for fifty percent. The greater the response rate, the lower the margin of error."

"What do you attribute this too," Caitlin asked.

Harmon shifted in his seat. He hoped Caitlin wouldn't play inquisitor. He wasn't worried about her taxing the presenter, but rather that she might excite Joe who could pick any presentation apart at the seams. But Joe only scratched his belly and yawned. One great restraint upon Joe; if this survey was deemed unfit, he was in line for some work.

Swanson attributed the high response rate to a very interested target group. The team had obviously tapped into an area of great concern, an area their associates cared a great deal about.

"If I could," the Chief Statistician interjected from his seat. "I would like to give thanks to Ms. O'Brian. Without her, we could never have made such an aggressive turnaround time. We were so backed up with work and, although we don't usually do this, Ms. O'Brian helped out with the intra-company mailing and collection. At great savings in both time and expense."

Caitlin, immediately alert to that began a question, but Harmon did something he could not have done just a month ago; he clapped for Riley and her great help. The pump primed, the rest of the team clapped, too.

Humble, Riley said it was a team effort, Joe and she together. Joe smiled and waved a hand to deflect praise, as if to say it was nothing. Riley nodded to that. Nothing was exactly what Joe had done.

Mr. Swenson got to the heart of the matter: the survey's twelve questions. Some of them control questions; three of them most critical to the project.

Question 3: I believe communication between associates is honest and effective.

Here a mixed response, approximately fifty-two percent answered always or most often. Forty-two percent answered sometimes or never. Not great, not terrible. Five percent without an opinion. Swanson said you always have your no opinion folks. The results not adding to one-hundred percent because of rounding. Everyone satisfied with that.

Question 6: I believe communication between associates and immediate supervisors is honest and effective.

A less positive response, approximately thirty-one percent answered always or most often. Sixty-two percent answered sometimes or never. Seven percent no opinion. Not so good. A question about the use of *approximately* and Riley with the answer. Most people think it means in the ballpark, but it really means not quite exact but very close.

Question 9: I believe communications between associates and upper management is honest and effective.

The bars showed a dramatically negative response. Nine percent answered always or most often. Eighty-seven percent answered sometimes or never. Four at no opinion. DNA-TMG had never seen such a negative response to this type of question. Oohs and ahs for that. The smoking gun found, the basis of quantification.

"So," Harmon asked, "what do you think this means for us, the People Team?"

"Well," Swenson said, "I believe it provides you with a very clear and strong mandate to recommend action to ameliorate this serious problem.

I will add this, we have access to historical surveys from across the business community and we cannot find anything like this. Such a negative response was not found in any enterprise, regardless of the type of business or the state of a business, even those that subsequently failed. We can share that historical data with you. I must say, combined with the high response rate this negative response is quite extraordinary."

Harmon looked to Riley. She winked. A conspiratorial wink that made Harmon turn away, as if seeing something he shouldn't have and not wanting to see more.

In his remaining time, Swenson went over some of the statistical methodology underlying the conclusions. Mean, median and mode; frequency distributions, correlations, factor and regression analysis; confidence intervals, norms, benchmarks. Lots more, too. The man liked his work. At the turn to theory, Joe took the opportunity to show off his knowledge, again surprising Harmon at the depth of his questions and interjections. How did he come by it all? Swenson surprised, too, mostly by the improbable contrast of Joe's esoteric knowledge and malapropian mischief. He had never before heard *à la mode* referenced in a statistical study.

"Thank you," Harmon said, relieved when the hour ran out. "I know Mr. Swenson is on a tight schedule and his time is up. Thank you for being so direct and concise."

The People Team had its survey and ammunition enough to build its case for change. Ammunition enough for some creative quantification, maybe even for a paradigm shift.

Time to turn to wording and packaging. The next challenge? The preparation of a persuasive report and presentation, up to the high standards of Preston P. Yates. That wouldn't be easy, but Harmon felt up to it. Something big happening, his own paradigm change. He wasn't as worried about failure as he was about developing a comprehensive plan to make AC&C a place where it was *Safe to Say*; reality proving less scary than his dreams. He even marveled a little at his former weakness.

Preparation

half an hour — a long week

Yates allowed a half hour for the People Team's presentation. Most extraordinary, his assistant usually apportioned his appointments in ten-minute blocks. Everyone agreed that such generosity was indicative of the importance the CEO placed on the project.

The team spent a week on the presentation: conceptualizing, outlining, drafting and finalizing. A long week of ten-hour days, personal and family needs in suspension, the team living the very words of Elizabeth of DNA-TMG.

Word choice and layout took most of the time. A long digression on font type and size, the debate over *Courier New* vs. *Arial* ran a day and a half and even sparked Fred's interest. Another debate centered on how to show emphasis, should it be italics or exclamation points? The discussions were spirited but civil, as if the team members had signed an armistice.

The final written report ran eighteen pages with four appendices of backup, quantitative and qualitative. Caitlin oversaw its physical production. Riley took charge of the slides. Joe, not involved with such trivial matters. He didn't mess with *floormating*.

Caitlin had the report laser printed on the highest quality paper, watermarked with the AC&C logo; she created a cover page with a relief of the headquarters complex highlighting an oversized *Golden Boy*; she hand-packaged it in felt binders, except for Mr. Yates's copy, which was bound in a real leather portfolio.

The Executive Summary formed the basis of the fifteen slides Harmon would present with the whole team in attendance for support and their share of, hopefully, the glory. The Team Members page, as approved, listed everyone in alphabetical order. Riley changed that so it listed Harmon first and separately, as suiting the team leader. The others might bitch after the presentation, but then it would be too late.

Presentation Morning

sleepless in new jersey — a friend

Harmon didn't need either of his two alarms. He was awake before dawn and lay still, not wanting to relinquish the safety of his bed, but knowing it couldn't last. He heard an early bird leaving for work, a car's trunk slamming and its doors closing an improbable number of times; he heard the garbage men on their rounds, clanging cans and talking and whistling. That wouldn't be a bad job, garbage man. Up early and done by noon. The rest of the day to yourself. A clear cut objective and union wages, benefits and security. Garbage man, a job to envy. The things you learned when you grew up.

He had slept maybe two hours. He tried imagining himself at home, walking again through the familiar fields to the creek that ran along the southern border of his parents' property, a walk that always relaxed him. He tried diaphragmatic breathing exercises, like the ladies in the typing room, focusing on nothing but his rising and lowering stomach. He even tried his mother's remedy: warm milk. Nothing helped.

Riley recommended he memorize the beginning to get him through the opening jitters, then let the subsequent slides serve as prompts, for a more natural, extemporaneous flow. Instead, he memorized his entire thirty minute presentation, even the little asides. Shaving and in the shower he repeated his presentation until, over prepared, he started stumbling.

He had no appetite for breakfast but forced an energy bar. He didn't want his talk punctuated by the hypoglycemic shakes. It was simple. Remember to breath and swallow. Why couldn't he do a thing as simple as that? He even worried about hiccups ruining his presentation. Could one imagine the disaster of that? He hadn't had hiccups in years.

There were horror stories of AC&C presentations gone bad and he relived them. A collection of most embarrassing moments: the speaker who forgot he stood behind a glass podium and played with himself through his whole talk, a performance Joe called *executive pocket-pool*; the panel participant who scooted off to the bathroom forgetting to take off his new fangled wireless mike, broadcasting his amplified excretions and exclamations to four hundred colleagues, sounding like some mix of intense torture and orgasm; the presenter who, suffering from a cold and using a vu-graph machine, sneezed on the glass and gave the audience a magnified view of his mucosal secretions. All of these came to Harmon, along with the premonition he was about to do worse.

***

He was in the office at 6:45. He wore his dark blue suit, just back from the cleaners with a razor sharp crease in the pants, his whitest white shirt with buttoned-down collar, his red striped tie that took the best knot. He had shined his shoes the way his father taught him, the Army way, setting a can of polish on fire and quickly suffocating it with the cap so the top layer melted and spread smoothly. He carried a second suit in his car, in case something happened to the first.

***

"God," Riley said, upon first seeing him, not hiding her concern. "You need to calm down."

"I'm trying," he said, not trying to hide that he was a wreck. Not having to hide it from her was a relief in itself.

Riley dressed nicely in a pinstriped pantsuit and moderately heeled shoes. Harmon had never seen that outfit before and knew she had purchased it just for this occasion and just for him. Such allegiance was a sacred thing.

"Are you okay?" she asked and reached over his desk and touched his hand. "Jeez. You're shaking." She smiled. Her impish one. "You're shaking, you know like Joe says, 'shaking like a dog pooping a peach pit.'"

"Thanks," Harmon said.

"But," Riley said, "Joe always says shittin'."

"What?"

"You know. Joe. He always says, 'Shakin' like a dog *shittin'* a peach pit.'"

"Well," Harmon said, "Joe's a classy guy. But either way, pooping or the other, thanks for the vivid image, that really helps."

"Let's go down to the cafeteria."

"You think?"

"Yeah." She turned and waved him to come along. "Let's get some tea in you and settle you down."

"Okay," he said. "That way I can run things by you one last time."

Riley stopped and dropped her chin to her chest.

***

The cafeteria was empty. Riley told Harmon to sit and she got his decaffeinated tea and her black coffee.

"Harmon, you're making way too much of this."

"But—"

"But nothing. You know this stuff inside out. You're the smartest one in the room—"

"But Mr. Yates—"

"Screw Mr. Yates, and the horse he rode in on. You know how to deal with him. Just like we talked about. Should we go over that?"

"No. I've got it. But what if he rejects the whole thing? What if he says the whole effort was a total waste of time and resources, end of discussion; *leave* and *get out*. What if he says that?"

"Then you know what you do?"

"What?"

"You get out."

"What?"

"Yeah. You get out and go off to your cabin in your beautiful mountains."

He smiled at that.

"Come on now Harmon. No more reviewing. No more stressing. Go into this meeting and tell the man the way it is. Show him you know the business. Show him he's not the only one in all of AC&C with cojones. You know about cojones?"

"Yes. I think so."

"Well show him the real Harmon. Like you've been the last few weeks."

"What do you mean?"

"I mean you've been terrific lately. You probably don't even recognize the change. I mean between now and when we started, it's amazing."

"You think I'm doing better?"

"Better? It's night and day. You're more confident and you're a leader. I see the way even Caitlin, a royal pain in the ass if there ever was one, follows your lead now."

"Thanks."

"Thanks nothing. It's the simple truth."

"Well. I'll do my best."

"And that will be great."

Yates Presentation

dress up — mechanical man — great job — a comment too many

The team gathered in the CEO's conference room. Everybody dressed for the occasion. Caitlin was in an expensive looking grey striped outfit. Joe was a new man altogether without his horse-blanket sport coat, though his black suit suffered some loss of dignity by its inadvertent white trim, from fraying around the pocket edges. Fred was in a charcoal grey three-piece, the vest too tight when he sat down. The fashion show spotlighted the importance of the occasion and added to Harmon's nervousness.

Riley set up the projector and clicked through the presentation to check the slides were in proper order. Caitlin placed Yates's leather-bound proposal at his place, carefully squaring it to the table's edge. That copy had been triple proofed against error of substance or order. Riley filled a plastic cup with water, made Harmon drink some and then took the seat nearest him.

Harmon stood at the front of the table, trying to get comfortable. No luck with that. He double-checked the order of his paper slides. His notes were on the edges in large print. Riley called his notes marginalia; she called him the *Marquis of Marginalia*.

The CEO's Executive Assistant came in and said, "Mr. Yates will be here in a moment. He's finishing a call."

New panic in Harmon. The man might be on time. He thought he had another half hour at a minimum, time for one last internal rehearsal. Suddenly, he couldn't remember a word of his opening remarks. Instead, words like *endogenous* and *exogenous* flashed through his mind, along with the thought that Mr. Yates would expect answers to every question. He felt totally inadequate. He wondered if he had shaved close enough. He stacked his slides and squared them, as if failure to square them might court disaster.

Riley got his attention, nodded reassuringly, then breathed and swallowed conspicuously, another reminder for him to breathe after each sentence and pause and swallow after each paragraph. Caitlin and Joe and Fred sat unnaturally still, Joe's hands empty for once: no comb, pocket knife, pipe or rope.

***

Yates entered with a poker face, his thoughts and mood inscrutable. He took his special chair. The room went silent, like a church about to begin a service.

"So," Yates said, drumming his fingers on his unopened proposal. "What do we have?"

Everyone turned to Harmon. The stage his alone. On the spot, this is what it meant to be a leader and a long way from sitting a tractor and pulling a farm implement or being a county clerk.

"I'm ready," Harmon said. A white lie. "Then let's go," Yates said. Riley brought up the first slide:

AC&C People Team
Report on Communications

"Mr. Yates," Harmon said, "before I begin, the People Team would like to thank you for your generous support of all our efforts. Without that support our work would not have been possible."

The team nodded agreement, Caitlin most aggressively. Yates nodded back to Caitlin, a personal recognition that brought a slight redness to her cheeks.

"Now," Harmon said. "I could say I have bad news and good news. But, what I really want to say is that we, the People Team, have discovered and documented," he nodded to the written report, "a problem that presents us with a great opportunity."

He felt his mouth drying. A telltale croak lurking. He glanced at Riley and she made another show of breathing and swallowing. He took the cue. He wanted a drink of water but thought it too soon, it would call attention to his fear. He nodded and Riley triggered the next slide.

Communications
An Organization's Lifeblood

"What is an organization's life blood?" Harmon's rhetorical question.

"Stop," Yates said. He fanned through his paper slides. "Listen, I don't want a fancy slide show. I don't want that." Yates looked directly at Harmon; *it's your show and I'm a man in a hurry.* "You say we have a problem and an opportunity. Then cut everything else. Tell me the problem. Tell me the opportunity."

In Harmon's chest the beginning of paralysis. But a new slide appeared on the screen, perfectly titled, as if Yates controlled the projector.

AC&C's Communications Problem

It was the sixth slide in the presentation. The skipped slides just pabulum that Caitlin and Joe and Fred had championed, but Riley argued against. Riley looked to Caitlin who kept her eyes straight to the screen, her backbone ramrod straight.

A willing automaton now, Harmon synchronized with the new slide and regurgitated its associated wordage.

"The problem we have discovered and documented goes to the heart of AC&C's most critical mission, necessitating a paradigm shift in our culture. That problem is a communications breakdown."

He looked to Yates.

"I'm listening," Yates said, but he made a circling motion with his right index finger. Hurry it up.

Riley skipped two more slides and brought up:

AC&C Employees Are Afraid To Speak Freely

The team had argued for days over that one, about freely vs. truthfully. Freely won because truthfully seemed too strong. Maybe that was a good thing because Yates reacted to freely.

"You're saying people are afraid to speak their minds?" He gave no indication he remembered Harmon's previous presentation.

"Yes we are," Harmon said, without equivocation. Equivocation would have required calm thought. "It is something," he quickly added, "that is a legacy of earlier management." He saw Joe grin. "It's something," Harmon said, "that is very harmful. But, with your support and leadership, we are confident we can fix it and reap the attendant benefits."

The room went silent for a moment, all eyes and attention on Yates, some instinctual understanding that he needed to agree to what he had just heard before things could proceed.

"Okay," Yates said. "Tell me more. Tell me more about the problem, with specifics."

Harmon did. He repeated the survey's highlights and selected detailed findings. How *seventy-eight per cent* of respondents believed even their constructive criticisms would engender recrimination. How *sixty-two percent* had actually suffered such recriminations. How *sixty-four percent* knew of flawed methods and procedures that hurt AC&C's performance but refrained from reporting such.

"In some ways," Yates said, "I knew this. But, in some ways, it is shocking."

Everyone nodded to that. A hint of relaxation infiltrated the room. Yates was in touch with their work; their work was good enough to engage the man.

"Go on," Yates said.

"We also have written comments," Harmon said, "from our respondents. It was optional, but some respondents provided them."

"Summarize them," Yates said.

"Yes," Harmon said.

A new slide came up.

> *Sample Employee Comments*
> **'I feel intimidated'**
> **'The environment is hostile'**
> **'It's a clique, and I'm not in it'**
> **'My boss makes me feel like I'm a maggot'**

"Okay," Yates said. "I'll make the assumption, for now, until I review your data, that there is a problem. What are you going to do about it? What are your specific recommendations?"

Harmon looked to the screen and its new slide.

> *Recommendation*
> **Make AC&C a *Safe to Say* Environment**

"Here's what we mean by this," Harmon said, speaking with increasing confidence, speaking directly to Mr. Yates, as if he were the only other person in the room. "We recommend that AC&C declare itself a *Safe to Say* environment."

"Safe to say?" Yates asked.

"Yes," Harmon said. "By safe to say we mean that any associate can make any responsible comment or suggestion for improvement without fear of repercussion. Actually more than that, we advocate an environment where all associates, regardless of level, are encouraged to offer their unique and valuable inputs."

He breathed and swallowed and allowed himself a glance at the team. Fred flushed with pride, *advocate* was his word, chosen after much deliberation.

"We also recommend a statement of policy that recognizes that each of us, with our diverse heritages and experiences, has important insights to offer and that such insights are valued and respected." His throat not so dry now. Still, as a precaution, he swallowed again. That made him feel more in control and more confident. He was breathing and swallowing on his own terms now. "And we further recommend that we establish and implement the procedures to turn this policy into practice."

"Okay," Yates said, nodding his head, indicating satisfaction to this point. "I'll need more details on this safe to say thing, but my immediate question is do you have justification for your recommendation? I mean financial justification? Or are you saying this is the thing to do and it will just cost me but contribute nothing to the bottom line?"

Everyone looked to the screen.

Project Cost Justification
Risk Assessment
Breakeven Analysis
Discounted Cash Flows
Best - Worst - Most Likely Cases

Harmon dreaded this part; the emphasis turning to numbers too shaky for his liking. He swallowed, took a deep breath and geared up his confident tone.

"As you directed Mr. Yates, the most critical measure of our project is NPV: the Net Present Value of future cash flows made feasible by our project. In the *Best Case Scenario* NPV exceeds one-hundred-twenty million dollars. *Most Likely Case* is seventy-eight million dollars."

The magnitude of the numbers scared Harmon. He knew what flimsy assumptions lay behind them, each arbitrary tweak changing the bottom line by millions. *Why go small,* unworried Joe had said. *It's all bullshit anyways.*

"How about worst case?" Yates asked.

Perfectly prepared Harmon said just what Riley had drilled him to say, what she so confidently guaranteed would work because Yates would *want* it to work.

"Worst case is still positive," Harmon said. "What you may find interesting is our breakeven analysis. As you will see in that analysis, even if we include all fully loaded costs, from the start of our project through implementation, and even considering future follow-up expense, we only need our communications improvements to reduce total corporate expense, *or* increase total corporate revenue by *one-hundredth of one percent* for this project to breakeven." Then the final gilding, "That's one penny saved per one-hundred dollars of expense or one penny increase per one-hundred dollars of revenue."

Harmon said no more, allowing the incredibly small level of necessary improvement to sink in. Yates was a worst case thinker and everything rode on those technically truthful but purposefully plotted numbers.

"Interesting," Yates said. "I'll want to see the key assumptions and supporting analysis." He tapped a finger on his proposal. "That's all in here?"

"It is," Harmon said. "You have it all."

"Page three of Appendix two," Riley said, her first words of the meeting.

Yates stared at her, then smiled. She smiled right back.

"Mr. Yates," Harmon said. "If any further support is needed we can turn it around quickly." He nodded purposefully to Riley.

Yates looked to Riley and then to his Executive Assistant. She shrugged her shoulders.

"Ms. O'Brian," Harmon said, nodding again in Riley's direction, "has been a great help in this project."

Yates renewed his smile. Then he tapped his forehead and returned to business.

"Tell me this," he said. "Do you have a specific implementation plan? A plan made up of action items linked to a detailed timeline?"

All eyes back to the screen.

Implementation Plan
Formulation of AC&C Safe to Say Policy
Announcement & Rollout
Follow-Up Surveys
Fine Tuning

"Okay," Yates said, to his assistant. "We'll study all that." Another task for her, another serving for her overflowing plate.

In a noticeably sympathetic tone Yates asked, "Who put this presentation together?" Everyone looked at each other, then at Harmon.

"The team," Harmon said.

"Well," Yates lowered his voice. "It's a job well done."

"Thank you," Harmon said.

"We really believe in our recommendations," Caitlin said. "I hope we conveyed that."

Her only interjection, perfectly and strategically timed to send the message that, although she was too classy to say so, she was surely at the heart of the team's work and recommendations.

Riley and Joe shared a smirk.

"We are convinced," Harmon said, "that better communications will lead to more efficient processes in every phase of AC&C's operations, from product development to marketing and sales, from order processing to implementation and customer retention."

"You and your team," Yates said, "have done a good job. I think I may have something here, a difference maker."

Yates made eye contact with each team member and stopped back at Harmon.

"This is the kind of commitment and execution I need to be successful in what lies ahead."

"Thank you sir," Harmon said. "On behalf of the whole team."

"Of course," Yates said, "I will take a more detailed look. I want to do my own counting."

"That's great," Harmon said, feeling affinity with the great man and his thorough and logical process. "Please let us know if there is anything more you need from the team."

"Rest assured," Yates said, "I will. After I study the numbers."

Harmon nodded.

"That's it then," Yates said.

There was a palpable sense of relief in the room, even triumph. Then silence. Yates didn't jump up as expected. Instead, he settled deeper in his chair and sat there with his hands folded in his lap, as if he wanted more, as if he were enjoying things for a change, taking a rare opportunity to indulge himself.

The silence became awkward and Harmon felt a host's duty to entertain. No slide for that, he went from the hip.

"Of course Mr. Yates," he said, "our proposal isn't all about numbers. We don't want to put all our faith in numbers."

"What?" Yates said.

"Yes," Harmon said. "You know what they say, if too much time is spent counting numbers, soon only numbers count."

Yates froze. He looked like someone had slapped him. Harmon knew he had said something wrong. He didn't know how wrong.

Yates stared at him, the muscles of his face tightening. He tilted his head and a little twitch started under his jaw. Judgment now in his hard eyes. Harmon expected an explosion, but the CEO just sat still. Harmon looked down.

"We need this room *now*," the assistant said. She tilted her head toward the door, an eviction notice.

Tension and silence all around as the team collected their stuff and hurried out. The assistant made eye contact with Harmon and shook her head.

Sunk Ship

why?

The People Team gathered in the cafeteria, waiting for Harmon. Everyone silent, in mourning.

"Why?" Caitlin asked, as soon as Harmon appeared and before he sat down. "Why did you say that thing about numbers?" She was swelled up with indignation, unable to contain herself.

"I don't know," Harmon said.

"Well you sure screwed up."

"I know I did. It seemed like, I don't know, I just wanted to keep Mr. Yates interested, to end the meeting smoothly."

"It shouldn't be such a big deal," Riley said. "It was just an observation."

"A mistake," Joe said. "Anything Yates can *conscrew* as criticism, that's a mistake."

"It impacts the whole team," Caitlin said. "That's why I'm upset. It endangers the whole project."

"Give me a break," Riley said. "The man can't take a little insight?"

"We're talking to him," Caitlin said, pointing at Harmon.

Riley reddened.

"I hope," Harmon said, "that I haven't hurt the team." He could feel hostility bubbling up all around him. All vestiges of camaraderie gone now, swept away by the sense of impending doom. His time as the anointed one so brief. "You think I should try and call and explain? Maybe to Mr. Yates's assistant?"

"Absolutely not," Caitlin said. "You stay away from her. Maybe I can help. I don't know."

"Everything else," Fred said, "went so well." He smiled and added, as if it would help, "I think you made a perfect presentation, until, you know, that little boo-boo at the end."

"A perfect presentation?" Caitlin said. "A boo-boo?" She snorted, twice, for the sheer imbecility of the remarks. "A perfect presentation that's gonna screw us all."

"I hope," Harmon repeated, "that I didn't hurt the team."

"Well," Caitlin said, "you did. You made it sound as if Mr. Yates, I don't know, as if he was some kind of a bean counter."

"God almighty," Riley said. "A big baby."

"Who's a baby?" Caitlin yelled.

"Both you and Yates," Riley said. "And it's were, as if he *were* some kind of bean counter."

"Listen you—" Caitlin started.

"Stop!" Harmon said. "I have to think about all this."

He left.

Unassigned talent

morning after — banished — guilt — avenger

The next morning he snuck into the office like a criminal revisiting the scene of his crime. He wanted to see no one and no one to see him, not even Riley. He had spent the whole night infected by the need to turn the day's events over and over, trying to figure some way to make things right, some way to relieve Mr. Yates's great disappointment. He tried to get his mind to fix on something else, but it wouldn't.

He played his messages. From Yates's Executive Assistant, time stamped at 11:17 p.m. the previous night, an order to see his direct supervisor the very first thing upon arriving and bring all his Leadership Team and Project Armageddon materials.

***

His boss had an officious look about her, as if she had something that must be done and would do it quickly, like ripping off a bandage to minimize the pain. She never raised her eyes above his tie.

"I don't know everything that happened," she said, "but Mr. Yates is disappointed with you and with your performance."

Though he knew something like that was coming, it still stung.

"You," the boss said, keeping her head down, looking at a document, as if needing to read what she was saying, "are being assigned to the UTP."

He didn't know that was coming. That was a punishment harsher than he expected. The *UTP* was a virtual corral, full of managers soon to be fired or more delicately put, downsized. A collection of the out-of-date, out-of-favor and out-of-chances. *UTP* was one of Human Resources' most imaginative euphemisms. It stood for *Unassigned Talent Pool*. It was a fate worst than an outright firing, for its slow death and stigma. An immediate firing at least meant that whatever you did wrong was something big. He felt dizzy, from the swiftness and severity of it all.

"You'll get your documentation by the end of the week."

Documentation meant a thick, sealed manila envelope, commonly called a *package* and full with the particular details of one's demise. First, a letter on official AC&C stationary, explaining that the recipient had been declared *non-essential*, the letter careful to note that said recipient was surely a valuable human being with a wonderful future, just rendered by circumstance non-essential to AC&C. Some flowery language employed, telling how just as the corporation was now going through a difficult transition in becoming a successful competitor in the global marketplace, said recipient was starting a life transition with his or her particular skill surely valuable elsewhere. There would be a section on all the help available during this difficult period of transition, worded to sound as if a whole world of support awaited but, distilled to the essentials, amounting to a few discount counselors and sixty days of telephone and copier privileges, ending with best wishes and good luck in the real world.

Harmon had seen packages delivered to colleagues before. Besides sympathy, and despite trying not to, he had always thought a little less of the recipient, believing they must have, for some reason, deserved it.

"Sorry Harmon," his boss said.

***

He took the staircase to the cafeteria and found Riley there, sitting in their corner, waiting on him. A faithful friend.

"I've been banished," he said.

"What?"

"Banished to the *UTP*."

"You're kidding?" Shock on her face.

"No," Harmon said, "I'm not kidding. My boss just told me. I'm getting a package by the end of the week. I just don't believe it."

"I believe it," Riley said. She was angry. "Because it's like this, whatever they preach most they practice least. Yates endorses a safe to say environment but can't take the slightest criticism."

"But I wasn't trying to criticize Mr. Yates."

"I know, but he thought you were and that's all that counts."

The way she looked at Harmon, he felt as if she were mad at him, that it was his fault that everything he'd believed in was a lie.

"He must be real sensitive to the number thing," Riley said. "I don't know, maybe his mother started him counting too soon."

Harmon looked out the window. The source of Yates's sensitivities a mystery far beyond him.

"What you spoke was the truth," Riley said. "But you made a mistake."

"I know it, but I'm still not sure—"

"You made the sale then bought it back."

"What?"

She explained what she had learned from salesmen, while temping at a furniture store. When you have the sale made you shut your mouth or talk about something unrelated and innocuous. Get back on-topic and you risk *buying your product back*. Once Yates was sold, Harmon should have engaged him about the weather or basketball or maybe about how good *Golden Boy* was looking. But he stayed on business and hit one of the man's sensitivities.

"My big mouth ruined everything," Harmon said.

"Listen," Riley said, "if the man can't take a little honest insight—"

"I just thought the numbers only counting comment was a good one. You know, maybe a little philosophical disagreement and something he'd find interesting."

"Where did you get that anyway, about only numbers counting? That was good."

"Someone I know said it."

"Harmon," Riley said, her voice softer now, no anger left in it. "Listen, this is not your fault."

She waited for his agreement.

"Listen," she said, "It's not your fault and maybe it's mine."

"It's not your fault," he said. "No way."

But she had already judged that it was, at least partially, and there was no changing her mind. Her guilt was firmly planted and already seeding a need for redemption.

"I don't know anymore," Harmon said.

"I know," Riley said. "And I should have known earlier. You're a fish out of water here and trying to get you to swim deeper was a mistake. My mistake and a bad one."

"It's not—"

"Listen," Riley said. "I'm just saying you should get out of this and find something that matches who you are. Somehow you got into this and it's not the life for you and pretending won't work. Forget about what other people expect of you. If you don't do that, you're going to be miserable."

"Going to be?" Harmon asked.

"You know what I mean."

"How about you," Harmon said. "I mean, doing this."

"Me? I'm just passing through. This isn't what I want. I thought I did but I don't and now I know it. I can play the game, you know, bullshit the bullshitters, if I want to. But I don't have much invested here. Not enough to make me fool myself."

"So this isn't for you?"

"Nope."

"So we have that in common."

"We do," Riley said. "And you know what my mama used to say?"

"What?"

"*La compania en la miseria hace a esta mas llevadera.* That means *two in distress makes sorrow less.*"

"I like that," Harmon said.

"One thing I know," Riley said. "What happened to you isn't right. And that Yates ..." Her voice turned lower and more intense with the mention of that name.

"It's okay," Harmon said.

He feared her reaction. The thought of Riley as an avenger was scary. With all that intelligence and energy and ingenuity swept up in revenge, anything was possible.

"What you said before," he said, "about this not being for me, you're right. So I feel better already. Everything's okay."

"Nope," Riley said. "Everything's not okay. I didn't mean that. It's one thing for you to decide this isn't for you. That's one thing. But, for you to work so hard, give your heart and soul, like you did on this project, then for someone to screw you, that's not okay."

"I just want to move on," Harmon said.

"Oh," Riley said, "you should move on. Me too. But ..."

Her voice tailed off but he could tell the need for satisfaction was already in her heart.

"But what?" he asked.

"The man needs to know something."

"What?"

"That what goes around, comes around."

PART V

Celebration

big plans—buttons—marching band—little me

"I believe," Preston P. Yates said, "in celebrating success."

His assistant nodded affirmatively, testifying to her boss' belief and seconding it. Caitlin bobbed her head enthusiastically. Riley, the other invitee from the now acclaimed People Team smiled. She had nothing against celebrating success.

"The People Team," Yates said, "has done important work. You have seized the moment and made a difference. I've asked you here as the Team's representatives, to take the lead in coordinating our celebration of success."

Riley put on a look of earnest appreciation. Now was the time to be practical.

Yates had glowing praise for Caitlin, who in difficult and trying circumstances had taken over the People Team, not an easy task, but she had responded courageously, just as he knew she would. Caitlin beamed with gratification. And, the CEO said, he knew how much Ms. O'Brian put into the effort. For someone so new to the organization, she had made a remarkable contribution and that's why he wanted her to share in the celebration and recognition. Riley lowered her eyes, as if the praise was too much for her.

Caitlin previewed the celebration plans. It would be an all-hands meeting in the big auditorium. They had a message so important that all headquarters personnel must hear it and share in the celebration. She looked to Yates after each sentence, to make sure he liked it. For leverage, Caitlin also wanted to communicate the message to everyone out in the regions. She planned to invite all the regional managers to attend in person and provide an 800 number for all worldwide associates to call in and listen. Yates liked all that.

Caitlin added, as if an afterthought, that the whole celebration would occur under the title of *Safe to Say*. That was another strategic linkage. All their ongoing efforts would be under that banner: *Safe to Say*. Caitlin emphasized it was a way to leverage their efforts. It was a synergistic approach.

Yates really liked that. Riley squirmed through it all. Yates directed his assistant to help make it happen. Synergistic was just the kind of thinking he wanted. When Caitlin said, for the sake of humility, that she was just following his example, Riley bit a little piece of her inner cheek off.

Riding Yates's approval, Caitlin provided specifics. To begin, she would have a pamphlet for every attendee. Buttons for everyone, too. She pulled a sample button out from her leather case and held it for Yates to see. *Safe to Say* printed in red on a white background, a little blue AC&C logo above it. Red, white and blue. She ceremoniously pinned the button on her lapel and handed two buttons to Yates's assistant. The assistant pinned one on. She didn't pass the other to Yates.

Of course, the highlight of any celebration would be Mr. Yates's remarks. After that, Caitlin had a little something extra planned. Several people would come up on stage, individually, to share their own safe to say moments. Concern on Yates's face at that; ordinary folks sharing his stage. But it had been carefully planned. Caitlin would lead off. To set the proper tone she would tell how the People Team brought the difficult legacy problem of poor communication to the CEO's attention and how, given past management's reaction to honest communication, the team was very apprehensive. But Mr. Yates not only accepted the message, but encouraged a deep dive into the problem. Following that, one of the interns would tell how she came to Caitlin about her experience as the only woman in the Technical Support Group and how she openly and safely told of the hostility she faced and how Caitlin worked with her to challenge the embedded culture. That would stand as an example of the inclusive new culture at work.

"All Good," Yates said. "As long as you have the agenda in control. Anything else?" He had the first tics of impatience about him: a finger tapping, an eye wandering. The discussion had veered too close to the day to day practicalities of execution.

Caitlin said there were other exciting things planned, along the lines of entertainment. They would have the local high school band to add pizzazz and excitement. Yates didn't look excited and his assistant quickly interjected that they didn't need to go into all that, as long as things were well in hand.

"One little thing," Riley said, her voice soft and low.

"Yes," Yates said.

"It just came to me," Riley said, "and I don't know if it's even a good idea."

"Let's hear it," Yates said, smiling at her.

"Well, I wondered if we should have a non-management person represented."

"An interesting point," Yates said.

"For the inclusion," Riley said. "So all our colleagues feel included. Like Caitlin said." She smiled demurely. Sacrifice sometimes necessary. There would be time for contrition.

"Yes," Yates said. "I like the idea."

"But who could we get?" Caitlin asked.

Riley's tongue twinged with *whom*. She didn't dare.

"I mean," Caitlin said, "we're talking about addressing the whole HQ staff in the big auditorium. Would he or she be comfortable doing that? I mean, we don't want to embarrass her or him."

Yates took on his thinking look and the room remained silent. He tapped his fingers on his desk, looked to his assistant and then to Riley.

"How about you Ms. O'Brian."

"Oh my," Riley said. "Thank you for your consideration, but I'm no public speaker. I mean, it would scare the daylights out of me." She pressed her elbows to her side and shivered to demonstrate.

"Yes," Yates said. "I can understand that." He even looked sympathetic. "But that could work for us. If you think you could do it?"

"Oh my," Riley said. She breathed deeply. "I don't know."

Yates smiled at her. A charm beam from a man who knew he was irresistible.

"I guess," she said. "With your support. I mean just knowing you think I can do it, well then, you know, I'd be willing to try."

"Just what," Caitlin said, "would you talk about?"

Riley said she could talk about how she, a newcomer and after all just a temporary, was nonetheless invited onto the team and given the opportunity to express her opinions and then ended up being heard and taken seriously even by Mr. Yates himself. "I mean," she said, "the thought of me just meeting with a man who's been on the cover of *Fortune* Magazine." She giggled a nervous giggle.

Yates smiled again. "You know," he said, "I think this is a great idea."

Caitlin nodded.

Yates turned to his assistant. "Make it so."

Hard To Say

disappointment — mom & dad — homeward bound?

Harmon knew his parents would be waiting for his regular Saturday call. If he missed, they would worry. He could try and fake it, not tell about his calamity and pretend things were normal. But he knew he couldn't pull that off. He wasn't much at deception. He braced himself for his bitter duty.

***

"Hello," his mother answered, her voice expectant. She knew it would be him.

His mother would only talk for a minute, then turn the phone over to his father, but she liked to hear her boy's voice. Amazing, how much she could tell just by the sound of his voice.

"Hi, Mom."

"Hi, honey. How are you?"

"Good."

"You're eating."

"Yep."

"Sleeping?"

"Yep."

"Taking a break? Not all work?"

"I'm doing fine."

"Harmon?"

"Yes?"

"Is everything okay?"

There was no fooling her. "I'm okay, Mom."

"You sure?"

"Yes."

He didn't want to tell his mother first. He didn't want her gasp to be the way his father found out.

"Well, okay, honey. Here's your father. He's anxious to talk with you. I'll say goodbye after."

Harmon could picture his father waiting impatiently for the phone. He drew a deep breath.

"Hi, Son."

"Hi, Dad."

If he could choose he would have preferred another session with Mister Yates. Facing Mister Yates would be bliss compared to this. His father didn't deserve this. His father didn't ask for much.

"So son, how was your week?"

Quick and direct as always, no small talk.

"Well, Dad, not so good." A monstrous understatement.

"Why? What happened?" His father's voice high with concern.

"It's a long story. Not a good story."

"Tell me."

"I might lose my job."

"What?"

"I'm probably gonna lose my job."

His father said nothing. Harmon could imagine his shock. He had never failed his father this gravely.

"What happened?"

"I made the CEO mad."

"Mr. Yates?"

"Yeah."

"How?"

"I made a remark he didn't like."

"That's it?"

"Well, pretty much."

"What did you say? It must have been bad."

"I said," Harmon looked to his apartment's ceiling, "something about arithmetic not being the only thing that matters."

"What?"

He told the story. His father disbelieving and why not? The story in its retelling sounded absurd, even to Harmon.

"You're sure that's all you said?"

"Yes."

"I can't believe he would fire you for that."

"Well it was in front of people. That wasn't smart. I should have known better. He likes numbers."

His father said he thought Harmon could still fix things, by going about it the way he would, by talking to Mr. Yates man to man. *Man to man? Harmon Wolcott* to *Preston P. Yates*? His father knew a lot about a lot of things but nothing about the ways of corporate hierarchy, nothing about the ways of a prince and his subjects. Harmon tried to explain how it didn't work that way, not with Mr. Yates. You didn't get a second chance. You didn't usually get a first. That self reminder, of his unique and blown opportunity, made him wince.

"But that doesn't mean you lose your job," his father said. "I mean, we've got so much invested now. You're whole career. You don't have to leave the company. That's so drastic. That's an awful price. There must be other opportunities within the company somewhere? Right?"

"Not really dad. Having the CEO as an enemy is the kiss of death. It's as bad as it gets."

"Why did you say what you said anyway? You must have had some reason?"

"I don't know dad."

It was a question Harmon kept asking himself. Why did he say what he said? Maybe it was his swelled head because things had gone so well and he was feeling like a big shot team leader and trying to play the part; maybe he was just enjoying the sound of his own voice; maybe a deeper thinker would say he was so afraid of success that he wanted to fail.

"I still think you could—"

"No, Dad. I think it's over. I know it's over. You'd have to be here." A flash of certainty in his voice. It was time to get beyond what happened, time to get to the future.

His father went grudgingly. He asked, "So what's next?"

Great disappointment in the question. Harmon knew that whatever was next wouldn't be good enough. He wanted to say, *dad I love you* and wait as long as needed for the reciprocal. He didn't. That kind of thing was forbidden between them.

"I've got sixty days, Dad. But I don't want to hang around. I thought, I guessed, that maybe, you know, I'd come home. At least for a while, or at least I thought so, you know, if it's okay?"

A long time before his father spoke. The silence significant. When he spoke, all he said was, "Okay."

The hesitation hurt Harmon. Maybe he should have expected it. Maybe he deserved it. Maybe it meant something different than he thought. But he felt embarrassed and a little cheated. He had anticipated his father's disappointment, but always thought of home as a sanctuary. His worst nightmares, the ones that prevented him going back to sleep, were of being all alone in New Jersey with no one waiting at home.

"Okay," his father said again and with a little more warmth.

This was a great shock for his father. Harmon heard his mother in the background, asking what was wrong.

"Your mother wants to talk to you," his father said and was gone.

"What's the matter," his mother asked.

He explained as briefly as he could, already tired of the telling.

"You want to know what I think?" his mother asked.

He wanted to know.

"I think that Mr. Yates is a bastard."

He had never heard his mother swear before. Never.

"Son, you know what else I think?"

"What?"

"You come on home. I mean just as soon as you can."

"Mom, I know you're disappointed—"

"Nope. Not a bit. Not in you. Maybe some for you. I know how hard you work and how important this is to you, but I'm not disappointed in you."

"I hope," Harmon said, "I hope …" He stopped, as if whatever it was, was too much to hope for.

"I'm worried Harmon."

"I don't want you to worry Mom?"

"I'm worried about you honey. I want you to be okay and the best way is for you to come on home. Everything else will take care of itself. Right now that's all I care about. I don't give a hoot in hell about that ACC or that Yale or whatever his name is."

Harmon's breath went out in a long, slow exhale. His mother couldn't even remember Preston Yates's name. Something reassuring in that.

"I'm worried about Dad," Harmon said. "Is Daddy okay?"

"He'll be fine. You worry about yourself." A new sentiment from his mother. She lived for his father's well being. "Your father will get over it," his mother said.

Was that hardness in her voice? His father must have picked it up, too. Harmon heard his footsteps, from the creaky wooden stairs that led up to his little office.

"Harmon," his mother said, "I want you back here. The sooner the better. You know I've got stuff for you to do. Stuff I can't get your father to do."

"I'm sorry, Mom."

"You got nothing to be sorry about."

"I've got to clean out my office and pack my stuff and settle the apartment. It'll take a while."

"Well, do what you have to do. Then come on home."

***

What would it be like to be home again? He and his father and mother in the old farmhouse. His old bedroom ready for him and everything unchanged. Would he revert to his boyish ways? Would he have chores to do? Would his mother still hang him a stocking on the mantel at Christmas? Would he sit in the back seat on the ride to the Friday night fish fry?

His mother would always welcome him and he believed she really wanted him home and he took comfort in that, but in his heart he agreed with his father that, a grown man now, he didn't belong there.

Truth Telling

big show — scared — avenger — left hook

The *Safe to Say* banner stretched across AC&C's atrium. Six-hundred managers packed the adjacent auditorium. It was a day of compulsory celebration, by order of the office of the Chief Executive Officer. Failure to appear would definitely harm your career.

On the stage sat the entire Leadership Team. Sitting with them, their special guest, Elizabeth of DNA-TMG, basking in the triumph of another culture set on the path to transformation. Yates's Executive Assistant was up and down and all around. She was master of ceremonies, her usual role at rallies, a duty to which she brought the passion of an evangelist. Once, during another celebration, she had screamed so loud she ruptured her vocal cords.

Riley sat in the auditorium's front row with the rest of the honored People Team, all except their disgraced and discarded former leader. Unable to sit still, she shifted in her seat and pulled loose threads from her sweater sleeve. She was all nervousness and determination, nothing less than truth and justice at stake.

Yates's assistant welcomed everyone and then the Central High School Marching Band paraded down the middle aisle, belting out the *Notre Dame Victory March*. Baton twirling cheerleaders came first, followed by drummers and trumpeters and a group of steppers recruited from the local YMCA. Once everyone assembled on stage another *Safe to Say* banner unfurled, followed by a blizzard of balloons. The band stopped and marched in place for a bit, then headed off to their bus, to wait for their show closing performance of *Happy Days Are Here Again*. The meeting itself was proprietary, for AC&C associates only.

Riley pictured Harmon, one floor above, taking the opportunity to clean out his office while assured of privacy. She had asked him to call in and listen via the 800 number. He promised he would. It was important he heard what she had to say. She hoped he wasn't listening yet, the whole circus would mock him. Even now, he could probably feel the reverberations.

"Wow!" the assistant screamed. "I think it's time to celebrate." Her vocal cords bulged like overtaxed cables. Might they pop again?

Celebration, the Kool & the Gang song, burst forth. *Celebrate good times, come on!* The assistant danced to the tune and with outstretched arms encouraged everyone to stand and wave their arms. Everyone stood.

Most made some effort at waving. *There's a party going on right here, a celebration to last throughout the years ... Everyone around the world come on!*

When the song finished, the crowd sat. The executive assistant introduced the Leadership Team. One by one the members jumped from their seats and stood fist-pumping and waving, each trying to best the other, as if trying to spike the needle on an enthusiasm meter. They all wore *Safe to Say* t-shirts over their dress shirts. The last manager introduced yanked his t-shirt off and waved it in the air.

The ceremony, the people, the stupid button on her lapel, it all disgusted Riley. The whole atmosphere was much more than she had anticipated. She used her disgust to try and stop her legs from shaking.

The executive assistant welcomed and thanked everyone again. The crowd quieted. Riley had noticed something about AC&C rallies—how easy it was to silence the crowd, and another thing—how slowly the auditorium filled and how quickly it emptied.

"Now," the assistant said, "and without further ado, let me introduce the man who made this celebration possible. The architect of the new AC&C and it's new *Safe to Say* culture, our CEO and one of America's visionary leaders, Mr. Preston P. Yates!"

Great applause. All the Division Managers stood and turned to honor Yates's entrance. He appeared from stage right with a wave for everyone. Riley went through the clapping motion, but her hands barely touched. She was a false cheerer.

Yates walked along the row of Leadership Team members, shaking hands with each, backslapping his favorite, the young Chief Financial Officer he had recently recruited. He singled out Elizabeth for a more intimate handshake, taking her hand in both of his. He took over the podium and opened his arms to embrace his whole flock. The audience clapped until he held up his hands in a stop sign.

"This is an important day for AC&C," he began. "An important day for all of us."

Head nodding and wide smiles up and down the Leadership Team.

"What the People Team has accomplished, and we will introduce that wonderful team in a moment, is quite remarkable."

He directed the renewed applause to the first row.

"This group has made a difference; they have seized the moment, they have filled unoccupied space."

Applause for that, too.

He told of the serious communication problem at AC&C, another of its insidious *legacy* problems. What, he asked, could be worse for an enterprise like AC&C, an enterprise that depended on the creativity and common purpose of all its associates?

"Nothing!" someone from the audience shouted.

"It's not important who caused this problem," Yates said. "That's not what I'm here for. See, I'm not a look-behinder. I don't drive by looking in the rear-view mirror. I'm a forward looking leader. I'm here to lead into the future. So I thank the People Team for bringing this serious problem to my attention. Without awareness there can be no improvement. So I celebrate the *People Team!*"

Maybe it was her imagination, but Riley thought she could hear the steady soft clicks of Joe's mechanical counter, adding up the CEO's *I's.* Yates directed the People Team to stand for more recognition. Another ovation. Riley thought in true wonderment, *all this for what we did? What did we do?*

Yates signaled for quiet, then said, "Caitlin, come up here!"

She came up quickly, smiling. She shook Yates's hand. He took her by the shoulders and turned her so the whole audience could enjoy her beaming face. Then he took the vacant seat reserved for him, in the middle of the Leadership Team, and immediately began a whispering conference with the CFO. The podium and the stage lent to his protégé, a new star in his orbit.

"Thank you all!" Caitlin said, too loud and too close to the microphone, vibrating eardrums. Her nervousness so obvious that it made Riley even more nervous. Recalibrated, Caitlin introduced the People Team, each member standing for recognition, Fred smiling, Joe embarrassed for once, Riley with a quick up and down. No mention of Harmon and no one seemed to notice, or care. It was as if he had never existed, as if some totalitarian state had expunged him from its history, even the mention of his name verboten.

"Our achievement," Caitlin said, "would not have been possible without the whole team."

Just the kind of thing a humble soul who carried the great burden of team leader would say and all the more aggravating for it. Riley focused on the red exit sign at the side of the stage. She stared at it until it blurred.

She thought of Harmon. He had told her of his decision to leave today and to leave nothing behind. There was no reason for a long goodbye. Finding a job within AC&C while carrying the stigma of the Unassigned Talent Pool was difficult enough, but to be exiled by Preston P. Yates himself, that made one an untouchable. Riley had asked him to stay until her presentation was over so, free of that burden, she could spend a few minutes with him. If nothing else, she wanted a proper goodbye. She was still afraid he would just pack up and leave, never to be seen again. She could imagine that.

Caitlin introduced her friend from Technical Support, a young woman so cool and composed in front of that huge audience that Riley felt ashamed of her own cowardliness. The intern told her story of sexism and Caitlin's courageous intervention, all the while her patron standing at her side, in total support. When the intern finished, Caitlin told how she tentatively informed Mr. Yates of the broader communications problems at AC&C and of his saintly acceptance of and firm commitment to fix the problems. She retold the event as if it might be memorialized as the seminal act in AC&C's miraculous transformation into the land of safe to say, as if the date should be a holy day.

It was almost Riley's time.

At the gym there was a saying: *money talks and bullshit walks*. The same sentiment in Spanish: *Mucho ruido y pocas nueces—much noise and few nuts, all mouth and no trousers, all talk and no action*. At AC&C she had heard a lot of flamboyant exits threatened. Disgruntled associates promising to sweep everything off their desk in one stroke, then walk out never to be seen again. In some of their fantasies they stood or squatted on their desks and, in an act of ultimate defiance, pissed all over them; in others they won the big lottery and told the boss to his face that he was a perfect asshole. All grandly imagined and energetically described, but never done. Maybe Caitlin would skip over her. Maybe she'd claim that in all the excitement she forgot little Riley. Part of Riley wished for just that, an easy but respectable way out.

Riley O'Brian.

Her name echoed through the auditorium. She prayed a fast prayer: *Dear God, if what I'm about to do is wrong, please strike me down right now, before I go up. If it seems fair and just to you, please help me.* Did God listen to those who prayed only when in desperate need? She sent a copy of her prayer to her mother. She would help if she could.

Not struck down, she stood up. Her time now. Talk or walk. Do it now or forever regret it. A secretary seated behind her, never her friend, stood up and straightened her collar and squeezed her arm. Riley thought it the most generous gesture ever.

A twenty step walk to the stage where she was about to address the whole auditorium: six-hundred professional people. It seemed like the whole world. Polite applause followed by dead silence because they were all waiting for her. She couldn't feel her feet touch the floor.

Bright and hot on the stage. Disorienting. She wished she had notes. She didn't need help for what was in her heart, but she had a flash of desire for the security of a written page of AC&C propaganda that she could recite and then make a quick, cowardly exit. Her instinct now for survival.

She made it to the podium, but it was too tall, up too her chin. There was supposed to be a step-stool for her to stand on. It wasn't there. The audience waiting, her chest tight, her breath short, her throat like sand paper. Yates's assistant saw her plight and found the little stool and brought it to her. An act of humanity. Suddenly, she popped up and was looking over the podium, as if she were a jack-in-the-box. Some in the audience laughed at her sudden elevation. A favor, because that made her mad, and with Riley O'Brian, anger and timidity couldn't coexist.

Looking over the podium at the assembled managers she felt, miracle of miracles, calm. Maybe fear was right there under the stage or podium, waiting to jump up and choke her, but right then she wasn't afraid. Maybe her prayer had been answered.

"The message," she started, then took a breath and started over. "*My* message is a little different from what you've heard so far. A different perspective you might say, but still a celebration of success. I, too, very much believe in celebrating success."

She swallowed and looked up, as if saluting the *Safe to Say* banner, but really looking to the second floor and Harmon. What was coming was for him.

"I've learned a lot from my experience with the People Team and that's what I'd like to talk about, how I've been so privileged. You probably don't know it, but I'm just a temporary. I've been so fortunate to be included in such an important project and to experience leadership at the highest levels."

Applause for that. She could feel the presence of the Leadership Team behind her, like someone reading over her shoulder. She imagined satisfaction on Yates's face.

"I feel especially privileged, to be able to talk to you and say what I've learned and say it straight because here at AC&C it is," she lifted her voice, "*safe to say!*"

Longer applause at that, allowing her to slow down and get her bearings. Following her own advice, she swallowed and took a deep breath.

"So, what have I learned? Well one thing is that real success means finding the right place for yourself. See, I didn't know if this was right for me. You know, such important projects and so many smart people. Could I fit in? Well, now I've seen things from up close, from inside out. During these difficult times I've heard the leadership publicly declaring their respect for people and lamenting the layoffs that hurt so much, just like they were losing family."

A collective, understanding sigh.

"And, like you, I've heard the inspirational words of Mr. Yates, stressing that people are what's most important. It's like our Human Resources department says, it's all about the people. So I guess what I'm saying, and I hope I'm not rambling because I'm very nervous."

A round of supporting applause and an opportunity to swallow and breathe.

"I guess I'm saying that a big part of success is finding out if a place is right for you. In doing that I've learned a lot about myself."

Signs of boredom now, coughing and shuffling and throat clearing, attention spans timing out.

"But I don't want to talk just about me. Instead, I want to talk about someone who's not here today. A hero of mine, you might say."

Choked up, she paused. She hoped again, that Harmon was listening.

"This man, he's a naive guy but I don't hold his naiveté against him. See naiveté can be defined a couple of different ways. One definition is *foolish, incredulous, simple*. I found that in the library here, in the *Oxford English Dictionary*. But I don't like that definition of naiveté, not for the man I'm talking about. The definition I like is *lack of worldliness*. See lack of worldliness can mean having a *concern with things of the spirit*."

Silence and confusion at this. She was talking fast but she needed to, to get it all said. "I don't have his spirit. Maybe I had it and lost it somewhere. See I've also heard our leadership in private, talking about stubborn retirees who resist their duty to drop dead and save the pension fund some money and discussing layoffs and the plan to *thin the herd*. That's leadership!"

A buzz now, the audience's boredom peeling away.

She turned and saw Yates still busy with the CFO, oblivious to her and her comments, conducting business while someone else presented, his usual behavior.

"Yes, our leadership team. Let's see, there's Mr. K, our director of marketing, though the only thing he's ever marketed is himself. And there's Ms. Griffin, our Human Resources and diversity guru, bet she doesn't know that when she's not around the boys get their laughs guessing whether it's she or her partner that straps it on."

Whispering and head-shaking among the Leadership Team, but the critical part of her plan still holding, her bet that the big shooters would be typically slow on the uptake, that years as the recipients of uninterrupted sycophancy would leave them unprepared for someone going off script and that they would be further paralyzed by Yates's presence, deferring all action to him. Without Yates's leadership, they would need time to *build consensus* on what to do about her.

"Now, instead of the real team leader, Harmon Wolcott, whom did we hear from today?" She had her full voice now. She looked down at Caitlin, wide-eyed in her front row seat. "We heard from our new team leader, and she is a true leader at something; she's the world's greatest ass kisser. Like it says in her appraisal, she's a role model. She kisses so much ass she blows her nose with toilet paper."

Stunned silence and then gasps and uh-ohs and some laughter. "Hey," someone from the Leadership Team finally said, in astonishment and admonishment.

"And now you're hearing from me, a lowly temp. How did that happen? Why am I up on this stage while a true team leader like Harmon Wolcott is not?" It felt good saying his name with such respect. "Huh? Because I know how to please 'em. That's why. It's easy. You wanna know how? Just keep grinning and saying yes." Not wanting this to end, feeling the power of the avenger, she changed her pose and tone, voice dripping with false sweetness. "You say, *it's wonderful working here,* smiling all the time, grin fucking the whole bunch of them."

Now Yates was looking up, suddenly aware something was amiss. Maybe the profanity woke him. Her time was running out.

"Now, at the top we have, of course, Mr. Preston P. Yates." It felt good saying his name with such contempt. "You see it's all about his leadership. Mr. Preston P. Yates showing the way, with his strategy and tactics for always getting the most from his human capital. A man who reveres counting numbers so much that, in his world, only numbers count." She heard frantic whispering behind her. The Leadership Team conferring with Yates.

"You know," she said, "after this, they'll probably need a serious team building trip, not like that last one, that cheap bowling alley bullshit. Anyhow, don't forget to wear your little buttons, that's an important part of changing the culture, here in the land of *safe to say.*"

Her microphone lost power and then Ms. Griffin was at her side. Another manager came from the opposite direction. It was Mr. K.

"Let's go," Mr. K said. Only at AC&C would he be the muscle.

She had done what she promised herself she would do. All she wanted now was to get off the stage and get away. But Mr. K grabbed her right arm and it hurt. He was tall and she couldn't reach his chin, not with any leverage, but his midsection was at the same height as her favorite heavy bag and staring at it tripped something in her. *Plant the right foot—bob to the left and twist the left toe, like you're stepping on a cigarette—keep the left elbow level to the floor... unwind to the right, legs and hips, twist your left toe to the right putting that cigarette out, uncoil like a mean snake with mean snake intentions, let go with the left hand, like you want your fist to go through the target.* She did all that and her fist disappeared in the soft stomach and wet air rushed from Mr. K as he bent over, coughing. Ms. Griffin jumped back, as if she might get some on her. No one else from the Leadership Team moved.

"Where's security?" someone shouted.

Riley exited stage left, fighting the great urge to hurry, forcing herself to take her dignified time and taking a purposeful look at Mr. Yates. She saw the shock on his face. Later she wondered if there wasn't just a hint of admiration there.

Salvation

future

She stopped in a corner adjacent to the Credit Union. The halls were empty and unnaturally quiet. She slumped against the wall. It settled on her, what she had done, and suddenly her shoulders throbbed and she was very tired but satisfied. She lowered her head. She had kept her covenant with God, her mother and Harmon. After a moment she walked to a stairway.

***

Harmon's bookcase, credenza and potted palm tree were already in the hallway. His office walls were bare and paint-prepped. No time wasted. Tomorrow the office would be ready for its next occupant. But he was there, at his desk, waiting for her, just as he promised. She stood in his doorway and they stared at each other.

"I can't believe you did that," he said.

"You listened?"

"I listened. But I still can't believe you did it."

"It needed doing."

Cardboard boxes flanked his desk, three full and stacked, one half full and still open. He had packed almost everything: books, mementos, awards, training class certificates.

"I just wanted to leave quietly," he said.

She knew he wished for a painless escape. A few handshakes and fudged consolations and out the door.

"Maybe I shouldn't have," she said, "but you deserved more."

"I don't know. But you sure did tell them." He laughed. "God! I never heard anything like it."

"Yeah," she said. "What does Joe say? You know, what he always says, sing 'em a hymn."

That was another of Joe's missives for upper management, whom he referred to as the collective *'em*. Really more of a chant: *Sing 'em a hymn* followed by *him … him, fuck him!* Said *for* upper management, but never *to* upper management. Riley had really sung 'em a hymn, and a good one.

They stayed quiet for a moment, sitting there like outcasts from Eden.

"You're fired," Harmon said. "I'm sure you know that."

"I already quit. I wrote the e-mail this morning and scheduled it to send during the meeting."

"You did?"

"Yep. So there was no going back. I also cashed my Amex check. Everyone on the People Team got $500, for our outstanding achievement."

"What will you do?"

"Something that means something. This will sound funny, maybe corny or clichéd, but maybe something with kids."

That surprised him until he thought about it and it seemed right.

"You didn't think I'd be interested in that?" Riley said.

"You know," he said, "we've never really talked about you. My fault. I've been so absorbed in all this."

"Yeah. Well, I have dreams."

"That's great."

"Making them come true would be great."

He waited for more but nothing more came. From the detritus on his desk he picked up a letter opener, its simulated wood handle ornamented with the AC&C logo and the words *Perfect Attendance Award*. He tilted the blade, to focus his reflection. He had hollows under his eyes. His mother would say he was too thin.

"I don't know how you did that," he said. "How you had the courage to do it. I mean I could never—"

"Well I had a special reason."

"You wanted a piece of Yates and Caitlin real bad, didn't you?"

"It wasn't about them," Riley said. "They deserved everything they got, but what I did was real hard to do and those two just aren't important enough."

Harmon squeezed his hands together until they hurt. He knew whom she did it for.

She sat down on the visitor's chair, yanked down hard on her skirt, crossed her legs and in one motion swiveled and kicked the door. It swung to the frame and hesitated. She glared at it and it clicked closed, succumbing to her will, just as he knew it would.

Their eyes met and then he lifted his face toward the ceiling, to hold the tears in. He thought he must look like some trained animal balancing a ball on his nose. He couldn't say it to her, and he couldn't explain it to himself, except that he knew she was the one person in this world that most lifted his heart. He was terrified to lose her and rather than risk that, he would have left things as they were and accept the meagerness of their business relationship forever, if all or nothing at all had not been forced upon him.

"Harmon," Riley said. "I was proud to do it."

It was all too much and there was no more holding back. His tears fell and he felt ashamed and sure that this was the last thing she would want to see.

"I'm sorry," he said.

She came around the desk. "Don't you say that." She touched her fingers to his lips.

He wiped his face on his sleeve and she finished that for him and took his hand. He knew they had crossed some important line and the best was still to come. He wanted to hold her.

"You know," Riley said, "they say the Adirondacks are especially beautiful this time of year."

The freckles along her nose glowed.

"They are," Harmon said.

She sat on his lap. He put an arm around her, and she took it and pulled it tighter.

"How about," she said, lifting his chin and staring into his eyes, "we escape on a get away from all the bullshit trip? Let's go to a mountaintop where we can really get to know each other in our own time and in our own place." She nodded to his photo of the log cabin still on his desk—the chimney still puffing smoke, the sky still blue, the mountain still white-capped.

"That," he said, "sounds great."

She leaned forward and kissed him. He kissed her back. She sat on his lap and they kissed passionately. She was so light, almost weightless. He had imagined this moment many times but never like this, never here in his office. She took him by the hand and pulled him off the chair and onto the floor.

They could hear the band start up again, downstairs. *Happy Days Are Here Again.*

"Now?" he said. "Here?"

"Here seems appropriate," she said.

Then all his troubles were swept away and only the present moment mattered.

About the Author

James Ward's award winning short stories have appeared in literary journals throughout the United States, in Canada, and most recently China and Africa. Safe to Say is his first novel. After a long and varied career in corporate America, he is delighted to be writing full time. He lives in New Jersey with his wife Barbara.

ALL THINGS THAT MATTER PRESS ™

FOR MORE INFORMATION ON TITLES AVAILABLE FROM
ALL THINGS THAT MATTER PRESS, GO TO
http://allthingsthatmatterpress.com
or contact us at
allthingsthatmatterpress@gmail.com